WINTER DAWN

Books by Alex Callister

Recommended reading order
Winter Dark
Winter Rising
Winter Dawn
Winter Falling

Alternative reading order
Winter Dawn
Winter Dark
Winter Rising
Winter Falling

WINTER DAWN

ALEX CALLISTER

For Tamsin and Ell

PROLOGUE

Anna

Central Park, New York

I HAVE A superstitious streak a mile wide. If you unravelled me end to end, spread me out on the floor entrails and all, there would be mile upon mile of black cats and magpies and if it lands on red and if I throw a six then he loves me, he loves me.

When I think about my superstitious self all laid out like an unwrapped Egyptian mummy, I feel a little ashamed, embarrassed by such awkward tawdry nonsense – it is not, after all, what I believe – but put my back to the wall and it is in the bone. Those thin white bones that are all that is left of my unravelled self. Even then, you could cut them in two or slice them end to end and there it would be, tattooed all through me like Brighton rock: Faith.

That is an ugly word these days. In the age of progress, there is little room for credulous belief. The ignorant suspension of disbelief. Faith in all its facets and I am not talking those modern men – Jesus and Mohammed. Man was making bargains with fate, chasing destiny, thousands of years before they came along.

It's what I am doing now as I wait. It is what I'm always

doing – making bargains with fate. I look up at the two birds flying side by side in the early morning sky. Is it a sign? It's grey in Central Park, that grey light that comes before the dawn, and dawn is not far away. I can already see all the way across the reservoir to the gatehouse in the distance. The winter solstice. The longest night of the year.

Lucky.

Soon it will be day and the sky will be blue. Not summer blue – the colour of his periwinkle eyes, so deep and rich they could be purple – but hard, winter blue. Pale and cold and so bright it hurts.

A breeze stirs the skeleton trees behind me. It is too early for joggers on the thin white reservoir track. The Jackie O Reservoir. Another woman who loved.

The water is dark.

Something makes me shiver in the early morning. A breath of anticipation or a premonition. The wind is whispering my name.

Anna, Anna, Anna.

Dark water. It spreads out around me, barely a ripple on the surface. So still I can see my face, strange and ghost-like on the mill pond, almost like another person behind my eyes.

He loves me. I tell myself over and over.

He loves me, he loves me.

There are footsteps on the path behind me. He is coming.

I cross the fingers of both hands and turn my face to the dawn.

CHAPTER 1

Winter

10 years later

I THROW MYSELF up the steps bent double. My long guns graze the stone. Bullets ricochet past me, my heart pounds and then I am at the top crossing the running track and hurling myself over the iron railings into the dark. The spikes catch on the underside of my hoodie and I tear myself free, slide down the steep lip of the Jackie O Reservoir and land, scratched and winded and panting just short of the water.

There are boots on the stone steps behind me.

They are coming.

Dark water laps my feet. Pitch-dark and ice-cold. I imagine hundreds of bullets thudding into my chest as I fall backwards into the water. I am drowning again in the dark.

My ankle buckles under me as I try to stand on the sloped edge; I wrenched it vaulting the fence. I grab at the railings for balance, and a hunter appears at the top of the steps. No more than ten feet from me. He is wearing body armour and a helmet and carrying an assault rifle in his arms. I freeze on instinct.

This is it, the moment of truth. Am I safe this side of the

railings? Is the reservoir the safe zone in tonight's game of
Colosseum?

His visor is shiny black – reflective. I can see nothing of
his face, but I know he is looking at me. For a moment, he
does nothing. We just stare at each other, but his M-16 stays
lowered and he looks up the track away from me searching
for the target.

I start to move, hand over hand, leaning backwards,
propelling myself along with my arms, while he walks beside
me. I turn my head to look back and they are all coming,
pouring out at the top of the steps onto the running track.
All dressed the same, all heavily armed, all well-equipped,
not shivering and bleeding in the dark and the cold.

I accelerate hard, the panic making me fast, lending
energy to my tired muscles. My biceps ache. Above me on
the path, the hunter is keeping pace with me easily. The
running track is smooth – he's not scrambling along a near
vertical slope covered in scrub.

We round the gentle curve. The stone walls of the south
gatehouse are near enough for me to throw a stone at and
there is no sign of the target, the woman I am protecting,
and the panic grips me again and I accelerate. Beside me,
the hunter breaks into a jog.

I slam up against the side of the gatehouse and reach for
the ledge. It is wider and lower than the one at the other
end of the reservoir. I let go of the railings and pull myself
up and ease along, out over the water, expecting at any
moment to hear them opening fire behind me. Just before I
round the stone corner, I turn my head.

All along the railings, as far as the eye can see, hunters
are standing watching me. Tens, maybe even hundreds of

them. They are still coming up the steps, spilling out onto the track.

I turn the corner and I am out of their sight.

There is a woman sitting on the little stone balcony waiting for me. Her knees are bent and her feet tucked up away from the water.

'This is it then,' she says.

I sit down, prop myself up against the stone and look out across the flat expanse of dark water. The reservoir surface is a silky, inky black. Manhattan's skyscrapers light up the night skyline. It is beautiful. Way ahead, out there somewhere in the dark is the north gatehouse. In front of us, the reservoir lies black and huge and impossible. Wind whips the surface. I shiver. A December night in New York, it is beyond cold. Cold in the bone. My breath catches and I feel it across every molar.

'The longest night of the year,' the Senator says. 'The winter solstice.'

'He probably thinks it's symbolic,' I say. 'A hunt in the depths of midwinter. A sacrifice to make the sun come up. It's been going on for millennia.' I lean my head back against the stone. I want to close my eyes. Suddenly, I am very, very tired.

'Tell me about Anna,' I say.

'She's been coming back to me all evening,' she says. 'In fits and starts. I've been remembering.'

'Don't fight it. Try and remember. What can be worse than being hunted?'

'Dark water,' she says. 'I already know what is worse.'

I look at her. Manhattan's lights reflect in her eyes. She is terrified of water, no question, but there is something else going on here.

'Anna loved the solstice,' she says. 'She thought it was lucky. The luckiest day of the year.'

I am silent. All the hairs are lifting on the back of my neck. What happened to Anna?

I stare down into the dark water and the fear rises. Maybe it was never that far below the surface; maybe on this longest of nights we are closer to our superstitious selves than at any other time. I can almost taste the fear. The primitive urge to get away from the water, to run, is so strong it claws up my throat, choking me with my own panic. A breeze blows in my face. I am cold to the bone, shivering and shaking in the dark.

I turn towards the east. Somewhere out there the sun is rising, its golden fingers creeping across the sky. Our time is nearly up. Dawn is coming.

CHAPTER 2

The Senator

8 days earlier

THE SENATOR STARED across the vast open space of her private office at the environmentally friendly bamboo Christmas tree and the Smart TV above a mantelpiece crowded with Christmas cards. The TV screen was showing an alien landscape, like a spaghetti western – the sky was very blue, the ground very bare. It reminded the Senator of a child's geography project – rock with bits of vegetation stuck on. Cold pricked her scalp, slid down the back of her neck, slid between her shoulder blades. She shivered.

Colosseum.

The latest, hottest reality TV show.

A global hunt to the death, live-streamed on the net. An adjudicator to make sure the hunters followed the rules. Not that there were many rules. A target was announced and a week later, the hunt began.

When it had first started, everyone had wondered why the Colosseum Adjudicator gave a week's notice. Why announce a target and then wait a week to start? Surely, it made everything much more difficult? Surely, the target, with a week to get away, would disappear? But it soon became apparent that the targets needed at least a week to prepare, and that even then, the hunt could end up being over ludicrously quick. Even the army general, holed up in Fort William, had been taken out in a matter of days. And it heightened the anticipation. The fun of it. The media went into a frenzy of horrified discussion the moment a target was announced. Possible tactics. Then came the tearful goodbyes, the talking heads. Like an extended obituary. Before you were even dead.

The other thing everyone wondered, apart from, *will it be me*, was who was behind it. The press speculated endlessly about the identity of the Adjudicator, a dark silhouette against the flaming backdrop of the Roman Colosseum. He was a mythical creature, the stuff of online legend with as much money as a nation state.

In the very beginning, the new pirate reality TV shows had been relatively low-key: the sex show that marked performances out of ten, the 'bride needs a groom' show that allowed voters to select a husband for the bride: *she has the dress, she has the church now all she needs is the groom*, the popularity contests in the jungle where the trials got increasingly explicit.

Colosseum was on a whole different scale. Like a global version of the show *Hunted* but with a fatal end. Professional hunters in body armour. A massive cash prize for the winning hunter.

The maximum realisation of human nature.

Oh, the irony. A show only possible because of the extreme technological advances of the internet age chose to hark back to the Roman Colosseum two thousand years before. Almost as if it was saying *nothing changes*. The emperors knew what people liked and so did the Colosseum Adjudicator. Blood sports for the masses.

Colosseum was an online phenomenon that ignored geographic boundaries and the rule of law because it could. Difficult to control. Difficult to police. You could arrest the hunters, although arresting the world's largest black-ops squad had turned out to be harder than expected. But what else could you do? Did you make it an offence to watch *Colosseum*? It was estimated nearly a billion people had watched the last hunt. It was bigger than the World Series. Bigger than ten World Series.

So far, there had been seven hunts: a judge, a captain of industry, a comedian, a general, a movie star, a priest, a banker. It was like that rhyme – a butcher, a baker, a candlestick maker, as if *Colosseum* was collecting professions.

Number eight, the youngest to date and the first woman, was still going. Avril, a YouTuber had barricaded herself into an emergency bunker in Croatia thirty-nine days ago. *Alone*. It was an odd location for a young American to choose, the Senator thought – Tito's Bunker in Croatia's Paklencia National Park.

No one had any idea why the Adjudicator had chosen Avril or, in fact, why any of the targets had been chosen. Avril was an influencer. A twenty-year-old with forty million Instagram followers, her every move slavishly copied, her opinion endlessly sought. It was said she could sell anything, but she was hardly a menace to society. Apparently, she interacted with social media every four and a half minutes, day and night. The world's most connected human had been stuck in a vault alone for thirty-nine days.

The Senator swallowed. She didn't know why this hunt was affecting her so badly. Maybe it was the woman thing – she had been championing the rights of women her whole career. Or maybe it was just Avril's youth. Or maybe it was the way she had walked so surely, so purposefully, to her solitary confinement.

Facebook was running a *Get Avril home for Christmas* campaign as if there was anything anyone could do. Every soldier in the world couldn't protect against a sniper. A lone hunter. Not that there was anything lone about the hunters after Avril.

The Senator looked down at her hand. It was shaking. Ever so slightly. Not enough for anyone else to notice. It shook against the polished wood of the meeting table. She was losing it. She couldn't focus, she couldn't sleep. Last night she kept waking up and checking to see if Avril was still alive. Still in there. She had got up from her bed, drifted down the corridor of her Long Island mansion to her study, rearranged the Christmas cards on the mantelpiece, all the while staring up at the unchanging scene, the closed titanium bunker doors in the mountain.

She looked round the table, the two-hour meeting was showing no sign of winding down – her campaign chief and the two image consultants were in full flow. Walter, her private secretary, was staring off into space letting it all wash over him.

'It is entirely your decision,' her campaign chief was saying.

Her gaze snapped back to him. He wasn't happy about something.

Entirely your decision. She knew what that meant. It was

his favourite phrase. Now he too was staring off into space. Respectfully. Conveying breathing space and time for her to think. Space and time for her to come to the right decision. Which was basically the decision he had already come to.

She could see them all reflected in the polished mahogany. The two image consultants, a man and a woman, were so similar they could be twins.

Now the twins were staring at the table like they could see their own perfectly manicured faces in its glossy surface. They were mimicking her. Subliminal behaviour to ingratiate. *I'm just the same as you.* They were certainly doing a great job with their own images – everything from their smooth foreheads to their carbon-neutral footwear had been carefully selected, scrutinised for any possible offence. Any possible flaw that might not play well on social media. They were so groomed and perfect and 'on message' they could have been created in a lab. Image consultant avatars.

On the mantelpiece, in front of *Colosseum*, a clock ticked.

What was her decision? The Senator's gaze flicked to Walter, looking for a clue. He was staring into the middle distance and wearing that expression she privately thought of as 'stuffed frog' – like the taxidermist had got to work and removed his innards and soaked him in preservative and mounted him on a plinth and at the last minute had inserted a pair of shiny glass eyes that stared out at nothing.

The image consultants weren't happy about him – he was British not American. It wasn't very patriotic. More British than the Union Jack, red buses and the Tower of London. Never out of a three-piece suit, mild-mannered, self-effacing, a tendency to quote Latin. A scholar and a gentleman. They had met at a charity benefit ten years before. The Senator had been the keynote speaker. Walter had been the representative from the British embassy. It had been a meeting of minds. A few months later, he had left the embassy and joined her permanent staff. Turned his back on his country to enter front-line American politics. Or if not the front line, then just behind it. He had her back like nobody else.

She replayed the last five minutes of conversation in her head. They had been discussing the newest addition to her private staff, a brilliant young political graduate, fresh out of Columbia.

It is entirely your decision.

What was entirely her decision?

'It is just that she is very young and attractive,' the woman image consultant said. 'And great skin.'

The Senator dragged her thoughts away from *Colosseum*. The image police were clearly not happy about her latest hire.

Young and attractive with great skin.

'Also, a major in political science from Columbia,' she said.

The image consultant woman looked at her colleague.

'We're not sure how it will play,' he said, flapping his hands. He had beautifully manicured nails. He flapped his hands some more.

Why the flapping? thought the Senator. Like she needed calming.

She could see her own reflection in the polished wood. Groomed. Styled shoulder-length hair, arching brows, red lips, suit in mid-blue. Her look was the culmination of hours of expensive consultants and laborious and occasionally painful beauty procedures. She looked good, no question, but she didn't look twenty-four.

'Are you concerned I will look old standing next to a twenty-four-year-old?'

They exchanged glances.

It wasn't that – she could tell at once. Their body language was all embarrassment. The woman cast a mute appeal across the table at Walter.

The Senator saw him come back. The glass eyes went sentient, life returned.

'We have an opening in Baltimore,' he said gently. 'You don't have to say you changed your mind. *Condemnant quo non intellegunt.*'

It was the pity that clued the Senator in. And the Latin. She rolled her eyes.

'You don't want a young girl from Columbia because of what happened last time. You think it will remind people,' she said flatly.

The woman jumped on it. 'We cannot be too careful.' she said. 'The press love an angle.'

The Senator sighed. She thought about the brilliant student she had hired for her personal staff and about her handsome husband hounded by speculation wherever he went.

'It is just that there cannot be a breath of scandal at this incredibly sensitive time,' the woman was saying. Her tone was upbeat. Relieved now the difficult message had been delivered.

The Senator glanced at her watch (expensive present from loving husband) and thought about a lifetime of sacrifice and the prize just within reach and whether she was going to allow them to bully her into this entirely unnecessary move and knew that she was.

'Fine,' she said. 'Send her to Baltimore.'

It was a very sensitive time, there was no doubt about that. In fact, that was an understatement. She was about to embark on the most gruelling two years of her life.

Tonight, the Senator was announcing she was running for President.

CHAPTER 3

THERE HAD BEEN endless debate about exactly when and where the Senator was going to announce her candidacy for the Democratic nomination. Many schools of thought. In the end, they had decided to go for her birthday at home.

It was a bold call highlighting to the world that she was now sixty. Why was sixty old for a woman but not for a man? When men were way more likely to drop dead in their sixties.

Home too was controversial. A colonial mansion that had been in her family for three generations with a sweeping Scarlett O'Hara staircase and a ballroom that could seat a hundred. But it felt right. It was the foundation of her support and sometimes, very occasionally, you had to go with your gut.

Tonight, she would have a political platform like never before. She looked round at her advisers. '*Colosseum*,' she said. 'Some things are unacceptable in a civilised society. Tonight, we could say something.'

It had been written on a note she had found on her desk this morning.

What are you doing about Avril? Some things are unacceptable in a civilised society.

The writing was just the same as the Senator's. It was almost as if she had written it in her sleep.

There was a shuffling from the image consultants. An unspoken something in the air. *Colosseum* was very popular with the voters. Everyone denounced it and everyone watched it. The world practically ground to a halt watching it.

'*Colosseum* is the single best thing to happen to the gun control cause in the last fifty years,' said the woman image consultant carefully. 'Approval ratings are at an all-time high. It has been trending for thirty-nine days straight. Bigger than any single mass-shooting surge.'

Mass-shooting surge.

So typical, they had a name for it. Gun control speeches were better delivered in the aftermath of a school shooting. They had analysed the timing for maximum impact. The decay rate, the fade. It was reckoned that the popular outrage lasted less time than the autopsies.

Live-streamed events needed stopping – that was the bottom line, and that ship had sailed back when they were all arguing about the independence of the internet and the individual's right to online anonymity. In touchingly naïve sincerity. Back when the internet was a cute novelty.

So how could you stop *Colosseum*? There was no physical way now to prevent the live-streaming. The only option was to make viewing *Colosseum* illegal. Prosecute every single person who watched it. Another minefield.

It was a natural and inevitable progression. The maximum realisation of human nature. Man coming full circle. The internet was the ultimate manifestation of human progress – an infinitely powerful network connecting every living soul on the planet – and what did those living souls do with it? Masturbate and watch hunts-to-the-death on TV.

At the same time probably.

She focused on the faces around the table. They were all looking at her.

'*Colosseum* needs to be stopped,' she said. 'It's time to speak out. Tonight. Before something happens to Avril.'

'It's all about freedom,' said the woman image consultant.

Freedom. It was a word beloved by the image makers. Freedom for the citizen to watch what they liked without fear of censorship from the State.

'It is a massive risk,' she continued, glancing sideways at her colleague. Her glossy hair swung slightly with the movement.

'And to achieve what exactly?' he said.

'*In absentia lucis, tenebrae vincunt,*' said Walter.

'Which means what?' said the male image consultant.

'In the absence of light, darkness prevails.'

'We should stick to the script,' said the woman. 'Sympathy for the family. We can't go anywhere near the second amendment. Not tonight.'

It was so easy to be portrayed as weak on national defence, especially when you were pro gun control. She had to be seen to be doing the right thing at all times. Strong. A commander in chief. And it was much harder for a woman – she knew that. It shouldn't be, but it was. She had spent her life in favour of gun control, and now, at its climax, she had to be very careful it didn't turn into a rod for her own back.

Freedom.

It meant absolutely jack. No one had any freedom. Least of all someone running for President.

The Senator looked out of the window.

'Fine,' she said.

The image consultants were moving on. Subject closed. They had something else on their minds. More important than *Colosseum*. They wanted to talk about whether they could get rid of her butler for the evening.

'It just doesn't look good,' they were saying. 'Sends the wrong message. We can't have any attention away from you.'

'Only for the announcement,' they said. 'We are not saying you need to get rid of him permanently.'

'He is an American citizen,' she said.

'But he doesn't look it,' they said firmly. And that was what mattered. Appearances. Not reality.

It had got to the stage where politics was a giant exercise in doing nothing. The higher you got, the more you had to lose. The higher the stakes. Until you were spending hours, days, weeks doing absolutely nothing.

'Worst case,' said the male image consultant, 'it plays soft on immigration.'

The Senator looked out of the window. *You end up doing the exact opposite of what you believe,* she reflected, *in an effort to fight your own stereotype.*

'At some point we do actually have to do something,' she said. 'When will that be?'

Walter smiled. The image consultants looked at her like she was losing it.

Had she spoken aloud? She was definitely losing it. She stared out of the window at the boating lake with the island in the centre. Why had she kept it? She hated water.

'Shall I talk to him?' said Walter. 'You know he will understand.'

'Understand I don't want to be tainted with his third generation mildly Hispanic blood?'

She went back to looking out of the window. She wished she was in New York. It was nearly Christmas. She loved New York at Christmas.

No one said anything. They didn't need to.

'Fine,' she said.

SOMETHING HAD CHANGED on the TV above the mantelpiece. The picture had shifted from an aerial shot and focused in on the blast doors. Bare rock towered overhead. Dark green pines covered the lower slopes. The Senator knew, if the sound was on, there would be nothing but the chatter of crickets. She could imagine the smell of pine and the fear.

'Turn the sound up,' she said. 'Right now.' Her voice was overloud. Everyone stared at her. 'Something is happening on *Colosseum*.' She felt her heart start to motor. Thumping in her chest. She really, really wanted this girl to survive.

She got to her feet and stood gripping the table edge. They all stared at the bare rock and the titanium door sealing the bunker.

'Is the door opening?' said the woman image consultant. She was on her feet too. They craned forward. The huge blast doors had sand piled in front of them, witness to the extreme dust wind. The bora. It even had its own name.

Slowly, slowly a crack was appearing between the doors.

'The doors are opening,' said the woman excitedly. 'I can't believe it. She's coming out.'

'Where are the hunters?' said the male image consultant. All thoughts of butlers were gone; Christmas had come early. He stood in front of the TV screen holding the controller and jabbing at the buttons. He reminded the Senator of a kid with a computer game. 'Can't this thing go any louder?' he said.

The picture widened right out. An aerial shot from a Colosseum drone. *Colosseum* seemed to have an endless supply of drones. It was how they televised the footage when they weren't using the hunters' headcams. Every time a drone was taken out, another one popped up in its place. This one took in the miles of crevasse and ravine and the narrow pass snaking up the side of the mountain.

She remembered Avril saying goodbye to her mother, an older version of Avril herself, and walking up the pass watched by a million drones and the world's media. *Colosseum* had made no attempt to stop her. Almost as though it knew where she was going. She'd been a strangely cheerful figure in her pink designer tracksuit, her long, blonde hair braided for the occasion.

They had hugged, mother and daughter, for perhaps twenty seconds. Tight, you could see the mother's fists balled round her daughter's neck and then they pulled apart and spoke a few words very close together, their foreheads almost touching and then Avril had turned and started her lonely climb up the narrow cliff face and her mother had looked after her with fierce eyes. And she had never left. She was still there at the bottom with the press photographers and the news anchors. Day after day, night after night. After the first twenty-four hours, someone had brought her a camper van.

The Senator wondered where Avril's mother was now. Did she know a kilometre up the mountain pass above her, something was happening?

The giant doors had opened from a crack to a small gap. They watched the opening. A figure in a dirty pink tracksuit was crawling out. Her braids were still in place. She got halfway out and sat back on her heels, hands over her face. Her body rocked.

'Why is she coming out?' said the woman image consultant. 'Is she mad? She'll be shot.'

They watched as Avril rocked backwards and forwards in a silent scream.

'What's wrong with her?' said the woman.

They stared at the rocking figure, at the rictus of pain running through her body. Something was wrong. She was suffering – it was as clear as if they could feel it themselves.

'Is she ill?' the woman said. 'Has she come out because she's ill? It's not like the Adjudicator will let her off.'

'She's blinded by the light,' said the Senator. 'It's her eyes. She's been in darkness.'

The Senator was right. After a while, Avril raised her head. Her hands came down from her face. She sat back on her heels and seemed to get her bearings. She reached behind her, patting the ground. The drone was so close they could see the dust on the dirty concrete under her fingertips. She was searching for the piece of paper she had been holding when she crawled through the doors. She found it and scrabbled in the dust, trying to pick it up. The drone focused in. Avril raised her face to the camera and held the piece of paper up to the world.

Five words had been written in spidery script by someone in total darkness.

Forty days and forty nights.

Her perfect golden face was white and emaciated, her eyes hollow in her head, but her hands were rock steady.

'What does it mean?' said the woman. 'I thought it was day thirty-nine today?'

The camera suddenly panned to the bottom of the mountain. A tiny figure was tearing up the narrow path screaming and running and waving its arms above its head. Avril's mother. A kilometre down the mountain below her daughter but moving fast.

The camera panned back to Avril. For a long moment, nothing happened. She looked up to the distant mountains, her message held up in front of her.

Then she toppled forwards onto the stone like a puppet with the strings cut. A moment later, there was the crack of a rifle as the sound caught up the distance.

The Senator put her hand over her mouth. She could feel her eyes burning.

Whatever Avril's mother had wanted to say, it was too late.

The eighth Colosseum target was down.

CHAPTER 4

I T WAS EVENING, the end of her birthday dinner and the presidential announcement was moments away. The Senator stared at herself in the bathroom mirror. She put her hand up to her cheek, the colour of the skin on her hands matched her face – she was made-up for television; her foundation was thicker than normal and slightly orange. Her nails were long and perfect and pink.

'We don't want the hands letting you down,' the make-up girl had said. 'There's nothing worse than face and hands that don't match.'

There is, the Senator had wanted to say. *Being hunted to death. Being shot on the side of a mountain. Pitching face-first into the dust. That's worse.*

But what could she do?

The inertia of politics. Once you were actually in a position to do something, your hands were tied by the fear of putting a foot wrong. And it was understandable – how many careers had been wrecked by an inadvertent word? A phrase spoken at random. Or worse, an attempt at candid honesty that had spectacularly backfired.

'You are pale today,' the make-up girl had said. 'Soon get some colour in your cheeks.'

The Senator's eyes looked glassy, her hand was shaking again.

The image consultants had been genuinely dumbfounded by their bad luck. A Colosseum death on the very day of the announcement.

'Why did she come out? *Why?* It makes no sense,' they had said, as if it was a deliberate attempt by Avril to sabotage their big day.

Now they would have to battle for every column inch. They had toyed for about ten minutes with postponement. It wasn't practical. There was a programme of events in place stretching from now to next fall.

The woman image consultant had paced up and down the Senator's office, irritation narrowing her features, cutting through the Botox, crinkling her forehead. Her colleague had stood where he was, thumping his fist into his palm, over and over.

The Senator peered at herself in the bathroom mirror. Hair: full and sleek. Make-up: perfect. Lashes: perfect. Lipstick: perfect and glossy with fixer.

'There's nothing worse than a great smear of pink lipstick on the teeth,' the make-up girl had said.

The Senator leaned forward and bared her teeth. Nothing. She scrubbed at the pristine white veneers anyway.

She glanced again at her notes. There was an autocue but she always had a backup.

Sincerest condolences.

What empty, hollow words. What could she say now that wouldn't look like a cheap PR stunt? She thought about Avril's mother running up the narrow path, falling to her knees in the dust beside her daughter. It was hard to picture her own immaculate mother breaking into a run for anyone. Certainly not for her only child. Always immaculate, always that mild, indefinable air of disappointment. That was before Alzheimer's had claimed all but the very essence of her. The Senator was finally going to do something to make her mother proud, and her mother would know nothing about it. It was typical of their entire relationship.

Her thoughts jumped immediately, defensively to her husband, as they had done for so many years. The contrast to her chilly upbringing. Soccer scholarship to college, a lifeguard at sixteen, the brain to match his impressive sporting credentials, the very definition of masculinity. Blond hair and blue, blue periwinkle eyes. They were husband-and-wife senators. The press would joke about whether the presidency could be a job-share.

The nail was mid-pink against the bright, white enamel. It made a squeaking sound.

She stepped back.

Breathed in. Breathed out.

She was ready for the biggest night of her life. She opened the bathroom door, crossed the landing and made for the stairs.

They had thought about whether to do the announcement on the staircase with a certain spontaneous informality, a new generation of politician – more casual, more informal, just mentioning it trotting down the stairs – but then there were the TV screens which would broadcast her making history even as she was doing it, and it was difficult to arrange a big TV screen spontaneously halfway up a staircase. In the end, they had gone for the ballroom, a small stage, a podium, a microphone and a huge TV screen behind. The end of her birthday dinner. A home crowd.

The fifteenth of December. It was a miserable time of

year to have a birthday – the trees, bare dripping skeletons, the weather dark, the sun low in the sky. Not the shortest day, she was a week away from that, but nearly. The low point of the year. Literally and metaphorically. 'A midwinter baby,' her mother used to say, 'is unlucky.'

It was a charity dinner of course. Even her birthday was an opportunity. Her husband had given her 50,000 acres of rainforest. Or to be more accurate, had saved 50,000 acres of rainforest on her behalf. Walter, her private secretary, had given her a real miniature Christmas tree in a red pot. It was ridiculous and she loved it. She had put her face in the branches and breathed in the real pine.

She looked down from the stairs. A string quartet of young students was playing in the hall beside the twenty-foot Christmas tree. Buskers. Impoverished. Painfully talented. The tree was fake. It had arrived in eight circular decorated sections and been assembled by men on stepladders. It looked fabulous, she had to admit. Like the perfect ones on the ground floor of Macy's.

The musicians were playing Elgar's cello concerto, but at the signal, they were going to break into the 'Star-Spangled Banner' in a totally spontaneous display of patriotism – youth moved by the moment and giving joyful voice to their emotions in their uniquely talented way. It was to be followed by a spontaneous outpouring of support on social media and, a slightly less spontaneous but more dignified, orchestrated series of announcements by leading supporters from business. The TV cameras were ready at the back of the ballroom. She could see their red recording lights already on through the double doors at the far end. She crossed the hall and went in the far door beside the mini stage.

She walked up the two makeshift steps to the podium. The steps were wooden wine crates under a white linen tablecloth. She knew because she had watched her campaign chief build them while the image consultants argued about whether she could step up nearly a metre tread in a tight skirt without looking ridiculous. She had seen the expression on Walter's face. There was something so ludicrous about the whole thing – appearance vs reality.

There were going to be no introductions. The whole vibe, according to the image consultants, was casual. Spontaneous. Like she had just been moved by the moment. Carried to the podium on a wave of public support. Manifesting her destiny and all that.

She wished Anna was here to see this. The culmination of all their hopes. It had been ten years since the Senator had seen her or really even thought about her, but she still came into her dreams sometimes. She felt closer tonight than she had for years.

They were all staring upwards now. A sea of faces. A mass of black jackets and white tablecloths and, here and there, a splash of colour from a silk dress. They had seen her come in and were waiting for the announcement. A home crowd. It probably wasn't going to be that much of a surprise.

She wasn't nervous. She didn't do nervous. She did planning and organising and practising until something was so familiar it made your ears bleed.

Waiters with trays of champagne were standing in the doorways ready to spring into action. The champagne looked golden against the cream walls. The waiters were staring. The room of white linen and the sea of faces blurred. She breathed in. Hairspray and perfume and lilies. Nothing from the Christmas tree in the corner, an identical baby clone of the huge one in the hall. She breathed out.

It was the biggest night of her career.

She focused on the sea of faces. They were staring upwards. They weren't looking at her at all; they were staring at the big screen behind her head. The room felt still, frozen, shocked.

Something was wrong.

Her politician's radar picked it up while her eyes scanned the crowd. There should be applause. She felt uncertainty start to creep over her, cold on the back of her neck until her whole body shuddered in the sudden chill.

She saw her husband leaning against the wall, halfway up the room. He had a strange flat look on his face that reminded her of something, but she couldn't think what.

There were gasps of shock and the room erupted. A moment before, it had been still, now it was filled with movement; people leaning towards their neighbours, hands over their mouths.

She turned slowly and looked at the TV behind her.

A huge logo filled the screen. A round building in flames – the Roman Colosseum – burning bright, and in front of it, the silhouette of a tall dark figure. The Colosseum Adjudicator had broken through her live broadcast to announce a new victim. It was quick. Too quick. In the past, he had let weeks go by before announcing another hunt. There was a picture of the new target and a name flashing across the centre of the screen. The words looked like they were on fire.

The new target was another woman. Older. Much older

than Avril but groomed. Immaculate. Her hair was full and sleek, her make-up perfect, her lips glossy with fixer.

The Senator looked out at the sea of horrified, whispering faces. Her eyes searched for Walter, scanning the crowd. Where was he? At first, she couldn't find him and then she picked him out, right at the back beside a waiter with a tray of champagne. In the half-light he seemed unreal, like a statue.

She turned back to the screen and stared up at the woman with the full, sleek hair, the perfect make-up, the lipstick glossy with fixer.

She couldn't take it in.

The new target was her.

CHAPTER 5

New York

A week later

24 hours to go

THE SENATOR WAS not nervous. Not at all. Not scared in any way.

Her eyes swept the hotel room (high end, business) on the Upper East Side that was doubling as a safe house. Swept the faces of the two men with her (strained, nervous) and returned to the document on the table in front of her.

Her will. Her final will and testament. Her final thoughts and instructions. Her last chance to say anything. To make any kind of a difference. The grey hotel room with its heavy brocades felt airless and claustrophobic. Like a trap.

She didn't do nervous. She did planning and organising and practising until something was so familiar it made your ears bleed. She had had a week. Not long. A vanishingly small amount of time in fact. It had passed in a blur of FBI and security.

She had been moved straight from her birthday dinner. Helicoptered out by the NSA. She hadn't even been allowed to go upstairs to change her shoes. The pile of presents was probably still there, the tables, the trays of champagne. Everything left in place forever like that house in *Great Expectations* with the mouldering wedding banquet. Only there would be no Miss Havisham in her house. Because she would be dead.

Funnily enough, in all the haste and the panic and the storm of noise, the thing that had hit her hardest was the thought of her butler. She was never going to get the chance to make it right. To talk to him in person, to apologise for making his ancestry any kind of a problem.

She was not nervous. Not at all. Not scared in any way.

She was the ninth target and the second woman. She supposed that should count for something. Some kind of a twisted blow for feminism and equality.

It wasn't so much that she was afraid of death, although it was surprising how childishly afraid she was, but there was something humiliating about being hunted for entertainment. As if everything she stood for counted for nothing. As if everything she had ever achieved, whatever that was, was irrelevant. All anyone would remember was how she ran, and how she hid, and how she died.

Her eyes tracked round the strange New York hotel room, looking in the corners, checking the angles. She had spent her life checking the angles, planning ahead. Now, at its very end, she couldn't shake the habit.

She turned to look at Walter, still in his three-piece suit, his scowling face poring over her final instructions for the hundredth time. And at her Head of Security, tears in the corners of his eyes. She turned away. The muscles in her jaw tightened.

There had been three safe houses in the seven days since the announcement and each time, the Colosseum Adjudicator had published her whereabouts for the world to see and speculate over. There was nowhere to hide. Apparently, he had eyes everywhere.

As a senator, her protection fell to the Secret Service and up until now, they had made a good job of it. Two agents man-marked her at all times, eight hours on, rotating shifts. The head of her protection detail had headed up the Vice-President's security team. He was well regarded. A high-profile senator with a lot of enemies, particularly among the gun lobby – the State took her protection seriously.

And then this happened, and normal rules no longer applied. An extra twelve agents had been assigned to her protection, along with a special agent from the FBI investigation into *Colosseum*. After the first safe house, deep in the Nevada desert, was a bust, they had added another twelve agents. Twenty-four agents plus her Head of Security in a ring of steel. It wasn't going to be anything like enough.

Her brain stalked round the problem, squaring it out, filing it down to its essentials.

The problem was this:

If enough people are prepared to risk their lives to take yours, it is very hard to stop them.

So what do you do?

The problem could be pared back to a simple choice – you hide or you fight. Both had been tried against *Colosseum* with zero success.

She added an appendix to the primary problem – enough people with enough money. Because that was what it came down to in the end. The Adjudicator seemed to have unlimited resources, and everyone had their price. She looked across at Walter and wondered what his price would be.

He was exchanging glances with her Head of Security. They had been doing it most of the week. They thought she hadn't noticed. She didn't know which was worse: finding out who cared or finding out who didn't.

After the three FBI safe houses, they were now back in New York in an anonymous hotel on 85th. A quiet tree-lined street, two minutes from Central Park.

Strangely, unlike every other Colosseum target, she had been given eight days not seven to prepare. Not that the extra day had made the slightest difference.

'The President has offered Camp David again,' said her Head of Security.

They all knew what had happened to the last Colosseum target to be guarded by the FBI. He had been shot by his own bodyguards.

'Tell me again,' she said. 'About this Brit.'

Walter looked up. His three-piece suit was slightly creased. It was the only outward sign of the week's stress.

'With the minimum of Latin,' she added, trying to smile.

'The best they have. Just come in from the field. In debriefing now. Been a year on mission below the Arctic circle.'

They have, she noticed, like he had abandoned his country in favour of hers.

She nodded. She knew this. Walter had been pushing the idea all week. A radical alternative solution. Counter-intuitive. A leap of faith. American might vs British cunning.

Her Head of Security had almost had apoplexy when he had heard.

She didn't feel very hopeful. What could one individual do?

What Walter hadn't said, because he didn't need to, was that someone from British Intelligence who had been undercover for a year was an outsider. No doubt, the Brit also had a price, but no one would have had a chance to offer it.

'The guerrilla defence,' he said.

She knew about this too. The vulnerability of heavily armoured troops. The defensive nature of highly mobile light infantry. Taken to its logical conclusion: one person had a better chance on the run than an entire regiment. In theory. Hypothetically. Of course, a lot hinged on who the person was.

'So British Intelligence?'

'Single-handedly blew up a Siberian nuclear facility.'

That didn't strike her as particularly impressive.

'And got out.'

OK, that was better. Able to blend in easily, melt into the background, a master of disguise. She was revising her image of a rugged marine and forming another. A will-o'-the-wisp. Unmemorable, unnoticeable in a crowd.

'An extreme sports fanatic. Trained in hostage retrieval, all forms of combat – armed and unarmed.' Walter looked at her helplessly. 'The best they have,' he said finally.

The best of the best.

And the Brits were great at that sort of thing, weren't they? Everyone knew that.

The clock was ticking.

On the TV, the Colosseum twenty-four hour countdown had started. In less than a day, she would be on the run.

She circled round the problem. American might vs British cunning. New world vs old. Head vs heart.

She looked at Walter.

She knew what Anna would say. *Sometimes, you have to go with your gut.*

'Fine,' she said. 'Make the call.'

CHAPTER 6

London

I N A RAINSWEPT London, the Best of the Best lay naked on a velvet sofa watching the painted faces on the ceiling move in and out of focus. The candlelight cast tall shadows. It looked like there could be cherubs up there or maybe they were demons – it was hard to say.

In real life too come to think of it.

Half the time you didn't know what was in your head and what was real.

Maybe they weren't cherubs or demons, maybe they were mythological creatures. One of them had a winged helmet. It could be scenes from Greek mythology. The white-haired godlike figure in the centre could easily be Zeus. He was watching now. Looking down on the action. He would probably approve – it was his kind of thing.

The Best of the Best stared upwards. Zeus was *definitely* watching. It always felt like someone was watching. The evacuation from Siberia had been so timely it was uncanny. The Best of the Best had a guardian angel out there somewhere.

The rainstorm battered against the tall, stone mullioned windows. Every now and then gusts of wind blasted round the sides of the old glass hard enough to make the candles flicker.

Rainbow stars exploded against the ceiling, filling the room with sparkling fireworks. Everything glittered. A woman crawled across the ancient Axminster towards the Best of the Best, her full lips open. She was also naked. Sweat gleamed between her full breasts. The air smelled of wood smoke and vanilla and sweat. The crawling woman put one hand up on the velvet sofa and then the other. The pink tip of her tongue peeped out between her lips like a promise. Behind her, a threesome was going for it. Two were standing and the third was kind of hanging between them.

It was all good.

There was a sudden burst of bright light, the crash of a heavy wooden door slamming open and a man stood on the threshold. He was dressed in military khaki and had a curl of wire in his ear. He surveyed the room, taking in the tangle of naked bodies, the heaving, thrusting tangle.

The Best of the Best sat up.

'Fuck off,' she said. 'I'm off duty.'

'Yeah,' said the man from GCHQ field support, 'about that.'

CHAPTER 7

The Senator

2 hours to go

NOW THE DAY had come and night had arrived and the Senator was still not nervous. Still not scared in any way. She had seen many nights in her sixty years and this one was no different.

She just had to live through it.

Her eye took in the silk bedspread, the velvet curtains, the brilliant white of the bathroom. The door to the en suite was ajar and the bathroom light was bright. It hurt her eyes. The Best of the Best was *late*. What if he wasn't coming? She had never expected to be in New York for the hunt itself.

'You don't think about death,' she said. 'It's so far away, it's an irrelevance. Away on the horizon. Almost out of sight. And then you start to know people who die. Just one or two, the hushed news, the horror of cancer, and suddenly, death is right there sharp as a pin under your nail, breaking through your reality.'

'But you push it away,' said Walter, nodding.

The Senator stared at herself in the mirror. At the blue suit (voter-neutral), the neat hair, the plucked eyebrows, the immaculate make-up. 'You push it away. Not something to think about, not right now. Then one day it dawns on you that you had one life, you can't go back and do it over and not long after that, you start to think about death. Until there comes a time when you can think about little else.'

Walter looked away. The Senator wondered if he too would cry.

'If you are a planner or a thinker, you want to deal with it,' she said. 'To understand it, control it, square it away, minimise it. A chore to be handled. A file on a computer, a rolodex of contacts, a will, details laid down, a plan. Even then, you can't really believe it, because the idea of the world without you in it is strange. Did you see that movie about a guy whose whole life was a reality TV show controlled by a producer and he didn't know?'

'*The Truman Show.*'

'That's what we all think deep down. Then you find out it's true, and the whole world is going to watch you die.'

Walter stared down at the table.

It was one of those half tables you only get in hotel rooms. Too shallow to be a desk but no use as anything else. The TV was showing the outside of the hotel. Every now and then it went to an aerial shot. They could hear the newscopters overhead, even through the soundproofed walls and inch-thick glass. A conference hotel. The Senator had been in many of them. Not really designed for a protracted stay but well soundproofed. The commercial customer appreciated that.

On the half table was a photo frame of her husband, his blue eyes smiling. It was from a portrait shoot during his first campaign for the Senate. The windows had been open and white floaty curtains blew horizontal across the big

warehouse space and he had stood in the centre of a
twittering crowd of photographers' assistants and stylists and
press secretaries, and laughed and laughed. And the room
had laughed back at him. His charisma was like a force field
around him. It sucked people in. Get too close and you
couldn't break away. You didn't want to. Everyone felt it –
men and women, young and old.

They had said their goodbyes nearly a week ago and
then said them again because the camera angle hadn't been
good and then they had said them a final time, and she'd
been able to hear some of the piece to camera her husband
had recorded eulogising his wife and her career and vowing
to dedicate his life to the pursuit of the man behind
Colosseum and the destruction of all reality TV shows that
had crossed the line into illegality. He had been a wreck, the
tears pouring down his face.

Then his security team had hustled him away. As if she
had an infectious disease. Like she was in quarantine. But
what choice was there? He had to survive to take up where
she was leaving off. He was her legacy. Her carbon copy.
Her soulmate.

'Look after my mother,' she had said to him, last of all.

'I don't think I'm going to tell her,' he said. 'I think it's
kinder.'

She loved him in that moment more than she ever had,
even in the white-hot heat of the early days.

'It's the longest night tonight,' she said now to Walter.
'Did you know?'

'Yes,' he said. 'The solstice.' He tried to smile. 'A time
of rebirth.'

'Or of death.'

'In Rome, they had Saturnalia,' he said. 'Their equivalent of the solstice. It was the time when everything turned on its head, the natural order of things was reversed. People swapped names and identities – the masters waited on the slaves and the Lord of Misrule was king.'

'Misrule? A trickster? Jokes and forfeits and riddles?'

Walter thought about it for a while. 'Yes and no,' he said. 'He was also a sinister figure, powerful. He could condemn someone to death on a whim, and the order would have to be executed. A bit like the Roman emperors themselves really.'

And like the Colosseum Adjudicator. He was more emperor than referee. Why had he chosen her? On a whim?

The Lord of Misrule.

*

ONE HOUR TO go.

'I thought they were going to close the skies,' she said.

'They will, at midnight. Maybe a bit before.' Walter was still looking at the table.

The Senator wondered whether they would have shut the skies earlier for the President if the President had been the target instead of her. Maybe they couldn't justify closing the skies above New York for anyone, not even the President.

The problem was, no one, least of all herself, had expected her to stay in New York. With a week to prepare, every other target had holed up in a nuclear bunker, got on a long flight, lost themselves in the Amazon rainforest. It hadn't helped any of them.

The media had speculated endlessly this last week about what she might do, where she might go. No one had even considered that she might not go anywhere.

She looked at Walter. He was staying too, and nothing she had been able to say in the last week had changed his mind. It reminded her of a laundry list:

10 things to do with sweetcorn

10 of the worst dance moves ever

10 people to have with you when you die.

The image consultants had done their best to get rid of him in the last few months. *It just doesn't look good*, they kept saying. *Your closest aide, not even American. Not patriotic. Like you rate the Brits more. Your private office must be American. It is non-negotiable.*

He had worked for her for ten years and she knew nothing about him. Did he even have a private life? He had got divorced just after they had met – she knew that. And now? She didn't even know.

'Are you seeing anyone, Walter?' she said.

He looked up. Straight at her. Met her eyes. He looked away.

'No,' he said.

Why had she asked that? It was so unprofessional, so inappropriate.

'I'm sorry,' she said. 'I shouldn't have asked.'

On the TV, the hour countdown had started. The British Best of the Best was cutting it fine. She had thought they would be far away from New York by now.

'And they are going to phone up, when he gets here?' she said.

Walter nodded. 'There's a ring of steel,' he said unnecessarily. They both knew there was a ring of steel. They could see it on the television. There had been a ring of steel since the Senator had arrived and the street had been closed for two blocks. All the way from Third Avenue in the west to First Avenue in the east. The hotel had been evacuated. The Senator wondered what had happened to the rest of the residents on the street. Most of it was businesses and offices anyway – the Central Post Office, an art gallery. She probably needn't worry. They would be able to come in to work in the morning, and it would all be over.

There was a knock at the door.

They looked at each other. Walter pulled something black and woolly out of his pocket and yanked it over his head.

The Senator stared.

A balaclava. It looked totally ridiculous on top of the three-piece suit.

He tiptoed to the door and peered through the spy hole. He backed away, hands raised and the door gave a click and swung open inwards.

A girl stood on the threshold in jeans and a hoodie. She had dreadlocks and a nose ring and a handgun with a six-inch silencer screwed to the barrel. She scowled at them.

'Never look though a spyhole,' said the Best of the Best.

She was tall and slim with slanting, green eyes and sharp, angular cheekbones. She held the door sideways on to the room and inserted the barrel of the silencer into the fisheye lens. She indicated the width of the door and tapped the spy hole on the other side.

'Kill shot,' she said. 'Straight through the eye cavity and

into the temporal lobe.' She considered the door. 'Particleboard,' she said reflectively, 'next to useless'.

They stared.

'You must be "the Senator",' said the girl. 'Cuter than I was expecting.' She jerked her head at Walter. 'Off you go, ninja warrior.'

'What?' he said. 'I'm staying.'

'Nope,' said the girl. She stepped up to him, spun him round, smacked down with the butt of her gun on the back of his neck and sent him sprawling through the open doorway. She kicked the door shut.

The Senator gaped.

The girl stalked over to the bed and looked up at the ceiling, her head tilted to one side. The handgun had disappeared somewhere about her person. She had a small rucksack like pro-mountaineers use on her back.

'Walter has been coming to my office every day for ten years,' the Senator said, keeping her voice neutral. 'I trust him completely – he never leaves my side.'

'I don't care if he's been coming all over your face for ten years,' said the girl, climbing on the bed. 'He's not staying.'

She bent down, pulled a long, white knife from somewhere around her ankle, straightened up and inserted the blade into the edge of the smoke detector. The cover flipped open, and the girl peered inside, then she was down off the bed and heading for the window. She threw the balcony doors open and stepped out.

The Senator exchanged a glance with her reflection. She went over to the balcony. Cold, damp air hit her face. She could hear the murmur of voices from way below, no traffic – the street was closed.

'How *old* are you?' the Senator said.

Right now, it probably wasn't the most tactful question, but the Senator wasn't feeling tactful. She was feeling like her last ditch, best chance had just fallen flat on its face.

The Best of the Best was standing on the thin, iron balustrade, looking up at the floor above. Ten floors up, and she was just standing there, balancing on an iron railing. They were above the tops of the trees. Strings of white Christmas lights looped their way between the lamp posts all the way down the street. The Senator could see paper chains in the windows of the building opposite.

'Twenty-one,' said the girl. 'Why? How old are you?'

'Sixty,' said the Senator. She turned to pick up the phone. She needed a backup plan, fast.

The girl jumped down from the balustrade.

'Before you do anything stupid,' she said, 'you might want to reflect on the fact that I got in here undetected which makes me better than anyone you have in the building, and that if I can get in, so can someone else as good as me.' She thought about this. 'Nearly as good as me.'

Undetected.

The Senator's Head of Security answered.

'Has the British Intelligence officer arrived yet?' she said without taking her eyes off the girl.

'No, Ma'am,' said the Head of Security. 'We'll let you know directly he arrives.'

The Senator put the phone down.

Which makes me better than anyone you have in the building.

The Best of the Best came back into the room. She disappeared into the bathroom. The Senator followed. The girl was standing with her back to the door, levering off the grill on the air-conditioning duct. It wasn't big enough to take a cat, never mind a full-sized human. It was empty. Just as the Senator had been expecting.

'Are you really the Best of the Best?' she said. It was completely and utterly unbelievable.

The girl went still. The Senator could see her in the mirror; she looked like she'd seen a ghost.

'So they say,' she said.

She pushed past the Senator and went back into the bedroom. She glanced at the TV. 'What time does this gig get started?'

'Don't you *know*?' said the Senator. 'Midnight.'

'Three safe houses in seven days?' said the girl.

The Senator nodded.

The Best of the Best stared off into space. 'Do you want my professional opinion?'

Not really, thought the Senator.

'I guess.'

'You're in deep shit. Completely compromised. This place is so full of cameras you could launch your own TV series. There is kit in the bathroom. Half your entourage have been got to. Maybe I could get round it with a bit of time and planning.'

'But I don't have time.'

'As you say. You don't have time.' The girl stood with her hands in her jeans' pockets staring at the TV, looking for all the world like a freshman in her first year at college.

'Is this the part where we accelerate the trusting process, the getting to know each other, so I can weigh up your skills and learn to trust your competence?'

'No,' said the girl, turning green eyes on her. 'This is the part where you decide how much you want to live.'

'I want to live,' said the Senator.

'I will need you to do exactly what I say, without question. Can you do that?'

Without question.

The Senator thought about this. She had been questioning things her whole life. It was who she was.

'I don't know,' she said truthfully.

The girl smiled. A shocking transformation on her sharp, angular face. 'Good answer.' She held out her hand.

The Senator stared.

'Winter,' said the girl. 'Nice to meet you.'

CHAPTER 8

'FIRST THING WE'RE going to do,' said Winter. 'Is get the hell out of here.' She hauled her rucksack higher up on her shoulders and went out through the balcony doors.

The Senator looked around. At her laptop, at her phone, at her credit cards.

Winter came back through the swinging velvet drapes. 'Come on,' she said. 'What are you waiting for?'

The Senator picked up her phone.

'Nope.'

'Shouldn't I let them know I'm going?'

'No.'

'But I can't just disappear.'

'That's exactly what you're going to do.' Winter looked her up and down. 'Have you got something else to put on?'

The Senator shook her head. She could feel Winter's eyes on her … on the blue suit, the silk blouse, the tailored jacket, the heeled court shoes. A uniform. Pretty much the only one the Senator had ever worn. 'I've got some sneakers,' she said, 'for when I go to the gym.'

Not that she ever went to the gym, but she wasn't going to admit that to the extreme sports fanatic.

'How fast can you run?'

The Senator stared. 'Is that a serious question?'

'Obviously. Can you even run at all?'

The Senator thought about it. She hated running. She never ran. In fact, she couldn't remember the last time she had broken into a run. Could she run if her life depended on it?

'Sure,' she said.

'Good,' said Winter. 'Get those trainers on because you're going to need them. We'll get you some clothes on the move.'

The Senator hurried out of her court shoes and felt herself shrink three inches. In the mirror, she could see Winter's eyes flicking over her. Down her legs to her ankles and back up to her face.

'Have you ever had a woman?' said Winter.

The Senator thought about this. She had had a husband and a career. She had never had a woman.

'No,' she said, putting one foot in a sneaker.

'Just an idea,' said Winter. 'To pass the time. It's going to be a long night.'

The Senator paused. She couldn't remember the last time someone had come on to her. Then she thought about what the voters would say about a sixty-year-old political veteran and a twenty-one-year-old girl. There was no doubt where public opinion would judge the balance of power lay. And public opinion would be a hundred per cent wrong. The Senator weighed what she had to lose against what she stood for. She picked up the remote and turned the TV to silent. She had spent her life standing up to coercive control. She couldn't let it go now.

'That was an inappropriate comment,' she said. 'Under

the circumstances.'

'Why?'

'Because I am dependent on you for my life.'

'Right.'

'I want an apology.'

'Why?'

The Senator stared at the wall. 'Do you understand the idea of coercive control?'

'Not really.'

'When you get pressured to do something you don't want to do.'

'That doesn't really happen.'

The Senator looked at her. 'Hypothetically, what would you do if someone tried to pressure you into having sex?'

'Are they cute, hypothetically?'

The Senator rolled her eyes. 'It is all about respect.'

'Right,' said Winter.

The Senator gave it up.

Winter turned suddenly and held up her hand. The Senator went totally still as if her body was already on high alert. It was like walking into a wall. It had gone very quiet, and the Senator realised why. The skies were silent. The no-fly zone was operational.

It was really happening. Right now, with one shoe on and one shoe off, in the middle of New York.

The thing about *Colosseum*, thought the Senator, was how unreal it was, how like a fantasy, or a horror film – somehow you couldn't really believe it. You kept thinking James Corden could walk in the door any moment and say, *Wasn't she a good sport?*

It was really happening.

The picture on the TV had split in two; half the screen was still trained on the hotel lobby and the ring of steel, but the other half had moved to a giant clock face, the live Colosseum feed. Somewhere, the hour was striking. In the hotel bedroom with the velvet curtains and the silk bedspread, the clock was on silent, the TV on mute, but somewhere out in the world, it was striking with heavy, echoing chimes.

Midnight.

Winter was staring at the screen like she'd never seen a TV before. The Senator looked closer. There was something strange about the picture. The hotel lobby was unchanged – bright white lighting, reception desk, tasteful minimalist Christmas tree, glass doors to street – the cameras had been trained on the same image since about ten minutes after she arrived, but looking closer, she could see clothes on the floor.

Then she got it.

Not clothes.

No one was standing guard. No one was manning the reception desk.

The soldiers who had been on guard in the lobby were lying dead on the marble.

The ring of steel had been crushed.

CHAPTER 9

T HE SENATOR STARED at the TV, at the bodies lying motionless on the lobby floor. She couldn't think.

'*Move,*' said Winter.

The Senator rammed the second foot into her sneakers and lunged after Winter out onto the balcony. The cold air hit her. She stood in her thin, blue, suit jacket, shivering. Winter was already the wrong side of the iron balustrade and disappearing downwards.

The Senator felt the fear surge. The frightened pathetic panic. *Please don't leave me.*

She rushed to the edge. Winter was getting up off the floor of the balcony below and climbing onto the balustrade.

Ten floors up.

Winter held up her arms.

The relief at not being abandoned was short-lived. The Senator peered down. She couldn't do it. She probably couldn't have done it when she was twenty-one.

She swung her leg over the balcony, first one and then the other to show willing. The stomach-churning horror of the last week had been replaced by an adrenaline spike of fresh fear, sharp as a knife in the gut. They were coming *right now.* She looked down into the street – it was full of black figures, body armour glinting in the Christmas lights.

A swarm of army ants. If they looked up, they would see her. She froze.

'Come on,' hissed Winter. 'Don't muck about.'

There was no way in heaven she could do it. *Colosseum* was going to have a really short hunt this time. She turned so her stomach faced the railings. She got down on her knees hugging the edge of the balcony. She slithered and slid and hung. The edge cut into her armpits, grazed her chin. Her legs dangled, cold air rushed up her skirt.

She dropped, and Winter caught and immediately released her, propelling the Senator forward. The balcony floor slammed up to meet her, shockingly hard, leaving her gasping and winded.

I did it.

She got to her hands and knees and felt grit through her thin skirt.

A hand in her armpit yanked her upright. Winter's bright green eyes were six inches from hers. She put her finger to her lips. The Senator nodded; she didn't need telling.

The balcony door opened onto an empty hotel room. The air was stale. The air of a room not occupied for a while. The whole hotel was unoccupied. A concrete castle to hide in, a concrete prison to get trapped in.

Winter opened the bedroom door onto a red corridor and looked out. The gun was back in her hand. They were directly below the Senator's room, one floor down. Winter beckoned, and they inched along the bright, silent corridor, slowly, slowly, until they reached the fire door that led to the back stairs which ran from basement to roof. A stone stairwell. Not part of the public areas. Emergency lighting and dust bunnies. Cold air hit them; the temperature was lower than the rest of the hotel.

Now the stone was echoing with the sound of footsteps from below. Several pairs of booted footsteps running up the stairs towards them. They were close, a turn in the stair away at most. The Senator shrank back into the brightly lit red corridor, but Winter's hand pulled her forwards through the door and into a cupboard in the stairwell. It was pitch-black and full of mops and the smell of bleach. There was no handle on the inside. Winter pulled the door to, just as the booted footsteps reached them.

Hunters in black body armour.

The Senator watched them pound past through a crack in the door.

Winter's face was frozen, a finger to her lips. The Senator really didn't need telling. The sound of boots receded. They had gone to the floor above. The floor she had been on a minute ago. They knew exactly where to go. They knew exactly what room she'd been in.

Winter pushed the cupboard door open. More booted footsteps were coming up the stairs. Another wave of hunters. From above came a deafening burst of automatic gunfire. It filled the stairwell, echoing down the walls, louder than an earthquake or a bomb exploding. Deafening. The Senator cowered back into the cupboard, ears ringing. They were trapped. Men below. Men above, blowing the door of her room to pieces.

'Come on,' said Winter. 'We need to move it. We need to get past before they come back out.' She didn't so much hear the words as read Winter's lips, see the urgency on her face.

Past?

The pounding feet of the second wave of hunters was just below them now. The Senator caught a glimpse of a black sleeve, and she tore up the stairs, hugging the wall.

Five flights later, her thighs were burning and her breath coming in great heaving gasps.

The gunfire had stopped. A door on the stairwell below them banged, and booted footsteps filled the stone space, hammering up the stairs towards them.

Winter was waiting on the next flight. 'They're searching the other floors,' she whispered. 'Very soon, they will check the roof. We need to move it.'

The Senator tried to accelerate. The ringing in her ears was easing off slightly, but the muscles in her calves burned, her head swam. She wished she were fitter. Her husband jogged every day, even in New York. She knew other senators and staff from her office who had run the New York marathon. She'd always thought they were mad. She'd never thought, one day, she might need to run up a building fast enough to save her life.

They were reaching the top – the gap in the stairs above them had a foreshortened look – and then they had arrived. There was a fire escape door to the roof, with a green running man above it. *The running man*, she thought. Like the book. The glass panel said *Break in an Emergency*. Was it an emergency? The Senator wanted to laugh. Her thighs were heavy with lactic acid. Her lungs hurt.

Winter opened the stairwell cupboard, yanked her inside and pulled the door to behind them. They waited in panting, sweaty, wide-eyed silence as the footsteps on the stairs got closer and closer. Winter had the gun out. There was hardly room for it with the long barrel of the silencer. It was unlike any gun the Senator had ever come across and she was an expert. What she had taken for a silencer was an extension of the gun. Making it the longest handgun the Senator had ever seen and, presumably therefore, the most accurate. The longer the barrel, the straighter the bullet flew, and the more accurate the shot. It was why sniper rifles were so long. The two and a half inch barrels on the average housewife's handgun couldn't hit a target in the same room. She knew – she had tried them out.

The hunters came into view through the crack in the door. They went straight to the fire exit. They were standing right outside the cupboard door – so close she could have reached out – looking at the roof access. They could see it was locked down tight, emergency smash-glass still intact. The Senator felt the tension in the still figure beside her.

There was some murmuring and disagreement, then one of the hunters smashed the glass and pushed open the fire door and all the alarms in the building went off. The Senator wondered why the gunfire hadn't set the sirens off before and felt the hysteria bubble up again. They waited, ears ringing with gunfire and sirens, half-crouched in the cupboard, watching the hunters disappear out through the fire door.

'Did you notice the headcams?' whispered Winter.

No, she hadn't noticed the headcams.

'Everything is being transmitted live.'

A moment later, and the hunters were back from the roof and tearing down the stairwell. Winter held up her hand.

Wait. Breathe. Wait some more.

Winter pushed the cupboard door open slowly and edged across to the fire door. She held her finger to her lips. They eased through, the Senator first and then Winter, closing the door slowly, slowly behind them.

The night air hit the Senator's sweaty face. She looked round. It was a whole other world up here. If she had pictured what the top of the building would look like, she would have got nowhere near. It was filthy, a shocking contrast to the pristine five-star interior. She had seen a documentary once about the wildlife that lived on the Brooklyn Bridge. The underside had been rusty and dusty, full of years of pollution. The roof of the hotel looked like that. Nothing was flat. There were air-conditioning units and huge metal ducts and railings and grass and other bits of scraggy green clinging to life in the inhospitable environment.

Just like her.

The air was ice-cold. It was a beautiful night. She wondered how high they were. Twenty storeys at least. The fire alarm in the building was muffled by the insulation, but now she could hear the street sirens. It sounded like every cop in the precinct was heading their way. She wanted to feel encouraged. But she didn't. What could they do? They couldn't defend her against teams and teams of heavily armed men. What would the NYPD do? It was a hostage situation in reverse.

Secure the perimeter – protect the public.

Secure the interior perimeter – remove any public.

Open channel of dialogue.

Winter had put the gun away and was threading a thin

cord around her waist. She clipped it with a metal carabiner like a mountaineer. She hauled the rest of the cord out of her rucksack and showed it to the Senator.

'High-tensile steel,' she said. 'You could hang a thousand kilos off this.'

She looped the other end around the Senator and yanked.

'Come on,' she said. She slung her rucksack onto her shoulder and walked to the edge.

The miracle that had got them this far looked like it was coming to an end. Was Winter going to try and lower the Senator down?

Below them, gunmen were searching the rooms, floor by floor. Soon they would know the Senator wasn't there. They would know she hadn't escaped out the bottom. She shivered in her thin, blue, voter-neutral suit. The warmth of the run had worn off. She was coming out in goosebumps. She started to shake.

Winter climbed up on the ledge.

The Senator joined her. They could see all the way along the rooftops of 86th Street. Dark shadowy rooftops, the edges lit up by the streets below. There could be hunters behind every air-conditioning unit.

The building opposite was a storey lower and a street away. Not an actual street with traffic. Not one of the grid streets. More like an alley. But still a huge distance. She looked at Winter.

'I can't,' she said. 'That's an impossible jump.'

Winter glanced over her shoulder at the fire door. 'It's actually quite easy,' she said. 'Because of the extra height. It's an optical illusion. I could do it on a skateboard.'

The Senator stared.

Optical illusion. Was she mad?

'I am going to jump and then you are going to jump, and if you fall, you will be attached to me by a rope and I will pull you up. Simple. No sweat.'

There was a brick wall all the way around the edge of the roof across the street. It was difficult to estimate from above, but it looked waist-height. If she missed, she would impale herself on it, a massive blow to the stomach, internal haemorrhaging, the works. Would it be better to fall short and go smack against the side of the building and hope Winter had the strength to take her weight?

'Won't I just pull you over the edge?'

Winter shrugged. 'Depends how good the lip is to be honest … and if I can still control the rope after taking the force around my waist and chest. You're not heavy though. Forty-five kilos I'm guessing. Should be OK. But preferably – don't fall short.'

The Senator looked across at the building opposite.

'I can't do it,' she said. And though it was only four little words, she was more certain of them than she had been of anything in her whole life.

Winter pulled her rucksack off her shoulder again and rummaged around.

'The problem is,' she said, looking back across the roof at the fire door. 'I really don't have the time to psych you up. We need to go. I was hoping not to have to use this so soon because you can't have more than one of these in twenty-four hours, and it's not advised when adrenaline levels are already elevated.'

She moved the Senator's jacket aside with one hand

and gripped her shoulder. 'Don't move, whatever you do,' she said, and stabbed down into the Senator's chest, through her silk blouse, through her cotton bra. The Senator felt the sharp, piercing spike of a fat needle then a burn like fire spreading out from her chest, down her arms, down her legs.

'Adrenaline,' said Winter. 'Hold still for God's sake.'

The needle pulled out and Winter stood, gripping the Senator's shoulder and watching her.

The Senator felt like the Hulk, too big for her skin and angry. She looked across at the building opposite.

Winter let go of her shoulder. 'Do you want me to do it backwards?' she said. 'Would it make you feel better?'

No, it would not make her feel better.

The Senator shook her head.

'You must roll, understand? Copy me. You are no good to me with a broken ankle.'

'Go,' the Senator said. 'I will follow.'

Winter leapt. Her elbows came high and her hair streamed out, one leg was bent and one leg straight like she was cycling in mid-air and then she landed and rolled instantly onto her shoulder and up again. Like a sideways roly-poly. The cord joining them pulled tight.

The Senator could do it. She knew she could do it. It was all in the mind. The fear, the danger, were just an illusion.

She leapt.

CHAPTER 10

THERE WAS A moment in mid-air when the Senator's brain went, *You can't do this*, and then the lip of the building opposite was rising up to meet her and she was going to slam straight into it and then she landed both feet together and hurtled forwards.

She tried to turn to take it on the shoulder like she had seen Winter do but landed hip, forearm, head. Her ear smacked down and she lay winded, ringing with pain. The shock was sharp. Her heart was racing in her chest. She was going to have a heart attack.

Through the roar in her ears, she could hear the street sirens. Legs wearing jeans straddled her. Winter rolled the Senator over like a ragdoll and fiddled with her waist. She was unclipping the line. Then she rolled her back again pulling the line free from underneath. Rough and ready.

The Senator levered herself up onto her hands, then her knees. Her pantyhose had had it. She rested on all fours, head hanging down, hair grazing the concrete. Her jaw hurt, her ears were ringing.

Winter yanked her up with a hand under the armpit and dragged her across the roof to some kind of metal duct. Square and aluminium and as big as a car, if the car was standing on end. Next to it was a metal box the size of a garage, one side entirely grill. Some kind of massive ventilation unit. There was dust and dirt all along the grill. A narrow gully like a valley stretched away between the duct and the ventilation unit. Winter pushed the Senator face forwards into the valley, and she fell – hands and then knees again.

'The headcams are the key,' Winter said. 'That gives us our edge. We need to get to a TV. Wait here.' And she disappeared around the end of the ventilation unit and out of sight.

The Senator eased awkwardly back on to her heels and propped herself up against the warm, sloping metal. Every bone in her sixty-year-old body felt broken. Her ears rang. Her chin stung from where she had grazed it on the edge of the hotel balcony. She couldn't believe Winter thought they had any kind of edge. The stupid arrogance of youth.

She stared up at the night sky. There were stars. You never saw stars in New York. She wondered if she was dreaming, having some kind of hallucination. She was warm again, the shivering had been replaced by hot, sweaty panic. Her heart was still racing, the panic charging round her body. That was the thing about adrenaline. The fight or flight hormone. Manufactured by the body to cope with extreme situations. And she had been given an extra load. A double helping, and it was amazing what it had done. Overridden her brain function. Sent power to her muscles. She could hardly believe she had made that jump, and maybe that was the point, no one else would believe she could have made it either. She understood now why they had waited to let the hunters break the seal on the fire door and check the roof. The searchers had to find the seal intact.

She rested her head against the warm metal, maybe she could stay here until the sun rose. Would she see the sun rise? It was seven hours until sunrise – 7.17 a.m. Hours away. An impossibly long time. She had had sixty years. They had gone quicker. Tears pricked the corners of her eyes. She knew what Anna would say. *Time to pray.*

The Senator was not particularly religious. Intellectually, she knew there was no supreme being directing the world's events and yet, it was hard, when the chips were down, not to appeal to a higher power – fate or destiny.

What would the Senator give to live? Just about anything.

Please, please, let me survive.

Who was she asking? Who was that prayer addressed to? Walter could have told her – Fortuna, the Romans called her or Tyche in the Greek, the fickle controller of unpredictable fortune, the personification of chance. She could bring you luck or not. You made a bargain with her every time you bartered for some result. It was what Anna would have done.

Anna had a superstitious streak a mile wide. She was open as the sky to any theory. 'It's obvious there is more we don't know,' she would say. 'I'm not talking about the religious fairy stories man has invented for himself but the fundamental lesson of history – be it gravity or molecular structure or the fact that the earth is not flat, there is always something massive we don't know. For our generation, that is religion. The human experience is extraordinary, filled with symbolism and significance and fate.'

'Your fate is my coincidence,' the Senator would reply. 'There is no higher force to appeal to.'

A silhouette appeared round the corner, as dark as the Colosseum Adjudicator – Winter was back.

'Who's Anna?' said Winter.

'No one,' said the Senator quickly. Had she spoken aloud? She was talking to herself again. Not good.

Winter pulled her to her feet. The Senator tried to see across to the rooftop of the building opposite, but the ventilation shaft was in the way. Winter hauled her stumbling and tripping round the metal duct, across a flat bit of roof to a chimney with a lid, like a submarine hatch. The lid was open.

'Service hatch,' said Winter. 'Bit of luck.'

The Senator peered down inside the long chimney. There was a thin metal ladder stretching down into the depths.

'Ladder,' said Winter. 'No problem.'

The Senator hated her. A sudden unexpected blast of visceral hatred. She felt like her mother now Alzheimer's had stripped away the veneer of manners and social graces. Her mother hated everyone. And she told them all on a regular basis. She had never been so happy in her whole life. Able to give free rein to her emotions at last, the perennial cloud of diffuse disappointment gone.

Now the Senator was in the same boat. Given free rein by the proximity of death. Liberated. And she hated this stupid, arrogant, overgrown teenager.

The chimney was only waist-high but awkward to climb. She scrambled and clambered in her pencil skirt until Winter got hold of her hips, yanked the skirt up hard and shoved her upwards. It was like being given a wedgie in the playground. She balanced on the chimney edge and peered

down. It was pitch-dark. There was a ladder there somewhere apparently.

'Go ON,' said Winter. 'Stop dawdling.'

The Senator rotated somehow on the lip, got a leg over
the edge into the dark and felt for the ladder. She got a foot
on the top rung then her other leg over and a second foot
on. The icy metal of the rail bit into her palm. Instantly,
Winter was climbing in beside her and yanking the lid
closed over their heads. The darkness was absolute. The
Senator froze.

'I'll go on ahead,' said Winter. 'I'm just fixing the lock.'

The Senator stayed right where she was, clinging to the
thin rail high above the yawning drop. How was Winter
going to go on ahead?

By climbing right over the top of her that was how.
Squashing her against the ladder, banging her face up
against the metal, smacking her ankle.

Stupid bitch.

For a moment, Winter's hands had been on the rung
above and Winter's feet were on the rung by the Senator's
waist and then she had swung down and past nearly
knocking them both off into the void. The Senator clung to
the thin rail, her heart hammering, her breath coming in a
half sob.

'Come ON,' hissed Winter. 'Let's go.'

The Senator could hear her disappearing down the
ladder fast. Almost like Winter was falling. She pried her
face away from the rail and took a step down and then
another and then another.

'*Hurry up,*' said Winter from below.

The Senator looked down. Winter seemed to be standing at the bottom of the shaft. Her white, upturned face was just visible.

The Senator imagined the hunters getting to the end of their search, going out onto the hotel roof, looking at the gap across the alley, making the jump, coming round the ventilation duct and finding a service hatch. Trying to lift it.

She hurried downwards, her long nails scraping the side as she gripped the metal, her forehead banging on the rungs.

There was the sound of a door being kicked in below her and the shaft flooded with light. She screwed her eyes tight shut, pressed her cheek to the ladder. When she opened her eyes, she saw she wasn't far from the bottom. She stumbled down the last twenty rungs. A door stood open on a maintenance area or storeroom. Broken air-conditioning units were stacked up against the wall. There was a mini fridge with its door missing and three service carts with mini soaps, mini shampoos, mini body creams and a pile of towels.

Another hotel.

Winter was standing waiting. 'We need to get to a TV,' she said.

The storeroom light was harsh and white – it had flooded the shaft.

Winter opened the door and they were in another long hotel corridor. Bedroom doors as far as the eye could see. The décor was blue. The lighting soft.

They stopped in front of a bedroom door halfway along the corridor. Winter fiddled with the handle. She had a thin bit of card in her hand, almost like a credit card. She fed it into the slot. Nothing. She slammed her hip against it. Still nothing.

The Senator could imagine the pursuit, the hammering footsteps, the clatter of armed men sliding down a service ladder, fireman style. Her neck prickled, she could feel the sweat breaking through the make-up on her upper lip.

The light above the key card slot went green.

'What if there is someone in there?' The Senator whispered.

'There isn't,' Winter said. 'You can tell from the handle if it's locked from the inside.'

The Senator looked at the gold-embossed number on the white door. Room 101. How fucking appropriate.

She whispered the words to herself.

How fuck-ing app-ro-pri-ate. Tried them out for size. She couldn't remember the last time she had sworn.

Winter pushed the door open and the Senator knew she was right. The air was cool and still and totally without life. The whole block had been evacuated. She remembered now.

Winter strode in and went straight to the window. 'Get the TV on,' she said, over her shoulder.

The Senator fumbled for the remote control. As soon as the heavy bedroom door had swung shut, the room had gone dark. The Senator wondered if the all-purpose access card would also work the lights, but maybe Winter didn't want that. She groped blindly for the remote control, picked it up, guessed where the 'on' button must be and pointed it in the direction of the TV.

The screen sprang to life, filling the room with bright, white TV light.

We hope you have a restful and relaxing stay at the Shangri-La

A smiling lady in a kimono beamed out from the TV screen.

The Senator sat down on the bed. It had a satin throw on it. It was cold and slippery beneath her.

She pressed the TV function and her husband's face filled the screen. It was like a sucker punch in the gut.

'Our prayers are with you at this difficult time,' said the news anchor.

She stared at her husband. He was supposed to be in hiding, and here he was being interviewed.

No doubt he was saying what they had agreed about gun control in a measured yet decisive way. Open, honest, authoritative. *Three voter ticks right there*, she thought. His hair was holding very rigid. Hair and make-up must have used a lot of spray.

10 people you want with you when you die.

She wished Walter was with her. He was the oil that eased the way for her senatorial wagon to come rolling into town. Sometimes she annoyed people and his gentle British manners made everything OK and his diplomacy smoothed things over when they needed smoothing over. Their working relationship was the rock on which her life was built. And he had been prepared to be gunned down at her side. She wished she had said goodbye properly. Taken the time. At least he wouldn't die as well now. She had the overgrown teenager to thank for that at least.

On the TV, the anchor had cut to some guest expert. A psychologist. A woman with long, glossy hair and red nails. Her hands and face matched perfectly.

'It makes you wonder,' the anchor was saying, 'what each one of us would do if we were a Colosseum target. Would you run, or would you hide? It is hard to know what any one of us would do. Do any of us really know ourselves?

Know what we are capable of?'

Could you ever really know yourself? the Senator wondered. Except maybe at a time like this. Self-awareness brought about by extreme terror. The cauldron of panic, the melting pot of despair peeling back every layer until there was nothing but your bare bones and the will to survive. Maybe everyone should give it a go. Cheaper than therapy. Let the Colosseum Adjudicator solve all your problems. They could do it for couples. Work as a team while you run for your lives.

'It's all about a positive mental attitude,' said the guest psychologist. 'It's an extreme survival situation reminiscent of the days when we were living in caves and being hunted by sabre-toothed tigers. The difference here is: the tigers have unlimited resources. Ultimately, everyone she comes into contact with is going to have a price.'

The Senator looked at the back of the dreadlocked head staring down into the street, at the slim neck, the hunched shoulders.

'What's your price?' the Senator said.

The dreadlocked head turned to look at her.

'What would be my price to hand you over to *Colosseum*?'

The Senator nodded.

Winter shrugged.

The Senator pressed the Smart TV function and *Colosseum* filled the screen. The last person to stay in this room had been watching it. They had come in here and taken their shoes off and sat down on the bed and typed 'Colosseum' into the TV's browser.

The Senator stared at the tiny images. *Colosseum* were

streaming the live feed from the hunter headcams – the picture was split into multiple tiny screens like a Zoom call. If you clicked on any of the images, you could make it pop up and fill the whole TV. You could jump from picture to picture, trying to find the action. *Colosseum* was very interactive like that. It was one of the things that made it so popular.

She peered at the little screens. One hunter was in the street. One hunter was in a red hotel corridor – the hotel safe house she had just been in. Several hunters were standing on a roof beside a metal ventilation shaft, and one was looking at a bedroom door in a blue hotel corridor. The door had the number 101 on it.

She didn't move; she didn't shout; she didn't react in any way. Beside her, the handgun with the long, black barrel fired once, twice, three times straight at the door. On the TV, the camera angle swung suddenly upwards, pointing at the ceiling.

Winter crossed the room and opened the door. The Senator could see a leg and the sole of a shoe. Cold drenched her from head to toe. She started to shake. Some kind of a reaction. She felt sick. The body was still moving. It was trying to get up on its elbows. Winter flipped the gun in her hand and smacked down against the hunter's helmet with the barrel and his headcam came loose. It hung down attached by a wire. She yanked the helmet off. The hunter was alive. He started to say something, and Winter smacked down again, and he lay still. She picked up an ankle and leaned back. The hunter moved about an inch.

The Senator leapt forward and picked up the other leg. It was wearing a heavy black boot. A soldier's boot. She put her back into it, yanking and heaving and dragging – trying to hold the door open at the same time. Together, they pulled the hunter far enough into the room to get the door shut.

The Senator collapsed against the wall. She was going to have a heart attack. Again.

The hunter's eyes were closed.

'Is he dead?' she said.

'No,' said Winter shortly.

She sounded distracted, her voice coming from a long way off. She was staring down at something. It was the hunter's phone. He had been holding it in his hand.

'Get your clothes off,' she said slowly, 'right now – everything you have on. Every stitch.'

The Senator stared.

'You're covered in trackers. You're lit up like a Christmas tree.'

Winter turned the hunter's phone so the Senator could see the screen.

On the black Samsung smartphone, a blue dot was flashing in the hotel room like a homing beacon.

CHAPTER 11

THE SENATOR STARED. She couldn't process it. *You are lit up like a Christmas tree.* She looked at the six-inch screen. She looked down at the man lying on the hotel-room floor. He had been carrying the phone. It was his phone. He had been standing outside the door looking at it. And there was a blue dot on it showing where she was. As if she was a destination on his satnav. How was that possible?

She looked up into the slanted, green eyes that were gazing straight at her at point-blank range and narrowing like they didn't like what they were seeing.

Winter pulled back and her hand came up and she slapped the Senator a sharp, shocking, open-palmed slap. The Senator's eyes pricked. Her cheek stung. She brought her hand up to her face. *You hit me.*

Winter's head swung to stare at the television.

On the TV, the hunter headcams were running across a hotel roof towards a circular maintenance shaft. The hatch was open.

'NOW,' hissed Winter, low and urgent.

The Senator scrabbled at her pencil skirt, yanking her jacket, the buttons flew on her silk blouse. She stopped at her underwear.

'Everything,' said Winter.

On the TV, a headcam was getting into the service shaft. As he disappeared down the ladder, he looked up. There were five or more faces peering down, waiting to follow him.

Winter yanked at her pantyhose, pushing the Senator over backwards. They fumbled together, fingers and thumbs. The Senator lifted her backside in the air, and Winter got her fingers around both waistbands, dragging them down her legs to her feet. Winter pulled until everything came free, and the Senator fell back in a tangle of bare legs and pubic hair. It wasn't dignified. It sure wasn't presidential.

How much do you really want to live?

Winter scooped all the clothes into the jacket, put the sneakers on top and knotted the jacket sleeves to make a tight bundle.

'Dressing gown,' she said, 'and wash your face.' She yanked open the door and it slammed behind her, leaving the room in darkness except for *Colosseum* on the TV and the headcams heading the Senator's way.

The Senator fumbled at the polished wooden walls, looking for the wardrobe. It was cunningly designed into the contours of the room, every square inch of space maximised. No handles. Nothing to disturb the sleek, smooth lines. And in the wardrobe would be a bathrobe. The glaring light from the TV reflected off the polished surfaces, turning the wood blue.

She could hear the hunter breathing at her feet. What if he woke up? Had he been shot? There didn't seem to be any blood. He didn't have a mark on him. She scrabbled at the polished surfaces, heart pounding. A sliding door. An ironing board, a tiny safe, a white, plastic, laundry bag – *all your clothes requirements catered for* – a hanging white towelling robe. She scrabbled at the hanger, scrabbled at the robe. The belt was wrapped three times tight round the waist. *Why?* She hauled it apart and got an arm into the sleeve, staring at the door. Her eyes were wide in the darkness; she was listening so hard she could hear her heart pounding in her chest, hear the sound her breathing was making – quick and panicked. *In out, in out.* She stopped breathing and listened.

Nothing.

The soundproofing had been as well thought out as the interior décor.

The robe was massive. Man-sized. Big man-sized. She knotted the fat belt and peered through the open bathroom door – an internal room, darker than the darkest night, carved out of a corner of the bedroom, all part of the maximised space aesthetic, like the interior of a luxury yacht.

She fumbled for the sink, fumbled for a tap. She couldn't even see the mirror. The water was ice-cold. She splashed it on her face – once, twice, three times. Her face was running away down the plug hole. The carefully created public image. She hadn't been without lipstick for twenty years.

She straightened up. Her fringe was soaking. It stuck to her forehead in great wet spikes. Her eyes stung with mascara. She reached blindly for a towel. Her fingertips smacked into cold tile. She found a towel and rubbed at her eyes. She went back into the bedroom and stood watching the door.

Behind her, from the TV, came the sound of hunters.

Suddenly, silently, with no warning, the lock clicked and the door swung open … and Winter hurtled into the room almost tripping over the body of the hunter. Her eyes gleamed in the TV strobe light. She slammed the door behind her.

'Moment of truth,' she said, striding to the television and staring at it.

On the screen, hunters were standing in the storeroom down the corridor looking about. They had their phones out. Hovering bright rectangles of light. Their headcams were picking up broken mini air-conditioning units, a fridge with its door missing, service carts with mini soaps, piles of towels. The Senator recognised a pile of towels. There was a lily embroidered in one corner. More and more hunters were spilling into the tight space. Like worker ants. They were only a few feet away. She tried to work it out. Twenty feet? Thirty at the most. Somewhere between the two. It seemed important to be sure.

The lead hunter opened the storeroom door. The picture from his headcam showed a blue corridor. The Senator stared at the TV screen and then back to the door. Then back to the TV. Now the lead hunter's headcam was looking at the bullet holes in the door of Room 101. A gloved hand came up and touched a hole as if curious. He was six feet away. Ten at most. Just the other side of the door. She stopped breathing. Again.

Winter was standing stock-still. The long, black gun was out, hanging by her side, pointing at the ground.

The Senator still wasn't breathing. She couldn't move. She was too scared to even turn her head. Her eyes swivelled from the TV to the door and back again.

On the TV, another hunter came out through the store-room door into the blue corridor outside their room and then another.

Winter had stopped watching the TV and was watching the door. Her gun arm was raised and her whole body was braced.

This was it then. The final showdown. *Butch Cassidy and the Sundance Kid, Bonnie and Clyde, Thelma and Louise.* She wanted to close her eyes, but fear wouldn't let her. She was going to die in a tangle of limbs and bullets. The slippery satin was going to get wrecked. Spray was going to coat the walls. The room would be full of red mist.

Silence.

Suddenly, the hunters whipped round and stared down the corridor, like predators getting a scent of something on the wind. For a moment, they were still, then the lead hunter began to run. Running away from them down the corridor in a thunder of booted feet. Soon all the headcams were hurtling down the corridor away from Room 101.

Where were they going? Who were they chasing?

The Senator felt Winter exhale, felt the tension ease slightly and realised she had been taut as her high-tensile line.

Winter held up the black Samsung phone. The blue pulsing dot wasn't in Room 101 anymore. It was moving downwards.

The Senator stared wide-eyed.

'Elevator,' said Winter. 'I put your clothes in the eleva-tor. They're following them.'

Winter hauled a bathrobe out of the wardrobe and put

it on. Her jeans and sneakers stuck out the bottom.

She climbed on the bed and smacked the smoke detector with the butt of her gun. Once, twice, three times. On the third strike, sirens started up, deafening and urgent, it was like being in the middle of an air raid. Exactly the same sound as the first hotel.

The Senator looked down at the hunter. He was breathing slow and deep; she could see the body armour going up and down. Would it wake him?

Winter started counting, slow and measured. When she got to fifty, she pulled open the door. 'Time to go,' she said.

All down the blue corridor, doors were opening and people were sticking their heads out. The hotel was full of people. Why hadn't it been evacuated? Surely the whole block on East 85th Street was empty? And then the Senator got it – they weren't on 85th Street. They had crossed at sky level to another street.

The Senator scuttled along the corridor, head down. The back stairs were full of moving bathrobes, the fire alarm deafening in the enclosed stone space. The night manager was telling people to keep calm. His lips were moving, but no sound was coming out. As they passed the fourth floor, they heard bursts of automatic gunfire. It sounded like the rounds were hitting metal, and the orderly shuffle of slippers on stairs turned into a stampede.

They burst out into a reception area with glass doors to the street.

The lobby was full of police lights from two cop cars parked up at an angle on the sidewalk, as if their occupants had leapt straight out leaving the engines running. The Senator felt an immediate, massive flood of relief. *The cops are here*. Until she realised how ridiculous that was. What could a couple of policemen do against hundreds of heavily armed and armoured men? Absolutely nothing.

This lobby had an environmentally friendly bamboo Christmas tree too. It was a giant version of the one in her office.

Winter dragged her across the marble to the rotating doors.

CHAPTER 12

COLD AIR HIT their faces. A blast of heat from the rotating doors had warmed them just as they went through. The street felt twenty degrees cooler. It was full of onlookers and white bathrobes. No one in New York was asleep. It was like standing on the stage at her birthday dinner again and having everyone looking. The stone sidewalk was icey beneath her bare feet. She started to shiver. Any minute now, someone was going to recognise her. Any minute. The Senator stared down at her cold feet and hunched her shoulders as if she could make herself less visible just by looking down.

Winter stopped and turned and the Senator cannoned into the back of her.

The trees all the way along the street were decked with fairy lights.

'I don't see a fire,' Winter said to the person next to her.

'It's *Colosseum*,' said someone. 'The Senator is still in New York.'

'Shouldn't be allowed,' said another. 'Look at all the people she is endangering. She should go to a safe house. There are lots of places she could go.'

The Senator felt naked, as conspicuous as a black bathrobe in a sea of white, but in the milling throng, no one gave her a second glance.

Winter was carrying a pair of sneakers under one arm. She passed them over. Black suede with gold writing, laces undone, the sharp chemical smell of shoe cleaner. The Senator hopped into one and then the other. When she looked up, Winter was already disappearing into the alley beside the hotel, and she hurried to catch up.

The alley was full of industrial trash cans. Cardboard for recycling was piled as high as her head. Winter did a quick scan up and down, lifted the lid on a dumpster and vaulted in. The Senator scrambled up the recycling heap, cardboard scratching her bare legs. She was naked under the bathrobe, and it gaped as she got one leg over the edge of the dumpster, blasting her with cold air. She could feel her core temperature plummet. She slid in and Winter pulled the lid down over their heads.

Inside was pitch-black and squashed. Street collections had moved to an environmentally friendly biweekly and the dumpster was nearly full, leaving a couple of feet of fetid air trapped between the black trash bags and the lid. The Senator lay for a moment, catching her breath with the roof just above her face.

The smell was unbelievable. Rotting food on rotting food. Something squashed up against her bare leg, smearing down her calf. She was naked, apart from a bathrobe, in a dumpster, and all she felt was relief at being out of the cold wind. She thought about them lifting the lid and the cameras and her make-up smeared face and found she couldn't care less. Her standards had melted away, along with her public image, burned up in the white-hot heat of terror.

Winter lay beside her, shrugging off the robe and pulling something out of her rucksack. She pushed it at the Senator. A flash of washing powder cut through the rotting haze – clothes. In the dark, the material felt strangely hard. Some kind of T-shirt, stiff and scratchy, and leggings. The Senator unbelted the bath robe and yanked the T-shirt over her head, braless. She lay back against the squishy bags with the plastic lid an inch from her nose and wriggled into the leggings, pantie-less. It was worse than braless. She probably hadn't been without underwear since she was five. The leggings felt synthetic like sweatpants but harder. They obviously belonged to Winter – they were inches too long in the leg. She folded them up and folded them up again. She took the sneakers off and put them on again properly. Too big. Her fingers fumbled with the laces in the dark.

'Where did you get the sneakers?' she whispered.

'Outside someone's door,' said Winter. 'They had about eight pairs out for cleaning. Probably designer.'

Winter shrugged out of her hoodie and passed it over. The Senator slid one arm in and then the other. It was warm from Winter's body and smelled of teenager. She wasn't about to complain. It was freezing.

Winter pulled something off her wrist and held it out. It felt like an elastic band. The Senator strained to see in the dark. What was she supposed to do? Winter snatched the band back, leaned up on her elbow, hauled the Senator's hair on top of her head and yanked it up into a ponytail. The band pulled tight. The Senator's eyes watered. Her hair was going to look ridiculous. Like a pineapple tuft.

'Ready?' said Winter.

'Ready,' she said.

Winter lifted the dumpster roof a centimetre with her head. Then she threw back the lid and climbed out and hauled the Senator after her. They walked down the alley. The hoodie was long and fleecy on the inside, it flapped open and the Senator's long nails fumbled to get the zip up. She pulled it up to the neck. Her fingers were freezing.

The front of the hotel now had four NYPD cars outside with their lights flashing. Uniformed officers were moving everyone up the street. A guy with a loud hailer was telling the crowds to get back. Someone was stringing up an emergency cordon.

Police marksmen were arriving and the crowds were gathering. Fleeing bathrobes met interested onlookers. Evacuation on the fly. Two different sites next door to each other. The police were hampered by the press of people pushing forwards, phones out, wanting to see the action. An officer shouted into his radio. The street cops shoved the crowds back harder. Sirens shrieked and the lights were bright. New York was wide awake. The sky was full of the *thud-thud-thud* of police helicopters, their powerful search beams arcing through the dark. Were they searching for her or for the hunters? What had happened to them closing the skies?

Winter and the Senator ducked out under the yellow tape, pushing their way up 86th Street going west towards Central Park. They were moving against the tide. Faces eager in the streetlights were heading for the action, not away from it. As if *Colosseum* was some kind of show to watch, some kind of spectacle. Like fireworks in the park.

'Get your hood up,' said Winter and the urgent voice was so at odds with their casual ambling pace, that at first, she didn't get it. Then she understood. It wasn't that Winter didn't feel the urgency; it was that Winter was worrying about how their flight looked. A discordant note – two people moving purposefully against the tide.

The Senator got the hood up. It was lined with fleece and smelled of washing powder and hid her face completely like she was a character off *South Park*.

She wanted to put her hand out to hold on to the back of Winter's T-shirt. *Don't leave me.* The urge to run, to get away from the press of people and the gunmen was almost more than she could bear.

They were travelling away from the hotel but slowly, so slowly. Every few feet, Winter kept stopping and staring until the Senator wanted to cry and scream and claw at her. They needed to get as far away, as quickly as possible. How did Winter not get this? It was obvious.

They walked the whole of 86th Street to Madison Avenue, and people were still coming.

The store windows were bright with Christmas, the streets full of fairy lights, and there was excitement in the air. Danger and street theatre and adrenaline. Like Mardi Gras. It was attracting spectators in their hundreds.

'Get back,' she wanted to scream. 'Why are you even here? So you can post how you were there in person, in at the kill.'

'Have we missed it?' A blonde girl was saying, gripping her boyfriend's arm. 'Is it all over? That was quick. I can't believe she didn't even last an hour.'

It had only been an hour.

Winter draped her arm around the Senator's shoulders, and they walked on, slow and casual, side by side, almost like they were a couple. She felt short without her heels – Winter's hip was banging against her waist. She stared down at her feet. The sneakers were too big. They looked like clown shoes. Winter's sneakers kept pace with hers. One two, one two, like they were doing a drunken three-legged race.

She stared at their feet and the sidewalk, crack after crack, trying not to think about pursuit, trying not to think about running footsteps behind, about hot breath on her neck. There wouldn't be any hot breath on her neck. She would be gunned down from a distance. Maybe she wouldn't even know anything about it or maybe that fraction of time between impact and death would stretch out for all eternity.

She had been in a car accident once on the freeway. A truck had pulled out of the slow lane – the car had spun, hit the central reservation, spun back, hit the truck, spun away across the freeway and come to rest a hundred yards further on, rammed up hard on the central reservation. The whole thing couldn't have lasted for more than ten seconds, but time had slowed to white-hot clarity, stretching out for ever.

She stumbled and tripped and righted herself. She stumbled again, and Winter held her up, an arm hard as iron around her ribs. Her heart was racing, speeding like a chainsaw whine in her ears. Would they come after her with a chainsaw? She imagined the hordes of onlookers, faces nightmarish under the street lights, the chainsaw raised high – shiny, shiny steel – the spray of arterial blood coating the buildings, pink mist in the air.

Every step, every footstep was taking her further away from the hunters. And that was all she wanted. All her hopes, all her dreams had condensed down to this single point, right here, right now:

Please, let me survive. Please, let me survive.

One step at a time, she thought. *One step at a time.* It went round and round in her head like a mantra.

'Where are we going?' she whispered.

'I dunno,' said Winter. 'I've never been to New York.'

I've never been to New York.

She was on the run with someone who had never been to New York. It was unbelievable.

They walked through a scaffolding tunnel. The whole of Manhattan was under scaffolding these days. The regulations were very strict. Boarded walkways to protect the public. Business as usual for the stores underneath. In this case, Starbucks.

Winter suddenly stopped dead. People pushed past them on either side like they were a little island in the tide of humanity. Winter leaned up against the Starbucks glass. It was still open. Christmas decorations hung from the ceiling. There was a poster for spiced apple cup.

'What are you *doing*?' the Senator hissed. 'We need to keep moving. I know where we are even if you don't.'

'I need to think,' said Winter.

She crossed one ankle over the other and looked down at her sneakers. She could have walked straight out of a music video: angular and young and very New York.

'We are going about this wrong,' she said. 'Never run. We need to know what is going on here. And I need a coat.'

She levered herself off the glass, and the Senator felt a surge of relief that they were on the move again, putting distance between themselves and the hunters, but Winter was squeezing through a gap in the scaffolding, hauling the Senator along with her and crossing the street in the middle of the block.

The Senator followed her gaze. She was heading for an all-night convenience store that was braving the gunfire and Colosseum apocalypse to sell snacks to the spectators. Winter had to be kidding. They couldn't stop. They had to keep going.

The heavy metal grill that came down to protect the store was a quarter of the way down as if getting ready to slam shut, but the door was propped open, and through it they could see *Colosseum* playing on an overhead TV in the corner.

The Senator dug her heels in, threw all her weight against the momentum. Her sneakers came off the ground, she smacked into a round, green trash can and then she found herself yanked across the sidewalk and over the threshold, her ribs crushed in a death grip.

CHAPTER 13

THE WHOLE STORE wasn't more than twenty foot. It sold candy and drinks and cell phone chargers and chips and earphones and anything else small and disposable that could be hung on a cardboard display from the wall. Its tinsel was definitely not recycled or environmentally friendly. The TV had the volume up high.

There were two customers – a man in a suit and a woman wearing a silver anorak.

Winter let go of her, and the Senator stumbled and fell against the open fridge unit. Tinsel drooped off one white corner. The Senator's knees hurt from the roof jump or from climbing down off the balcony. She didn't know which.

'Good work for still being open,' the man in the suit was saying. 'Everywhere is shut. Apart from Starbucks. Where are you meant to get cigarettes?'

The storekeeper looked across at the Senator from behind his high counter. A long, hard look. He was black with tight-cropped grey hair. Anywhere between fifty and seventy. It was hard to age him out of context. Was it OK to think that? Was it racist to think he was hard to age? She didn't know. She could just hear the image consultants going, *Keep off race at all costs – it's a minefield.* Just about everything was a minefield according to them.

He stared and the Senator's racing heart thudded. Was she still pumped up with artificial adrenaline? The floor was cold beneath her. The leggings didn't provide much insulation. Her knees ached. Under the leggings, they would be bloody and grazed. She could feel the broken skin rubbing and sticking against the strange rough material.

The storekeeper's gaze flicked back to the TV in the corner. His hands groped blind in the cash register, his eyes fixed on the screen. The hunters were firing hard at a closed elevator door. The corridor was deserted except for the black-clad figures. More and more were appearing, charging down the corridor. Where were they all coming from? The Senator imagined them surging across the rooftop, swarming down the access shaft. Piling up like black sand until every bit of space was full.

'Can you believe it was all over so quickly?' said the woman. 'What a let-down.' She was wearing a huge silver anorak over her leggings and was buying Virginia Slims.

'That's what happens when you pick a woman target,' said the man in a suit. He had just paid for his cigarettes and was standing to the side watching the screen. 'No offence. But how long was Miss Bleeding-Heart-Liberal going to last against a load of assault rifles?'

No offence, thought the Senator.

'Is your friend OK?' the storekeeper said to Winter. 'What's wrong with her?'

Winter shrugged. She was rifling around in the candy display below the cash register.

'You gotta take her outside. She looks like she's gonna be sick.'

Winter shrugged again.

The Senator's nerves stretched taut and terrified. She felt as exposed as a snail without its shell, stuck and slimy on the dirty, cold lino. She was too afraid to speak, too afraid to do anything but stare, and Winter said nothing. Her posture was distracted, the slant of her head said, *Nothing is more important than chocolate right now.*

How was he not recognising her? She had one of the most famous faces in New York. Even in leggings and a hoodie, she should have been recognisable. And yet, she was not.

Winter was rifling around at knee-level now. She tilted her face towards the Senator and winked one green eye. And the Senator got it. It was inconceivable that someone on the run from *Colosseum* would be sitting on the floor of a convenience store only a couple of blocks from the hunters. It wasn't that she looked different – it just couldn't be her. Presumably her feckless twenty-one-year-old protector knew that. Presumably she knew that only too well. *Never run*, thought the Senator. *Stand there in plain sight while everyone runs past.* It was a master class in subliminal messaging.

The Senator stared at the lino. It was ripped and stained and grey and smelled. She wondered about the smell. Where was it coming from? Like rotting meat. Almost like he had a dead body under the floorboards but slightly sweet. It reminded her of that flower. What was it called? She couldn't remember. Anna would know. She could see it now – white, delicate petals clustered like wild cherry blossom.

Corpse flower.

So named because it mimicked the smell of a dead body

to lure the flies in. That would be her soon. A dead body to lure the flies in. Rotting in the ground. There was a hanging display of Christmas-tree air-fresheners. She could smell them, sickly sweet and artificial in the air. They didn't smell of pine. She tilted sideways and her head swam and she blacked out for a moment because when she came to her cheek bone hurt and her face was pressed up against the filthy lino. The smell was worse close-up.

'Get her out of here,' the storekeeper was saying, decision in his voice and urgency. No doubt he had seen it all before. He had seen it all before and just come to the conclusion he was going to be spending ten minutes scrubbing sick off his lino.

Probably make it smell better, thought the Senator.

'Alright,' said Winter. 'Keep your hair on.' But she didn't make a move. She leaned up against the counter, watching the screen.

There were so many hunters in the corridor looking at the elevator doors now that they were having to back up. The action kept flicking away up the corridor as their headcams turned to see who was behind them. Confined space, metal doors, people piling up – it was a health and safety nightmare. They were going to end up shooting each other in the back … if they didn't get hit by ricocheting bullets.

'Why don't they just open the door?' said the woman in the anorak. Her tone was scornful, like she couldn't believe they hadn't thought of it for themselves. *Some people are just sooo stupid.*

'Fire alarm,' said the man in the suit. 'All the elevators lock down for safety and you have to take the stairs.'

'No sign of the cops,' said the woman in the anorak. 'Where are *they*?'

Nowhere, thought the Senator. Crowd control. Getting everyone to safety. Not rescuing the person trapped in the elevator that was for sure. But then what could they do? It would probably take every member of the NYPD. What was the average officer armed with? A handgun and a stab jacket. No match for the hunters with their assault rifles and body armour.

The Senator wondered what it would be like to be trapped in that metal elevator. Trapped in a steel cage hearing the gunfire and knowing it was only a matter of time before the hunters broke through. She had heard of rabbits dying of fright. Their little hearts stopping. Would that have happened to her?

'It was a bit of a disappointment when he chose her,' the guy in the suit said. 'Not that she isn't annoying, but what chance does a woman that age have when all's said?'

'Makes you wonder what the cops are doing,' said the woman in the anorak. She had finished paying and was backing out the door, her eyes on *Colosseum* every step of the way.

What could they do against a small army? Policing was, after all, by consent. There were 42.3 cops for every 10,000 New Yorkers. She knew that for a fact. No kind of odds.

'They should just shoot everyone wearing a headcam,' said the woman.

It wasn't going to be long before the professionals arrived. In fact, given the helicopters, they had probably already arrived and were already surrounding the perimeter. The Senator wondered if Winter realised that. Even so, they wouldn't storm in. Observe and assess. The hostage situation in reverse. And here was where New York was a much better location than the rainforest or the desert. There were professionals here to hunt the hunters.

Winter was piling candy bars on the counter. A Kit Kat, a Snickers, Hershey's Cookies n Creme. As an afterthought, she picked up a chocolate Santa from a display of Santas and stood him on the counter. He wobbled and fell over.

The Senator couldn't remember the last time she had eaten chocolate. She had been vegetarian all her life, but it wasn't that. She had a naturally thin body type, but as it got older and the skin got saggier, fat looked like tiny beads strung out under the loose skin and appearances were everything. You could read the entire life story of a person in the way they wore their hair, their nails, their clothes. Everyone wore a uniform, everyone belonged to one tribe or another, projected a particular message. What message had she been projecting at the start of today? Blue suit, silk blouse, heels – clever, competent, rich. She looked down at her current outfit: hoodie, leggings, ponytail – drunk, desperate and poor.

Her media image. The image consultants had written pages on the subject. Everything was stage-managed to give the right impression. Thousands of dollars spent perfecting the look. And there was far less wiggle room for a woman. Her husband was chiselled and, therefore, sexy with voter appeal, at the same time as the image consultants were pencilling her in for her third facelift. She didn't so much resent it as accept it as a necessary evil. It was what you were prepared to accept for the bigger picture. It was more correct to say she resented her acceptance.

She rolled her eyes. What was *wrong* with her? Even now, in the hot, sweat-soaked final hours of her life, she couldn't stop analysing.

'Any minute now,' said the storekeeper, staring at the screen, and he was right.

The firing had stopped, a crater the size of a small person had opened up. *It was amazing how long the elevator doors had held really*, the Senator thought. The lead hunter braced himself, feet and hands, trying to lever the gap open. Somebody produced a fire extinguisher. They wedged it in the opening. Headcams peered through the gap. The whole world craned forwards.

'She will already be dead,' said the guy in a suit. 'A bullet will have hit her. No way could she have survived that.' He sounded regretful – it was disappointing not to see the final coup de grâce. Not to see the light leave her eyes.

The Senator was used to being unpopular, she was used to being trolled on social media – it was the lot of the female politician – but nothing had prepared her for this. The casual interest in seeing her die.

She closed her eyes and felt the pricking in her sinuses. She was exhausted.

'Holy cow,' said the guy in the suit. 'I don't believe it.'

'She must be in the elevator shaft,' said the woman in the anorak. 'Can you believe it?'

The Senator opened her eyes. The hunters were in the elevator and it was empty. One of them was holding up a blue suit jacket. The headcams tilted upwards. The access panel in the ceiling had been removed. An open black square gaped down at them.

The Senator tried to think about how Winter had had

time to do that.

A hunter jumped up and hoisted himself into the opening. A full-body pull-up. They watched him disappearing, elbows straightening, legs swinging.

'I don't believe it,' said the man in the suit again.

All over the world, people were saying the same thing to each other. *I don't believe it.*

'Who would have thought it?' said the guy in the suit. 'More to her than meets the eye. Am I right? Maybe it isn't all over.' He had a spring in his step now. Like he'd just got some really good news. He stood up against the counter, watching the screen. There was nothing but black elevator shaft on the TV. He couldn't keep still. 'I'm going to go back out and see if there is anything to see,' he said.

'They won't let you through,' said the woman in the anorak. 'I just came from there. It's locked down all the way from 85th. You wanna get home – you get a much better view on the TV anyway. It's like the Super Bowl.' She followed the guy in the suit out, watching the screen the whole way, and the door that had been propped open slammed behind them, and the bell above it clanged.

The store was quiet for a long moment. Long enough to hear the shriek of sirens going past, muffled now that the door was shut. The emergency response massing. Long enough for the storekeeper's lined face to turn the Senator's way.

'You can hide in the back if you like,' he said.

CHAPTER 14

THE LONG, BLACK barrel of Winter's gun was pointing in the storekeeper's face before the Senator had even registered that she had moved. Winter had been standing to the side, watching the TV while the hunters were breaking into the elevator, propped up against the counter, blending into the night-time scene, fading into the background, but now she was front and centre and radiating menace.

The storekeeper raised his hands. They were steady. 'The Senator has nothing to fear from me,' he said.

'When did you know?'

'Just now,' he said. 'She is unrecognisable. I saw the clothes in the elevator, and I saw the look on her face, and she doesn't look drunk. She looks frightened to death.'

Still here, thought the Senator.

'If you had anything to fear from me, I would have pressed the panic button and not said a word. The first thing you would have known was the cops bursting in.'

Winter stood stock-still.

Outside, police cars were going past. How long before someone came into the store? Any minute now, someone would walk in and see a tableau – a dreadlocked youth in jeans pointing a gun at a storekeeper who had his hands up. A very recognisable scenario. Unmistakable.

The Senator could see the muscle definition in the bare arm holding the gun at full stretch. The arm was taut and hard and a pale golden brown.

A hundred years went past.

The arm lowered.

'You got a PC?' said Winter.

It was not the question the Senator had been expecting.

The storekeeper nodded. His hands came down but Winter scowled and they went back up. He jerked his head towards a door behind the counter meaning *in the back*, and Winter nodded, meaning *lead the way*, and he shuffled sideways along the counter and Winter turned and yanked the Senator up off the floor, her eyes never leaving the storekeeper, and they both followed.

*

THE BACK ROOM was small and windowless. Cardboard boxes were piled five high, to the ceiling. Basically, a storage facility. But it was clear it wasn't being used as such. Or it wasn't *only* being used as such. There was a futon and a two-ring hob and a flat-screen TV mounted on the wall. The futon had that dishevelled, rumpled look that said it spent most of its time as a bed. On the wall directly opposite the futon, the TV was playing Fox News with the sound off.

What were they doing here?

'We need to do some research,' said Winter, almost like she had heard the question. 'Find out what's going on.'

Wasn't it obvious what was going on?

In the corner, a PC screen flickered with monochrome CCTV images. The screen was split into six. The Senator looked closer. It was the store. Blueish grey, like it was underwater. Six screens for a store no bigger than a garage.

The storekeeper ran his hand over the back of his neck. 'Sorry about the mess,' he said.

She was running for her life and he wanted to apologise for the mess. She searched her politician's repertoire for a response. She'd had a lifetime of saying the right thing. Finding the words.

She had nothing.

She leaned against the doorframe.

'Computer,' said Winter.

The storekeeper turned to the desk in the corner with the PC and the CCTV and tapped two-fingered on the keyboard. Now he was out from behind the counter, she could see he was small, the same size as her. His shirt was hanging out of the back of brown, polyester pants. His shoulders had a slight stoop. He was wearing carpet slippers. *Sixty*, she thought. *Old.*

The six mini-screens and the CCTV vanished and up came the multi-coloured Google search box. There was something odd about it. She looked closer. The word was decorated with tiny Roman gladiators.

Thanks a bunch, Google.

The storekeeper turned his head, a question in his eyes, and Winter stepped forward. Her body blocked the screen as she leaned in. There was a slight gap where her T-shirt didn't reach her jeans. She had the slim hips and long legs of adolescence. What the Senator's mother would have called 'coltish' with an air of disapproval, although whether it was the long legs or her daughter's lack of them that was unsatisfactory was never entirely clear.

Winter was typing fast. She straightened up and the PC came back into view. Google had vanished.

The screen was showing mountainside. Rocky. Like a child's geography project. A blonde-haired girl on her knees, holding a message up. The crack of a rifle. The body slumping forwards, strings cut.

The Senator staggered. She felt cold and grey and nauseous. Her hand started to shake. Then her leg. *Why* did Avril come out? Her mouth filled with saliva. She was going to be sick. Her thigh muscles ached. She slid down the wall just inside the door. Everything was shaking.

'You're coming down,' said Winter, without turning. 'From the adrenaline shot. Going into shock. It was to be expected. Close your eyes. You are no use to me if you can't run.'

The Senator shut her eyes. The room spun. Her heart rate accelerated. She opened her eyes. She was never going to be able to keep them shut.

'I need to see all the past runs of *Colosseum*, not just the most recent.' Winter said to the storekeeper. 'I need to know what happened the other times.'

'You didn't see them?' he said.

'No.'

'You must be about the only person on the planet.'

'So it seems.'

'That was Avril,' he said. 'Number eight. A week ago. She did the best so far.'

The two heads leaned forward. The back of his neck was shiny brown with sweat, his grey hair clipped short to the head. Winter's hair looked darker in this light. The Senator imagined what her dreadlocks would feel like to the touch. Like rolls of spun wool. What would happen if the hunters came in now? Winter had put her gun away somewhere. They would be trapped. A split-second warning as the bell rang above the door and then the firing would start, and it would all be over.

'I thought Walter would be here,' she said.

'Was that the guy in the balaclava?'

The Senator was silent.

'He never left you. He was sitting against the door.'

'What?' Panic gripped the Senator. 'How do you know?'

'Particleboard,' said Winter. 'Like I said. I only clipped him. He would have come round quick.'

The Senator got to her feet. Her head swam. Her knees ached. 'We have to go back.'

'Funny,' said Winter. 'That was an hour ago. Would he want you to waste his sacrifice?'

The Senator turned to the storekeeper. 'What happened at the start?' she said. 'To my private secretary?' He stared. 'Older guy? Three-piece suit?' She could hardly get the words out.

The storekeeper's eyes were wide. 'I don't know,' he said. 'I'm sorry. I was serving.' He put his hands in his pockets. 'There was someone there, outside the hotel-room door in the beginning, I think.' He shrugged. 'I'm not sure, sorry.'

'I have to see it,' said the Senator, rounding on Winter. 'I need to see it. The headcams. They must have caught everything. We can rewind.'

'I don't think that's a good idea,' said Winter.

'I want to know if there is any hope.'

'No,' said Winter. 'There isn't any hope. And you will distract me from what I am doing.' She kept on typing. 'We need to know what is going on here.'

The Senator looked over Winter's shoulder at the screen. She seemed to be in a chatroom.

'I have to know what happened to him,' said the Senator. She put a hand on Winter's shoulder. It felt hard under the cotton. She took her hand away. What could she say to this overgrown teenager? There had to be a way to connect. 'You know that part when you asked if I could do everything you said without question?'

Winter stopped typing.

Time spooled away. Somewhere a clock ticked.

'OK. Fine,' Winter said and looked up. Close to, her irises were bright green, almost fluorescent. The Senator wondered if they were contacts. 'It's not going to be difficult to find. It will have been in the opening seconds.'

The Senator planted her feet firm and clasped her hands together and breathed in and breathed out. Her heart rate was motoring. 'I have to know,' she said.

Winter pulled up *Colosseum* and dragged the cursor back to the beginning.

The very start.

Midnight.

A dark van interior. Hunters were sitting on bench seats waiting. The ten-second countdown started, then they were bursting through the back doors and out onto 85th Street and running up towards the hotel. They charged through the main entrance, pounded across the lobby, past the Christmas tree, past the bodies lying on the marble and then they were leaping up the stairs. The Senator remembered.

She had jumped off a balcony and hidden in a broom cupboard. The hunters pounded past the cupboard.

Winter hit the track pad and the image paused, a perfect still of the stairwell. A hunter's-eye view. 'Are you sure?' she said.

The Senator thought about it. She wasn't sure. Watching Walter die was going to be harder than she would have guessed before this evening.

'Yes,' she said.

Winter pressed play. The headcams pushed through the swing doors from the stairs and into a brightly lit, red hotel corridor.

A figure was sitting on the floor against a bedroom door, his knees up and his arms resting on his knees. His empty hands dangled. He got to his feet and turned to face the hunters. He had taken off his balaclava, but you couldn't make out his face. He was just a man in a three-piece suit at the end of the corridor.

The hunters pounded up to him. A headcam looked down on the top of Walter's head – the hunter was taller. For a moment, nothing happened; the hunter was nonplussed. He could see the situation, but it was making no sense.

What the hell is this? you could see the hunter was thinking. *A civilian. No threat. But in my way.*

The headcam came up to look at the number on the hotel-room door. Checking the room. You could see the thought process. It was the right room. The hunter raised his gun. An assault rifle, an indiscriminate automatic weapon capable of firing 600 rounds a minute. The Senator knew plenty about them and the damage they inflicted.

Bodies were a mess after. Chewed up. A short burst with the dial set on automatic meant thirty bullets in the target straight off. She remembered how heavy they were, how difficult to control. How the recoil could break your arm.

She wanted to shut her eyes. Time stretched out, mile upon mile of it, stretching away, leaving her in a wasteland, a no man's land of anticipation. Not for her own death. But for somebody else's.

Then the butt of the gun came up and caught Walter hard and fast on the head, and he keeled over sideways onto the floor.

'I *don't* believe it,' said Winter.

On the screen, firing had started. Pinholes of light were appearing in the hotel-room door. Two, three, four hunters were firing. Full rounds set to automatic. They stopped. A booted leg came up and kicked the door at waist-height and went straight through in a cloud of greyish plaster dust.

Particleboard, next to useless.

'What happened?' said the Senator. She could hardly breathe. The words were stuck in her throat like she couldn't get them out. 'Did the bullets hit him?'

'No,' said Winter. 'Any bullet fired from an M-16 would have gone straight through the door and possibly through the wall and out onto the street.' She shook her head in disbelief. 'I think he survived.'

CHAPTER 15

THE SENATOR FELT her whole body exhale. As if every muscle had been tightened to breaking point and suddenly released. Her heart was hammering, but a sort of strange warmth was filling her. On the screen, hunters were scouring the bedroom, pulling open the wardrobe, kicking through into the bathroom, black-clad figures pouring into the room. She could see her court shoes lying where she'd left them. She stared, transfixed.

'That's enough,' said Winter, closing the replay.

The Senator backed away, felt the edge of the futon against her calves and sat down heavily.

'He knew you were watching,' said Winter. 'He knew you had the TV on. He went to his death knowing you knew. Maybe you should think about that.'

The Senator thought about courage and about everything she would do to avoid being in the position she was in and tried to picture volunteering to be in it. Tried to picture doing it for someone else, and she came to a sudden, clear understanding of her private secretary and what was motivating him and felt ashamed that she had never guessed. The knowledge bloomed in her, like a bright golden swirl. So warm and contained and perfect, she could have touched it. How had she never realised? But maybe she had realised, maybe she'd always known. That first night when they had talked for hours – there had been something.

She picked up a Kit Kat and inspected it, smoothing her thumb over the packaging. Four fingers of chocolate, she could feel the ridges. According to the image consultants, there were several PR reasons why you had to be careful not to be seen eating a Kit Kat in public. Some ancient association with orangutan fingers and the rainforest which was so old no one could even remember the details but was still there in the collective psyche, something to do with Nestlé powdered baby milk and free samples, which again, no one could remember, and finally, the ever-present worry for any female politician faced with long cylindrical food – *do not look like you are giving a blow job.*

Bananas and Mars bars were totally out of the question. In fact, food generally was a minefield according to the image consultants. Vegetarian, vegan, carnivore – there were pros and cons politically to every position.

She stared at the red bar in her hands then put one long, perfect nail into the gap between the third and fourth fingers and ripped a jagged, uneven line. She broke it off and peeled back the wrapper. Her mouth watered. She stuffed it in. One bite and in. Then the next finger and the next. Nothing in her entire life had ever tasted so good.

'Get the sound on the TV,' said Winter, without turning. 'While I do this. Find out what's happening.'

TV. Right.

She stared round, looking for the remote. Paperwork was piled on every surface. She picked up a stack of bills from the futon and there it was, stuck down the back. The

volume came back full blast. Fox News was coming live
from the temporary studio set up on the Central Park tennis
courts.

Something caught her attention and she looked down.
The bill on the top of the pile she was holding had an
embossed crest. It was rough under her fingers. *Not a bill.* A
court order for eviction. She turned it over and read the
charge sheet. The storekeeper was due in court just after
Christmas.

Merry Christmas, she thought.

She wondered what the chances were of his having a
decent lawyer. It was years since she had practised any kind
of law and never at this low a level. She thought about good
intentions and what she had always planned to do and how
they had got lost and diluted over time, ground down by the
need to maintain a public image. To do nothing and say
nothing.

Her husband was on the TV again.

Now he was in some kind of a concrete shelter with
screens and phones and people looking busy behind him.
She could read the subtext as clear as day – *look at me rising to
the occasion, look how presidential I am, look what a commander-in-
chief I would make.* His hair was still brushed in that preppy,
careless way designed by the image consultants to convince
voters of his rugged masculinity and no-nonsense style.

'I am in close communication with the Director General
and everything is being done at this time to tackle *Colosseum*,'
he was saying.

The Senator could practically feel the approval ratings
surge.

'What would you like to say to your wife if she is watching now?'

He looked deep into the camera lens.

'My darling, I love you, and I am praying hourly that we are reunited.'

Strangely, she didn't get any kind of warm hit from the words like she usually did.

'Well, that's a comfort,' said Winter, without turning her head.

'He's doing what I asked,' the Senator said. Not that she needed to justify her husband to this overgrown teenager. 'He is going to step into my place. He is doing what he needs to. Keeping our dream alive.'

She was relieved to find she could still analyse his political performance, break it down by voter categories, estimate how it would play with each demographic.

'If you say so,' said Winter.

The Senator got to her feet. She felt light-headed. A blood sugar surge.

'Could I use your bathroom?' she said.

The storekeeper nodded. 'Of course,' he said. 'Through there.' He pointed at the small, grey door in the corner. 'Sorry, it's a bit of a mess.'

The room wasn't big enough to call a bathroom. It was a toilet with a basin and a tiny hand-held shower with a plastic curtain. It was smaller than her wardrobe. Half the white tiles were cracked. Someone with an unsteady hand had tried to touch them up. The single bulb was bright. The Senator gripped the edge of the basin and stared in the mirror. She wouldn't have recognised herself. It was no wonder no one else was.

Two facelifts and years of Botox had left her face smooth and flat and ageless. Paint it with make-up and it

could still be called attractive. Without make-up, it looked
unfinished. Like a blank canvas waiting to be drawn on.
The hair sprouting out of the top of her head in a pineapple
ponytail and the hoodie made her look younger. Much
younger. About three decades younger. It was surprising.

The Colosseum makeover, she thought.

Was it only a week ago she had been looking in the
mirror in her marble bathroom about to announce she was
running for President? There was no trace of that woman.
None at all.

Now she could get a good look at the leggings she had
borrowed from Winter, she could see they weren't ordinary
sports gear. The material was dense and fibrous, almost like
woven plastic. It felt cold under her fingers. She shifted the
waistband higher. She hated not wearing underwear.

She pulled off some toilet paper and ran it under the tap
and scrubbed at the black mascara smears under her eyes.
The cheap toilet paper balled, disintegrating, leaving a trail
of tissue. She looked like she was wearing heavy black
eyeliner. She splashed cold water on her face and sat down
on the toilet lid. It wasn't that the bathroom was a mess; it
was just old. The grouting was cracked, mould clustered in
the corners. She pulled the shower curtain to her face and
gagged at the smell. Her nails blazed pink and perfect
against the off-white curtain. Polished SNS perfection. She
wondered what her real nails looked like under there. They
hadn't seen the light of day for twenty years. She pictured
them translucent and yellow and weak, like something
under a stone that made you recoil instinctively, although
you couldn't really say why.

Her skin was stretched taut over thin, bony fingers. She

stared at the perfect nails. The only part of the public persona that remained. She tapped one on the side of the basin. *Clickety clack.* The dull, warm sound was plastic, not the chill of china ceramic.

She stood up and peered in the mirror, smoothed her eyebrows. When she put her hand up the contrast jarred.

There's nothing worse than hands and face that don't match. It makes you look like a fake.

How right that make-up girl had been, although maybe she hadn't expected the mismatch to be fatal. Would anyone notice? It was back to subliminal messaging. What could you read from a perfect manicure? Money. That was the most obvious thing. It was an expensive habit. A manicure every three weeks. That was seventeen and a bit manicures a year. Nearly a thousand dollars a year on nails. And that was just the start of it. What else did it say? I am interested in appearances and don't do much in the way of domestic chores.

I am rich. I am kept. I am feminine.

Here was something she could do for herself. She picked up a pair of rusty toe clippers from the side of the basin.

The Senator remembered the summer there had been an attempt on her life at a fund-raising event. It had been a member of staff – the student from Columbia whose legacy had so worried the image consultants. She remembered how her security team had coped, how she herself had coped. There were no similarities. It was like comparing a puddle with the ocean. And why was that, she wondered, when the threat of death was exactly the same? Maybe it came down to the shooter. The student was more to be pitied than feared. She knew what Anna would say. *You can only be killed once – it's the same thing in the end.* She had come close that night, stared down the barrel of a gun. An actual bullet had been fired. Was it a question of confidence? She had had total confidence in her security team.

Now? It was up to her.

She squeezed the clippers until the SNS cracked and hacked at her manicure. The polished chunks landed in the stained sink. Where the SNS had flaked off, her real nail was revealed. Thin, almost translucent. It showed her age. That's what her bones would look like, she thought, when they peeled back the skin. Her teeth were probably the same behind their spotless white veneers. She watched the chunks of polish disappear away down the plughole.

Now her nails were rough, jagged, broken versions of their old selves.

Like the rest of me, she thought and smiled.

Anna

10 years ago

WIND IS BLOWING across the dark water. The ducks squawk and flap. Out of nowhere, clouds have arrived. It is not even dawn and the early promise of the new day has vanished, banished by the sullen sky. It feels like a storm is coming. I shiver in the wind.

Nothing must spoil this perfect day. Not the weather, not the cold, not her. Destiny approaches. I hear his footstep on the path.

The wind is calling my name.

Anna, Anna, Anna.

Do you believe in love at first sight? That moment that feels like Christmas morning and the jolt? The jolt that is tangible, the shot of pure adrenaline, a sudden sharp thump in the gut?

No?

'The thunderbolt' – that's what Hollywood calls it – *I never really expected the thunderbolt,* says the hapless hero and you know, as sure as Hollywood is Hollywood, the meet-cute is just around the corner. The bolt from the blue, the lightning strike and the hero is caught up in a crazy, mad, dazzled whirl and you think, before you've sailed these waters, *You'd never catch me acting like that.*

I remember the first time I saw him. There, across a crowded room. The perfect ultimate romcom moment. Destiny in all her glory. There is no such thing as coincidence. Fate came thundering into town that day and I felt it like a bulldozer in the back.

Apparently, there is an entirely rational explanation for this condition – the brain produces dopamine, a hormone associated with the reward centres, which lights up your pleasure receptors. You crave the rush. And there's more going on. Cortisol, the stress hormone, is elevated. Similar to the body in fight or flight mode, making the brain sharper, cleverer, more able to focus on its single-minded purpose. You can spend hours at a time, in a sea of daydreams, surfing the pleasure wave, scheming and speculating and hugging the thought of the beloved to you like a precious secret.

People call you dangerously unstable, but you don't care. That's the other thing. Love makes you blind as well as crazy. You convince yourself black equals white. You convince yourself you are right and everyone else is wrong. Reality becomes suspended, everyday items take on superstitious significance. Two magpies means *he loves me*, a raindrop getting to the bottom of the window means *he loves me*.

Above all, you want to be the one he loves. The only one.

He didn't love her, the girl from Columbia. I know because I watched him kill her. I watched him shoot her between the eyes, like he had been doing it his whole life. I remember the noise and the bustle and the clinking of champagne glasses and the years and years before anyone realised anything was wrong. I saw her slow-motion fall. I saw the glass dropped by the woman next to her. It hit the floor, base-first and broke clean at the stem and the golden liquid flew into the air and came to land in a shower of droplets. I saw it all because I was watching.

The wind is calling my name.

Anna, Anna, Anna.

CHAPTER 16

THE BACK ROOM was quiet. Quiet enough to hear the shriek of sirens going past in the street. The emergency response massing. Winter was still on the computer. There was no sign of the storekeeper. He must have gone back out front.

'How can we stay here?' the Senator said. 'He knows.'

'Yeah,' said Winter, without turning. 'Surprising. Nothing gets past the small shopkeeper.'

'What if he has gone to get someone? Everyone has a price.' It had been on Fox. The guest psychologist had said it. *Everyone has a price.*

What was Winter's price?

'You don't know much about people, do you?' said Winter.

The Senator didn't know what to make of that. She would have said she knew a lot about people.

On the PC screen, the emaciated figure of target six was crawling up the stairs of the nuclear bunker he and his team had been sheltering in. He had gone in a huge, cheerful guy and come out a wreck. He had crawled out of the bunker alone and been taken out by a long-range sniper before he reached the top step.

That was the thing about bunkers. It was very tempting

to hole up somewhere. Counter-intuitive to stay out in the open. In reality, the safety was all an illusion. You weren't safe; you were trapped.

The Senator's restless eye roved round the room. A microwave. No fridge. He probably didn't need a fridge what with the industrial-sized units in the front of the store. There was something sad about the idea of him keeping his few bits of food out in the open for late-night drunks to pick over. No sign of a wife. She looked at the nearest cardboard box. According to the lid, it held five hundred Santa car-air-fresheners. She tried to imagine how many of them he could possibly sell and what sort of profit margin they might have.

Some of the cardboard boxes were ancient. Maybe he wasn't doing that well. Times were hard for the small-business owner. Business rates and rising rents. A place like this was probably open 24/7. So that meant he had to employ someone else, with all the paperwork that entailed. Unless he did it under the radar. She glanced towards the open doorway. Unless he tried to do it all himself. Banked on a few hours' sleep between 4 a.m. and the commuters at 7.

And she thought her workload was tough.

Now target three was on the screen. His hunt had been the quickest. He had been shot by his FBI bodyguards after three hours. They had put down their weapons and offered to slug it out like some kind of trial by combat, but he had refused.

So they shot him.

His was the only Colosseum death so far not to have been broadcast live. A short delay to let the bodyguards escape. And they had.

The futon was hard. The Senator wondered what it would be like to sleep on. The room didn't even have carpet. It had a rug which stopped short of the skirting board. The whole room was smaller than her bathroom. It was an uneasy thought. All over America, people were living in cramped windowless rooms like this one. Getting by.

It wasn't that she didn't come face to face with ordinary people – she came face to face with them all the time – at campaign rallies and party fundraisers and outdoor public events, she just didn't go into their homes, see how they lived. She spent her life purporting to stand up for the common man and she had no idea about him.

Although once you were in the running for a presidential nomination, you didn't do a whole lot of sticking up for anyone. Life became one long exercise in appearances. It was the same for her husband. A young, idealistic student – nuclear disarmament and workers' rights. Somewhere along the line, he had got distracted. She wondered when that was.

On the screen, the very first Colosseum target was running through English countryside. Winter must have gone back to the beginning. The Senator remembered the first hunt. It had been breaking news and everyone had watched. It had turned into a long-distance run. The target had been a comic. Frank someone. Prime-time TV, his own show on CBS. Not English countryside, she remembered now. *Welsh.* The Brecon Beacons. Nature's ready-made assault course. Winter was jumping backwards and forwards through the hunt looking for wide-angled shots as if she was only interested in the scenery. There was something about the sparse vegetation and rocks that reminded the Senator of Avril's mountain. It was strange, the Senator thought, that like Avril, Frank had decided to hide in bleak hostile terrain thousands of miles from home. She watched him stumble and pick himself up and stumble again. It was hopeless. He was a drinker and a smoker, overweight and unfit. *Play to your strengths*, she thought, *don't maximise your weaknesses*.

The Colosseum fitness programme. Terminally successful.

On the TV, Evan the news anchor was getting ready to interview another guest.

'Well,' said Evan. 'In an extraordinary turn of events, the Senator appears to have escaped the net that was tightening around her.'

The security expert was shaking his head. 'Frankly,' he said, 'it is as much of a surprise to me. At sixty, she's the oldest Colosseum target to date. The odds were already against her and then there was the controversial decision to stay in New York.' Evan the anchor was nodding. 'Right now, all the world and probably *Colosseum* are wondering where the hell she has gone.'

'Is it possible,' Evan said, 'that the whole thing was an elaborate bluff and that she was never in New York at all?'

The security guy looked thoughtful. 'There is pretty strong evidence she was here at the start. Certainly, *Colosseum* themselves thought so. They swarmed on that hotel if you remember, Evan, like a plague of army ants.'

Strange, the Senator had thought of the exact same analogy.

The storekeeper was back, standing in the doorway.

Her heart thudded like she'd had another shot of adrenaline.

'I've locked up but not brought the grill down,' he said.

'Fine,' said Winter.

'And now they are bottled up, almost as if she had planned it that way,' Evan said. The screen panned to the FBI shields surrounding the hotel. 'Is it checkmate?'

The security guy looked sombre. 'We have seen this before, remember? In the desert. And the rainforest. *Colosseum* found a way both times.'

The Senator remembered Ian, target two, who had had facial alteration surgery. He had been caught in a Mexican village on the edge of the desert in a simple white-washed room with a brightly coloured beaded curtain instead of a door.

Winter sat back suddenly and half-turned. In profile, her face looked very perfect.

'The previous hunts,' she said. 'People hid in remote, inaccessible places and they were still found?'

'Sometimes not for weeks,' said the storekeeper.

'Right. Just when the hunt was going cold. The hunters picked up the scent.' Winter stared into the middle distance. 'When they came past us on the stairwell, not one of them was holding a phone. They already knew where you were. Then, we gave them the slip and they needed a bit of help. Out came the devices.' She paused like she was replaying the scene in her mind's eye. 'Someone is directing the hunters, masterminding events.'

The Senator shut her eyes. *The Adjudicator.* Not impartial like a referee, more like a ringmaster. It just made it all so much more personal. He had personally selected her.

'Why did you get eight days to prepare and every other target only got seven?'

The Senator shrugged. 'Because I am older? Or maybe there's something special about tonight. It's the longest night of the year after all, the winter solstice.'

Winter was silent. 'That feels significant,' she said eventually.

'But it makes no sense,' said the Senator. 'The Adjudicator would have had to *know* Avril's hunt would be over by tonight, and I don't see how that's possible. Avril could have gone on for weeks.'

'When you look at it,' said Winter. 'There are a lot of things about *Colosseum* that make no sense. And the biggest one, apart from who is behind it, is why is he doing it? What is it all for? What is the point? It doesn't make money. Let's face it, it's not exactly an advertising model. The risks are enormous. What is going on here?'

The Senator stared. It had taken someone unfamiliar with *Colosseum* to stand back and see the blazingly obvious. What the hell *was* going on? They had been so caught up in the horror of each hunt that they had never stopped to ask the obvious question.

'Money,' said the storekeeper. 'It must make a fortune. Everyone watches it.'

'How?' said Winter. 'Am I missing something? He has all the expense of organising the hunt and broadcasting the live feed undetected. Something which would take millions. He has the prize money. Maybe the hunters even get paid and they don't take in a penny. And just think of the logistics – the risks are massive and what does he get out of it? What's in it for him?'

'Is it all an elaborate attempt to hide one particular murder?'

Winter shook her head. 'No one goes to this much trouble for one murder. Think. What does *Colosseum* achieve?'

'It gets everyone talking? Everyone afraid? The whole world is watching. The whole world is afraid of being chosen?'

Winter frowned. 'It reminds me of something. I just can't put my finger on it. Almost like a game. A riddle. Like those old-fashioned escape room challenges where you have to solve the puzzle and break out. Do you get that?'

The Senator stared at her jagged nails. 'No,' she said. 'I'm stuck on terror.'

'You're feeling better,' said Winter.

Not really, thought the Senator.

But she was. She could feel some slight cognitive function returning. She was no less terrified, but now, it seemed that there might be something more going on. A problem to solve. A puzzle. There was a chance that there was a reason for all this, that *Colosseum* wasn't just mindless sport, that there was more to it. Even a million-to-one chance was still a chance. And then there was Walter. The image of him sitting, unarmed, against her hotel-room door, burned into her skull. It was unbelievable. It was the bravest thing she'd ever seen.

CHAPTER 17

O N THE TV, Evan the anchor was teeing up another interview. They were still broadcasting out of the temporary facilities put up for the concert in the park. They probably couldn't believe their luck. A ready-made TV studio less than a mile from the action. The picture shifted from the street to the studio and the new interviewee – a blonde woman. She didn't look like a security expert.

It was Avril, back from the dead.

Then the mists cleared, the picture resolved itself and there, under the harsh TV spotlights, was Avril's mother. No longer howling her misery on a Croatian mountain but groomed and made-up in a TV studio less than a mile away. The brown roots that had started to show through during Avril's hunt were gone. She barely looked forty.

There was an intro, a montage of Avril's final moments: the two women saying goodbye, Avril's final Instagram post. The music rose to a crescendo. The Senator felt her eyes prick just like she was supposed to.

'Thank you for being with us. This must be a very hard time for you,' Evan said.

Vulture, thought the Senator.

The camera homed in on Avril's mother, no doubt hoping for tears.

'Yes,' she said.

Silence.

Evan scrambled to fill the live TV void.

'How d'you think the Senator is feeling right now?'

For a moment, Avril's mother didn't answer. She looked straight at the camera and the Senator held her breath.

'I hope she is feeling strong,' she said.

Evan smiled the fake TV smile that news anchors use when a live interview is not going according to plan. 'But probably terrified,' he said.

'Strong,' said Avril's mother. 'I hope she is rising to the challenge.' She leaned forward and looked down the barrel of the TV lens. 'If she is watching this, I want to tell her to rise to the *challenge*.'

'Curious,' said Winter. She pulled up Avril's hunt on the PC.

Avril and her mother were saying goodbye, forehead to forehead. Winter rewound and played it again. Then she rewound and played it for a third time. She sat back, staring at the screen.

'Why did she come out?' she demanded.

'Maybe death was preferable,' said the Senator. 'She was buried alive in there. Maybe she started seeing things. They said the electric had been out for twenty days. Can you imagine? She had been grubbing around in the pitch-dark for twenty days. No wonder she came out. Probably anything was better than waiting to starve to death.'

Winter scowled. She pushed away from the screen, she pulled in close again. She went back to Avril's final moments. The message held high, the mother pounding up the path, Avril collapsing face-first in the dust. Winter muttered under her breath. Avril seemed to be affecting her more than all the others put together. The storekeeper stood with his hands in his pockets.

Winter spun round. '*Why* did she come out?'

The Senator shrugged helplessly. Nobody knew. She shuffled her feet in the massive sneakers. 'She couldn't stand it. Can you imagine what it was like for her? Someone like that? Never alone. She probably went mad.' She felt her eyes prick. She didn't know who she felt more sorry for – Avril or herself.

Winter pushed back from the desk, stretched out her legs and looked at the screen. 'It wasn't that.' She snapped upright and rewound the footage to the same point again. 'Look at this.'

The Senator watched Avril, her pale face lifting to the hills, her piece of paper held high.

'Look at her hands.'

They were filthy. The nails broken and black with dirt.

'She didn't have anywhere to wash,' said the Senator. Her sinuses were starting to burn.

'They are rock steady,' said Winter. 'She knew exactly what she was doing. There is no way she wasn't in her right mind. She was sending a message to the Adjudicator.'

'Forty days and forty nights,' said the storekeeper. 'What does it mean?'

'It was the time Jesus spent in the desert being tested,' said the Senator. 'She was trying to tell him that she had served her time. Enough was enough.'

'But it wasn't forty days,' said the storekeeper. 'It was only thirty-nine.'

Winter was silent.

'Is it like that book? *The Thirty-Nine Steps*? Some kind of riddle?'

'No,' said Winter finally. 'It was meant to be forty. That's why you ended up with the extra day.' She looked into the middle distance as if she was picturing Avril in the bunker. 'No connection with the outside world. Total pitch-darkness after the electricity failed? How would you gauge days and nights passing?'

They stared at each other.

'She just made a mistake,' Winter said. 'That's all.'

'She thought she'd been in there forty days?' said the storekeeper.

'Exactly. And then she came out. Like it was a pre-arranged thing. Like *Colosseum* had said to her, *Here's your challenge – solitary confinement for forty days and forty nights*. It explains why, in all the time she was in there, the hunters made no attempts to get to her and why the Adjudicator knew her hunt would be over by tonight. What did her mother say? The Senator must *rise to the challenge*. Don't you think there is something very odd about that? Those words. Like she was expecting you to have some kind of challenge, like her daughter. And her being here tonight. Less than a mile from the action.'

'No,' said the Senator. 'There is absolutely nothing odd about it. That is the press all over. They probably can't believe their luck. They actually have a temporary TV studio right in Central Park, right by the action. How handy is that? Nothing better than the previous victim's mother to provide a bit of pathos. Next, they'll be asking her how she felt climbing up the path and not making it in time.'

'Not that,' said Winter. '*Rise to the challenge*. She said that deliberately. It's not a coincidence she used the word *challenge* twice. There is something going on here. *Colosseum* knew where Avril was, but they didn't attempt to stop her. They could have got to her inside the mountain, but they didn't. *Why* didn't they? The running guy. They could have taken him out, but they didn't. Like he was doing some challenge. What was he doing in the Brecon Beacons?'

'Hiding?'

'You don't go to Pen y Fan to *hide*.'

The Senator looked blank.

'He was doing the Fan dance. The SAS selection test march.'

'How do you know?'

'Because I've done it.'

'But what does that *mean*?'

'It means that there is something else entirely going on here. These aren't hunts at all. They're challenges. It means that there is a way to win.'

CHAPTER 18

WINTER PINNED THE Senator with her green gaze.

'So the key question is: What is *your* challenge?'

'I don't know,' the Senator said. 'The only time I've heard from the Adjudicator was the night of my birthday. I was on stage about to announce I was running for President.'

'I thought so,' said the storekeeper.

'I looked round at the big screen behind me and saw him standing there and my name in flames.'

'Not good,' said the storekeeper.

The Senator had to agree. *Not good.* As life lows went, it was right up there.

'Very cinematic,' said Winter. 'He probably had his announcement planned for the next day but Avril jumped the gun and he grabbed his chance to crash your birthday party. Very dramatic. Like the wicked fairy in Sleeping Beauty.'

'Well he hasn't been in contact since; he hasn't said anything directly or indirectly; he hasn't set me any kind of challenge.' The Senator stared at Winter. 'I wish he had. At least there would be some hope. Some kind of way out.'

'He might have told you and you missed it,' said Winter. 'It might be really obvious.'

'How?' said the storekeeper.

'Well, look,' said Winter. 'The fat guy ended up running the special forces training course, the cowardly guy was challenged to a bare-knuckle fight, Miss Social Media was supposed to spend forty days and forty nights alone. It's not rocket science. Think about it. What would *your* challenge be? What is your biggest flaw?'

'I have no idea,' said the Senator. 'I am practically perfect in every way.' She tried to smile. 'I can't swim. Is that any good?'

Winter didn't smile. She turned her back on the Senator. 'What would her challenge be?' she said to the storekeeper.

'I don't know,' he said.

'What is she known for?'

He looked uncomfortable. 'I'm not sure,' he said. 'No offence. Nothing really.'

'*Nothing?*'

He shrugged. 'She's a politician. She's known for being in politics. They are all the same when it comes to it. Lots of talk and no action.'

Lots of talk and no action.

'There has to be something. He must have told you somehow.' Winter stared at the TV screen, at the street with people pushing forward and the cops trying to hold them back. 'We need to find out how they communicated with Avril before her hunt began. What they said to her.'

'Why?'

'They probably use the same method each time. It's probably how they told you.'

'How can we find that out? She's dead.'

'By going and asking her mother.'

'You have to be joking?' said the Senator. 'They know I am alive. They know it was a trick – the hunters are out there right now looking for me. Think about the crowds, the gunfire, the screaming. We can't walk into a TV studio in Central Park and expect to get away with it. We might as well paint a giant target on our backs.' She looked down. Her feet were scrabbling like crazy in their borrowed sneakers, her toes turning in on themselves like they used to when she was a child and her mother was angry. She could feel the panic rising, the hysteria. It was going to swallow her whole like a great snake dislocating its jaws.

'We already have a giant target on our backs.'

'So let's just stay put.'

'What do you think I've been doing here?' Winter waved her hand at the screen. 'How did you think this was going to end? That you would sit here until they got you? We are going to get to the bottom of this. If there is a path through the maze, we will find it. And the person most likely to have some answers is less than a mile away.'

'Can't someone else go?' said the Senator.

'She hasn't said anything to the FBI or anyone else. There has to be a good reason for that, and the most likely one is fear. She is not going to tell some random person.'

The storekeeper's eyes were wide and white in his sombre face. 'You need to get as far away from here as possible,' he said. 'While you can.' He checked his watch. 'Two a.m. This is your chance. Take my car. Go. You could be five hundred miles away by morning. You could have been half way to Canada by now. I don't know why you stayed.'

Winter shook her head. 'It's counter-intuitive. I don't

have time to go into it. It comes down to pattern recognition. Humans don't act randomly. We would think we were fleeing in a random direction, but all the time, we would be making choices, decisions which could be anticipated, be followed by someone who is skilled and trained. Basic military training covers combat strategy, placement of troops, moves and counter-moves. Then the best learn to forget it all. Forget strategic deployment, forget everything they have ever learned and try not to act on instinct. It is almost impossible to act randomly.' Winter frowned as if something had just occurred to her. She stared at the far wall.

The Senator wondered what she was seeing. 'Is that the kind of training you had?' she said.

Winter's eyes came back into focus. 'Yes. Except it went beyond hunting. More like being hunted. It is the kind of training you get in very specialist branches of the military.'

The Senator tried to remember the biography of the hypothetical British agent of her imagination from before Winter broke in on the scene and smashed her preconceptions to pieces. She could hardly remember what that fantasy man had looked like.

'You become the target. They find your biggest weakness and then use it to try and break you,' Winter said.

'What's the point of that?'

'To face down your weakness and rise from the ashes stronger than ever. Purged. The theory is: It makes you invincible.'

'And does it?' said the Senator.

'I wouldn't know,' said Winter. 'They never broke me.'

CHAPTER 19

THE CHRISTMAS STREETS were crowded. Wall-to-wall pedestrians heading for the action. In the distance, there was the sound of gunfire; close-up, sirens wailed. A police helicopter hovered overhead. Excitement was everywhere, you could smell it in the air – human phero-mones broadcasting a subliminal message. *Something is happening, the whole world is watching and we are right in the thick of it.*

The Senator felt exposed – she was a snail without a shell again. No longer stuck on cold lino but out in the open. If the store had been bad, this was worse. Any minute now, someone was going to recognise her and the game would be over.

'Which way to Central Park?' said Winter, stopping short.

She was on the run with someone who didn't know where Central Park was from Madison Avenue. It was unbelievable. But then she knew New York as well as anyone. It was her city. Time to rise to the challenge.

'Next left,' she said, 'brings us out at Engineers Gate.'

Winter strode off and the Senator found herself hurry-ing to keep up.

They were moving against the tide of people still pressing on towards the Shangri-La. The one-way traffic was gridlocked. They kept on down 90th, past the railings of the Cooper Hewitt, past the Church of the Heavenly Rest on the corner. She stared up at the carved Gothic cross.

She remembered having arguments with Anna about religion back when they were still talking. Back before she disappeared from her life. 'We are carbon structures and then we die and our bodies break down and that is the end of it,' she'd say to Anna.

'All the more reason to use the time we have well,' Anna would reply.

That was back when they were still talking.

Fifth Avenue was as bad as Madison. Horns blared. Up ahead, they could see the dark expanse of Central Park and, above it in the far distance, the skyscrapers of the West Side. Police sirens screamed as they tried to force through the press of cars. They picked their way between the stationary traffic.

Any minute now, thought the Senator. *Any minute now, someone is going to recognise me.*

They reached the other side of Fifth Avenue. The stone pillars and metal bollards of Engineers Gate were ahead and then they were in the park, quieter than the street but not deserted, and the Senator breathed out.

The temporary TV studios were set up on the tennis courts diagonally across the park, on hand for the concert stage. A collection of prefabs easily brought in and easily removed. The courts were shut all winter. They might as well be used for something. A little extra revenue. Like the Christmas market and the ice rink that came and went.

Ahead were the twin stone staircases up to the Jackie O

Reservoir and the running track. The bronze head on Mayor Purroy Mitchel's memorial gleamed.

In Memory of John Purroy Mitchel. Mayor of the City of New York 1914 –18

Difficult years to be mayor. Dead at thirty-eight, he had achieved more standing up for his beliefs than most people managed in a full lifetime.

Leaves crunched underfoot, icy cold. She was shivering in her new coat. She had borrowed it from the storekeeper and given Winter back her hoodie. She pulled the frayed cuffs up over her hands. The temperature was falling under the clear sky. She looked up at the stars and tried to remember. How did it go? The clearer the skies, the colder the temperature? Clouds were like a blanket keeping the air warm.

She peered ahead. It was darker in the park with pockets of light from the art-nouveau street lamps. She could feel a hunter behind every bush. In every shadow, every creak or snap of twig. Was it safer to stick to the shadows, stay off the track or take the quickest route? She didn't know.

'In the shadows or up on the running track?' she said.

'Track,' said Winter. 'We need the speed.'

Winter took the stone steps two at a time, hauling the Senator behind her. The black reservoir came into view. The Senator shuddered. She could feel the cold hovering over the huge body of water. Fear shivered up her spine. She hated water. Dark water was the worst of all. There was something in there waiting for her. What was it? She didn't know. She didn't even know where the thought had come from. She shut it down, slammed it behind the door in her head.

They turned northwards and broke into a run. There was globe lighting every few yards, the track snaked ahead almost as bright as day. It was popular with celebrities: Madonna, Jackie O, the Senator's husband. She remembered seeing it in a *Welcome to Central Park* promotion. She wondered what had happened to the police unit that patrolled the park at night. Probably, they had been pulled into crowd control like everyone else.

After twenty seconds, her limbs were heavy and awkward. Her body felt huge, thudding and lumbering along, jarring with every stride. Her breathing was coming fast and shallow, the air choking cold in her chest. Every breath made her want to cough. Beside her, Winter was totally silent, her long stride covering double the ground.

The track was 1.58 miles. She knew that because her husband often went round that bit extra so it would be a perfect two miles, powering along, his security team blowing behind him. He felt free, he said. He didn't even give it up when he became too famous to walk the streets. He just went earlier and earlier, running in the grey light before dawn.

She wished she had joined him. Maybe if she had, she wouldn't feel now like she was having an asthma attack.

She found herself jumping between patches of shadow. Speeding up through the lit sections, slowing for the dark. Every now and then, the path was lit up by a sudden, brilliant white spotlight and she froze, heart pounding. She wondered what had happened to the no-fly zone. Maybe public safety had overridden the operational concerns. The NYPD vs the FBI.

Directly across the reservoir, on the West Side, she

could see the stage and the big screen. The stage jutted out over the water with the screen thirty foot above. They had been left over from the concert in the park and used as an impromptu set for the Thanksgiving fireworks. It had been such a success that there was already talk of repeating it next year. The fireworks had gone off from floating islands, and the Manhattan skyline of twinkling towers had reflected in the water. It had been magical. Now the big screen was dark, but she could still see Manhattan lit up for Christmas all along the West Side.

They rounded the north-east curve of the reservoir and the first of the two northern gatehouses loomed ahead of them. A square stone building. It had been built to look like a mini Gothic castle in the 1860s. Back then, it had served a function. Now it was decorative, a landmark on the reservoir, a rendezvous point for lovers or runners meeting up to circle the track.

They jogged past the second northern gatehouse, a miniature pumping station. The blank, blind windows and doorways of the defunct building stared out. It said *1864* in copper letters above the heavy iron door.

Ahead, they could see the tennis courts and a collection of metal trailers and a prefab that, from a distance, looked like the trailers behind a fairground. A chain-link fence surrounded the tennis courts – a no-go zone for the general public. The whole thing was lit by huge stadium lights like a sports arena.

The Senator pointed. She had no breath in her lungs to speak, and they left the path and crashed through the scrub and dead leaves. The sandstone building of the tennis club was there below them in the dip.

Welcome to the Central Park tennis centre, it said on the door.

They stood in the shadow of a tree, thirty feet out from the chain-link fence. The Senator leaned up against the trunk, her lungs heaving. They could see security moving between the trailers. A giant generator hummed. The broadcasting lorry had its engine running.

Winter's eyes swept back and round, back and round. She reminded the Senator of a deer snuffing the air, poised for flight. Except there was too much menace in her stance. Like the deer might turn around and behead you. The Senator wondered about the specialist military training that hadn't broken her. What would they do to a young woman?

The bark was scratchy against her cheek. Drifts of leaves came halfway up her calf. Under here, the leaves had been protected from the rain and they still had their crackle and crunch. Or maybe it was the hard frost the forecasters had promised. She could see the white plumes of her breath curling away from her.

Winter seemed to make a decision. 'We can't wait,' she said. 'In and out, quick and dirty if need be.' She waved her hand at the trailers in front of them. 'One in five chance of finding her first time – we are just going to have to get lucky.'

The Senator shook her head. 'One in one chance,' she said. 'She will be in there.' She pointed at the prefab furthest from the court entrance. 'That's the temporary green room, where you hang out before you go on. Unless she's still broadcasting live obviously.'

'How d'you know?' said Winter.

The Senator rolled her eyes. 'I know TV. That is hair and make-up.' She pointed at a slightly smaller trailer. 'That is the studio, that is production and *that* – she pointed at the prefab – 'is the green room.'

'OK,' said Winter. 'If we meet anyone, I'll do the talking.'

They set off towards the gate in the chain-link fence. About halfway there, they were spotted by a security guard in a hi-vis yellow vest. He came away from the gate to intercept them, walking across the grass with his hands in his pockets.

'Sorry, ladies,' he said, and there was no recognition in his eyes. 'No access for the public.'

They kept on walking. The Senator waited for Winter to speak but she didn't. They walked right up to the guard and Winter reached out as if to steady herself and then he seemed to fall against her neck.

'*Crikey,*' she said and staggered. 'He weighs a ton.'

He fell with a thud onto the grass.

The Senator looked round wide-eyed, heart pounding. 'What did you do to him? Did you kill him?'

'Don't be ridiculous,' said Winter.

I'll do the talking, thought the Senator.

They slid through the gate and onto the court. It was slippery with rotting leaves. She glanced back. The guard was lying in shadow but out in the open. They had about thirty seconds before someone noticed.

They half walked, half ran across the brilliant floodlit court to the steps of the prefab green room.

The door was closed. It had a metal push handle. Cheap and flimsy. The Senator stood in the shadows, shivering.

'Here goes,' said Winter.

CHAPTER 20

THE SENATOR HAD been in plenty of temporary green rooms and knew what to expect, but it was still a surprise – a subverting of expectations. It was like walking into a living room that wasn't quite right – sofas, coffee table, pot plant in the corner, but the floor was dirty, the coffee table scratched, the wooden blinds plastic. Like a department store window display or a stage set. Fake.

This one was particularly tired – it had been there since the concert in the park. It had probably started out minimalist chic, but now it was just tatty. The black leather sofas were battered, the magazines dog-eared. The water dispenser in the corner had run out of water and old, empty containers were piled up at its base. A four-bar electric heater glowed red hot on the wall. The room was warm, the air slightly stale. A digital display showed the minutes remaining till the end of the TV segment. It was 2.25 a.m. Five minutes to the ad break.

There was only one person in the room. She glanced up as the door opened.

Close to, Avril's mother was less fresh-faced. She looked like a misshapen version of her beautiful daughter. Like Avril viewed through wavy glass. Her forehead was stretched high and smooth. The TV make-up was thick; it was stuck in the vertical lines beside her mouth. It wasn't quite blended down the neck. The hand that held a paper coffee cup was lighter.

Avril's mother saw them both and focused on Winter. Their respective status was clear – a twenty-one-year-old woman trumped a sixty-year-old, any day of the week. It was the other way around with men. A sixty-year-old man always had seniority. Stripped of her political status, people were responding to her at face value. Which turned out to be zero. It was interesting.

Avril's mother looked at Winter as if she was expecting something, and the Senator realised she had mentally grouped Winter with the other beautiful young things that worked in television. She had assessed her, come to a reasonable judgement based on age, looks and outfit and was now waiting for some kind of instruction. It was the external messaging all over again.

Winter was coming to the same conclusion.

'Hi,' she said. 'We didn't meet earlier. I work with Evan. I need to ask you one or two extra things.'

'I just wanna help,' said Avril's mum. Away from the cameras, her voice was shockingly trailer park. *Wanna.* Like a built-in whine. She might have clawed her way out on her daughter's coat tails, but there was no mistaking where she came from. She was wearing a fuchsia-pink tracksuit and gold bangles. Poorly educated white trash. Republican, the Senator would bet her life.

'Did the Adjudicator tell her to go into solitary for forty days and forty nights? Was it a challenge? Did he tell her where to go? How did he communicate with her?'

Avril's mum flinched. It was almost as if Winter had slapped her.

She stared.

The trailer was still. Then she was on her feet, rocking with rage and momentum.

'Who *the hell* are you?' she said.

'I don't have time for this,' said Winter. She moved, and a second later, Avril's mum was sitting back down on the black leather sofa with a white blade a millimetre from her face. It was the same blade Winter had used to flick the cover off a smoke alarm about a hundred years ago.

The Senator felt her throat close. She could see Avril's mum tearing up the mountain, up the rocky path. Shouting, shouting into the wind.

'NO!' she said. It was almost a wail. She shoved Winter aside. 'For God's sake. She has just lost her daughter.' The tears stung in her eyes and she blinked hard. 'I am so sorry,' she said to Avril's mum. She got down, awkward, on her bruised knees in front of the sofa and picked up the mottled hands. 'I am so, so sorry. I was going to do what I could to stop *Colosseum*. I know it was too late for Avril. I am so sorry.'

She saw understanding hit the face in front of her. The blue eyes stared. This close, the Senator could see the black mascara clogging the lashes, smell her expensive perfume.

'Christ,' whispered Avril's mum. 'What are you doing here?' She looked at the door as if she was expecting a band of hunters to burst in. 'What is your challenge? Is it here in New York?'

'I *knew* it,' said Winter.

'I have no idea,' said the Senator.

'What?' said Avril's mum.

'Did you hear what happened to Walter?' the Senator

said. 'Was it on the news? Do they know anything here?'

Winter rolled her eyes.

'Who's Walter?' Avril's mum looked confused.

'The guy who tried to stall the hunters outside her hotel-room door,' said Winter. 'Three-piece suit. Glasses. Not our top priority right now.'

The Senator could feel her eyes starting to prick again.

Avril's mum glared up at Winter. 'Who *is* this?' she said to the Senator.

'This is what James Bond looks like these days,' said the Senator. 'The Best of the Best.'

'Downgrade,' said Avril's mum.

Now it was Winter's turn to glare.

'Your man is in NYU,' Avril's mum said. '*Extradural haemorrhage*. Whatever that means. They tried to get an interview but he was in theatre.'

'Skull fracture,' said Winter. 'Smacked the temporal artery I expect.'

'I need to speak to him,' the Senator said.

'He'll still be in theatre,' said Winter. 'Code black – emergency neurosurgery. They'll have to deal with the blood clot to relieve the pressure on the brain. He won't be conscious for hours.'

'How do you know?' said the Senator. 'Have you seen it before?'

'Yes,' Winter said.

'And what happened? Did they survive?'

'Absolutely,' said Winter. 'Right as rain.' She didn't meet the Senator's eyes. 'So give it to us now.' Winter said to Avril's mum. 'What did the Adjudicator say to Avril? Did he tell her she had to spend forty days in solitary?'

Avril's mum crumpled, aged a thousand years in a split second. 'She nearly made it,' she said. 'One more day. If only she had waited.'

'Was it a challenge? How did he communicate it to her?'

'Don't you know?'

Winter shook her head. The Senator kept quiet. Avril's mum stared at the wall. There was some internal battle going on.

'OK,' she said. 'You're right – it was a challenge. A task. He sent her a message. An email to her private account.'

'Before or after the announcement?'

'At the same time. Only we didn't notice because she was too busy watching her notifications go ballistic.'

The Senator remembered the day of Avril's announcement. *Colosseum* had posted all over Avril's social media: her Instagram stories, her Facebook page. Everywhere.

'Government-grade electronic interference,' said Winter.

'So it was a while before we got around to noticing an email.'

'And how many people would have had that email address?'

Avril's mum shrugged. 'School friends, family. That sort of thing.'

'OK,' said Winter. 'And what did it say?'

'*My first is in threat,*
My second is in hide,
My third ends your debt

deep down inside,
My last is twice in a closed room
hidden underground,
Who am I and where am I found?
None are in Bunker but there you must go
Forty days and forty nights alone to pay what you owe.

Tell anyone and we will have to kill them (sorry)
Love Colosseum'

They stared at Avril's mum.

The four-bar heater on the wall buzzed.

'I *knew* there was something else going on here,' said Winter. 'This whole thing has felt like an escape room puzzle from the start.'

'But what does it mean?' said the Senator.

'It's a riddle,' said Winter. 'You take the first letter from the first word, T from threat. Second letter from the next one – I from hide, T ends debt and O is the letter that is twice in room. Spells TITO. Pretty basic. Final couple of lines give the terms – *forty days and forty nights alone.*'

Avril's mum scowled. 'Not *that* basic. Took us most of the week.'

'No comment,' said Winter.

'So, what happened when you worked it out?' said the Senator. 'Who owns Tito's Bunker?'

'The Croatian government,' said Avril's mum. 'It is part of a national park.' She looked away. 'They were amazing. We didn't tell them about the challenge, we just said we wanted to use it and they opened it up for us. They worked non-stop for forty-eight hours, checking it was functioning –

the air filtration units, the generators. Stocking it with food. It hadn't been operational since the 1970s.' She petered out, thinking about that awful final week. 'She was afraid of the dark,' she said.

There was silence.

Outside, the background noise of the generators kept up a steady hum.

'Love *Colosseum*?'

Avril's mum nodded.

'Unbelievable,' said the Senator.

'But she still told you even though he said not to?'

'She had too. She needed help and she couldn't hide it from me. I'm her mother. She was only a baby. How could she have pulled it off by herself? The Adjudicator must know she told me. He must have guessed. I am as good as dead anyway.'

'Join the club,' said the Senator.

Avril's mum snorted. It wasn't a laugh but it nearly was.

'I definitely didn't get an email from *Colosseum*,' said the Senator. 'I clear my inbox every day, and it is not the sort of thing you would forget.'

'Check now,' said Winter. She looked at Avril's mum. 'You got a phone?'

Avril's mum handed it over.

The Senator stared at Avril's laughing face on the home screen for a moment, then she logged in and scanned her email. 'Nothing.' She went back two weeks. Still nothing.

'Are you *sure*?' said Winter, scowling.

'Yes,' she said. 'There's nothing here.' She checked her public email just in case. Still nothing.

'Unless someone deleted it,' said Winter. 'For some

reason. Who has access to your private emails?'

'Nobody,' she says. 'You have to be very careful about that sort of thing as a politician.'

'What about your husband?'

'OK, yes,' she said. 'My husband and Walter, of course. But that's it. Literally, no one else. I could bet my life on it. And why would either of them delete it?'

'I have no idea,' said Winter. 'And it's not relevant anyway. All that matters is that you never received it. We don't know what you are supposed to be doing.'

Outside the *thud-thud-thud* of the emergency generator choked and stopped. The sudden silence was shocking. They hadn't been aware how loud it was until it wasn't there. A massive background noise that they had tuned out. They stared at each other in the sudden ringing silence.

Winter crossed to the window in two strides and peered out through the slatted blind into the night. The long, black gun was back in her hand. She went very still.

Outside, there was a sound like running feet.

'They're coming,' said Winter.

'They're *always* coming,' said Avril's mum.

Winter yanked open the door.

The air poured in, bitingly cold.

There was gunfire and it was getting closer.

CHAPTER 21

THE TRAILERS WERE in a pool of bright light. There was nothing but trees and darkness beyond the chain-link fence. It gleamed under the powerful overhead lighting. The Senator could see her breath, snowy white in the crisp air and Winter standing stock-still on the top step, listening and Avril's mum shivering in her pink.

There were shouts from somewhere behind them. Security guards.

They crept down the steps and slid round the green room prefab, jumped across the lit space to the next-door trailer – *hair and make-up* – and hugged the metal sides, staring out through the fence at the blackness beyond. Everything was still.

'I wish they would just hurry up and catch her,' said someone from inside hair and make-up. It was so clear, the speaker could have been standing beside them. 'At this rate, we will still be here for the breakfast show.'

There's nothing worse than hands and face that don't match, thought the Senator. *Except people discussing your death like it was an inconvenience.*

She looked at Winter. She was still in that hunted-deer pose with the black gun up by her face. The Senator couldn't tell if Winter was listening to the conversation inside the make-up trailer or listening for approaching hunters. The sound of gunfire was getting closer. The Senator could almost hear the running feet. Her leg started to tremble. Just the one. She pressed her face up against the metal side of the trailer. She had expected it to be warm but it was ice-cold and damp with condensation. When she took her cheek away, it would be wet.

Suddenly, there was the sound of the trailer door being thrown open. A metal handle hitting a flimsy metal trailer side.

'Get out,' said a man's voice, breathless and urgent. 'We're evacuating. The hunt is coming.'

For a second, there was silence, then a screech of chairs and a stampede from inside as mugs hit tables and feet hit floor and scrambled for the exit.

A moment later, two make-up girls in T-shirts and jeans came round the corner, skidding on the wet court as they ran for the gate. They took no notice of the three people standing in the shadows.

'Come on,' said Winter. She set off after them, closing the gap so it looked like three young make-up artists making a run for it, and the Senator and Avril's mum scrambled after her, slipping and sliding on the wet leaves.

They bottle-necked as they came to the gate and then they were through, past where the guard had been lying. There was no sign of him. The waiting trees had a dank, dripping look. The gunfire and noise were coming from behind them and people shied away, heading deeper into the park away from the street. Studio execs, make-up artists, technicians, security men crowded together on the Gothic bridge up to the running track, trying to get away. The boards rang with clattering heels. No screaming, just urgent, desperate flight.

Something had changed behind them – the sound from the tennis courts was different. The chain-link fence rang with tearing metal. Hunters were inside the court. There was a sudden burst of automatic gunfire. *Assault rifle*, thought the Senator.

Winter broke from the fleeing crowd, dragging them off the path into the shelter of the trees, and they lurched to a halt and stood half-crouched in a drifting bank of leaves, listening to the sounds of the city, the sirens and the thudding of their hearts.

Never run, thought the Senator.

It was counter-intuitive. Every fibre of her being was burning to run, to throw herself down the path with everyone else. Instead, she was forced to stillness, panting and listening.

She glanced at Winter – she was crouched, every muscle tense, almost vibrating. She hummed with tension. The Senator swung round, staring into the dark, trying to make out movement between the trees. Beside her, Avril's mum was wide-eyed, breathing hard. Why had she stayed with them? She should have run with all the rest. Winter put her hand on the Senator's arm to hold her still. *Not watching*, the Senator realised. *Listening*.

Under the trees, the leaves were still crisp and dry, away from the trees, under the open sky, they were sodden. Something or someone was creeping over the falls of crisp leaves under the trees.

She saw the truth on Winter's face a split second before.

'RUN,' Winter said, and there was no mistaking the fear.

They exploded out of the undergrowth with a massive cacophony of sound, hurtling blindly through the scrub like pheasants breaking cover. Behind them, the footsteps started to run. The Senator could hear her breath coming in great wheezy gasps.

The reservoir loomed ahead, black and empty in the night. A void of cold air. They ran up the grassy bank and onto the running track that circled the water.

White beams of helicopter searchlights arced across the park.

They tore down the straight in a flat sprint, the terror of being chased lending them speed. Winter in front, then Avril's mum, gold tassels flying, then the Senator. How could they possibly hope to outrun soldiers? They couldn't for long, but off the start, they had a tiny advantage. Body armour and assault rifles were awkward – it would take a little while for the hunters to hit their top speed. And they couldn't run and fire. It just wasn't possible.

They passed the giant screen and the stage put up over the water, rounded the end of the curve and saw a building ahead – the Gothic stone building of the south gatehouse. The twin of the northern gatehouse at the other end.

The air was catching, cold in her throat, her lungs heaved. She had never had an asthma attack, but now, in the cold air, she couldn't breathe. She coughed and choked and wheezed, fighting for every breath like she was dying.

Winter stopped suddenly and turned and yanked the Senator over to the railings. Winter got an arm around her shoulders and an arm behind her knees and picked her up. For a moment, the Senator felt the panic – *put me down* – then the iron railings were scraping against her back and she was being dropped the wrong side.

She staggered on the edge, staring down into the dark water.

Fear, pure and sharp, arrowed through her, draining her of strength. It was numbing, worse even than the fear of being hunted. Drowning and dark water. The ultimate nightmare. She froze, unable to move forward, prevented by the railings from moving back.

The Senator felt the iron posts behind her. Cold through the thin coat.

Winter put one hand out and vaulted the railings and then she was pushing past the Senator. 'Come ON,' she hissed over her shoulder.

The Senator edged one step sideways and then another. Beside her, she could feel Avril's mum doing the same. Winter reached out and grabbed her bodily and yanked her the remaining couple of feet to the stone wall of the gatehouse. The Senator crashed headlong into the cold, wet stone. It knocked the air out of her.

A decorative ledge no wider than a single brick ran round the outside of the building. Winter edged along it, away from the path. She gripped the Senator's leading wrist, dragging her behind. The Senator felt tears sting her eyes, prick her sinuses. She stumbled and shuffled and edged her way along to the corner of the building and round.

The back of the gatehouse was built right out over the reservoir. Deep, dark water lapped the brickwork a metre or so beneath her feet. She hugged the face of the building, cheek pressed into the stone. She was not looking round at the water.

There was a tiny balcony on the reservoir side, entirely hidden from the track. It stuck out over the water. The Senator climbed heavily up and over its edge and clung to the wall, panting and wheezing. Avril's mum landed beside her, knocking her against the stone. Winter was already there, facing outwards, scanning the dark. Suddenly, she put a hand over the Senator's face, covering her mouth, stifling the sound of her wheezing. Winter's other hand closed over Avril's mum. She was holding their faces with both hands. The Senator tried to control her breathing. Her heart was pounding in her ears. Over it, over the sound of the breeze across the water and the distant hum of the city was the hammer of running feet on the path. They had only just made it around the corner in time.

The feet slowed and stopped. Right in front of the gate-house. Only a few metres away from where they were. Foreign voices. Speaking Russian. It sounded like one was asking a question and another one was answering it. They were so close the Senator could hear every word.

The hunters were standing on the path in front of the gatehouse. Not chasing. They knew where the target was. Her legs began to shake and she felt Winter clamp down tighter across her mouth. Now the footsteps were moving around on the gravel. A whimper rose in her throat and she choked it off, pressing her forehead into the stone. The first voice was speaking again. The sentences more emphatic, pauses as if he was on the phone asking a question and then waiting for the answer. Then the footsteps were moving again, not on gravel but on grass, up and away, and then there was silence.

The Senator clung to the stone. She dug her fingertips

into the grey mortar. It was cracked and crumbling. *Built in 1864*, she thought.

'What the hell?' said Winter.

The Senator lifted her head off the stone and looked up at her. 'What did they say? What happened?'

'They knew we were here,' said Winter. 'And they left us. I can't understand it. The Adjudicator told them to stand down.'

'How do you know?' whispered Avril's mum.

'Because I speak Russian.'

The Senator remembered the resumé of the fantasy agent.

Just back from a year in the field, below the Arctic circle. Single-handedly blew up a Russian nuclear facility.

'But why? Why would he do that?' she said. 'He didn't tell them to stand down when they thought I was cornered in an elevator.'

'I don't know,' said Winter. She stared out across the water. 'He is directing events, controlling the gameplay. More like a dungeon master than a referee.'

There was silence. Avril's mum shifted, got her back to the stone and slid down until she was on the balcony floor. The Senator got down beside her but didn't turn. She crouched, facing the stone, her legs shaking.

Winter pulled off the wall. 'We have to go,' she said, and there was something new and upbeat in her body language. Determination and momentum. Like the way was suddenly clear. 'We need to let him know there is a problem.'

Just like that, thought the Senator.

'Who?' said Avril's mum.

'The Adjudicator. The head of *Colosseum*. The Dungeon Master.'

'What problem?'

'It's like a *Call of Duty* campaign without a mission. She never got her challenge.'

'So what? Why would he care?'

Winter rolled her eyes. 'Because she can't rise to a challenge she never got. A lot of effort has gone into all this.' She waved her hand to indicate the reservoir, the park, the Senator. 'This is a clever man, not some mindless thug.'

The Senator didn't know if that made it better or worse. 'So how do we tell him?'

'We call him.'

The Senator stared.

'We get hold of one of their phones.'

'You have to be joking?' said Avril's mum. 'Have you seen their body armour? You couldn't take a single hunter, never mind a pack of them.'

Winter scowled. 'No one said anything about *taking a hunter*. It would be far too dangerous with civilians in the mix. I left a hunter phone in a dumpster in case we needed it and now we do. We couldn't have it with us. *Colosseum* are tracking their hunters.' She turned to face them. 'We have got to get in the game, get one step ahead. These are challenges and we don't even know what ours is. This is where we stop running and fight.'

Fight. It was inconceivable. No one had ever been able to fight *Colosseum*.

CHAPTER 22

'I'M IN,' SAID Avril's mum.

'Guess again,' said Winter.

'Don't you think I have the right?' Avril's mum got to her feet, hands on hips.

Winter shrugged.

'No one on the planet wants to fight *Colosseum* more than me.'

'Sure,' said Winter. 'Doesn't mean you can.'

Avril's mum stood silent, swaying slightly, dealing with the strength of her emotions. She was going through the same internal checklist the Senator had. *How can I connect? What can I say?*

'Are you worried I'll be killed?' she said finally.

Winter shrugged again, a more eloquent shrug.

'I'm as good as dead anyway,' said Avril's mum. 'They will guess I've told you.'

Winter said nothing.

'And I can help you,' said Avril's mum. 'Maybe I will remember something important.' She paused. 'Maybe there are things I haven't told you.'

Winter had put a hand on the edge of the balcony like she was just about to vault it. She turned back. 'Are there?' she said.

'Maybe.'

Winter narrowed her eyes. Time stretched out. 'Get rid of your phone,' she said. 'If you're coming. They could track us through you.'

Avril's mum pulled out her phone and hurled it over-arm into the night. 'Happy?'

'Fine,' said Winter. 'The very first time you get in my way – you are gone.'

'*Fine*,' said Avril's mum.

But Winter was already swinging over the balcony edge. One leg, one hand. Second leg, second hand, then she was gone, back the way they had come with Avril's mum right behind her like she wasn't going to let her get away. A moment later and they had disappeared round the corner and the Senator was alone with her cheek still pressed against the stone.

She could feel the weight of dark water and the silence behind her and the huge block of cold air. Sweat was creeping over her body. Black, nameless, abstract fear. The fear of your own imagination. It was hardly possible that dark water could be as frightening as being hunted. As having to perform some kind of challenge while armed men hunted you down. But it was a different sort of fear. One was real and immediate, the other was a spiralling descent into madness, panic clawing at her sanity, scrabbling to keep hold of reality. Was it something to do with Anna? She had been coming back to the Senator all evening and now she felt closer than ever. A ghost on the wind. Why did dark water remind the Senator of Anna? What had happened to her?

The wind rippled the surface. She could feel it and the

terror rose through her like a tidal wave of panic and she scrambled back the way they had come, scrabbling at the corner, slipping, regaining her balance and shuffling along the ledge to the bank and the long grass and away from the dark water.

The running track was smooth and pale and lit like it was day. Bright globes every few yards snaking away into the distance. Chains of light like a garden decked out in lanterns.

The Senator felt her brain crash against her skull, every footstep hurt. They were running again. Not sprinting but jogging fast, and she was exhausted. She wondered what time it was and why she hadn't thought to sleep in preparation for this evening. Whatever she had expected, it wasn't this. An exhausting marathon of endurance. Beside her, Winter was loping along and Avril's mum was padding soft and silent in her gold sneakers.

They took a left-hand path over the ornate bridge. The entrance to the park on 90th Street and Mayor Mitchel's monument were ahead. They had done a full circuit. This was where they had come into the park earlier. An hour ago? She had no idea. Time was passing strangely. Spooling away from her on this longest night. Like those childhood dreams where you ran and ran and couldn't get away.

The trees were thinning and visibility increasing. The closer they got to the steps above Mayor Mitchel's gold head, the more they would be seen. She slowed and stopped and they stood in the shadow of the trees beside the track, Winter on one side and Avril's mum on the other. They were both looking at her and she realised neither of them knew where to go.

'This is where we came in,' she said, pointing ahead. 'We have done a full circuit. But it is very open.'

'We can't wait,' said Winter. 'We can't stay still. I don't know why they left us. But they can't be far away.'

They crept out of the shadow of the trees, backs prickling, ears straining to pick up footsteps behind them, and scuttled down the steps that led to the street. Mayor Mitchel was still there, right where they had left him.

Fifth Avenue was busy. The Smithsonian blazed with pink light. Police sirens blared, trying to get through the traffic.

They hit 86th Street and started up towards the hotel. Everyone was still going in the same direction. Avril's mum shivered in her thin tracksuit. Winter was looking sideways at her.

'We need to get you something else to wear,' she said. 'If you're staying. The pink is very obvious.'

'It's Moschino,' said Avril's mum in a tone that suggested she thought it closed the conversation.

'Right,' said Winter. She shrugged off her hoodie and held it out.

Avril's mum stared for a moment then pulled it on.

They passed the Starbucks and the convenience store and the Senator had a sudden powerful feeling of nostalgia, almost a longing for the back room, as if she had lived there all her life. She could remember every cardboard box, every Christmas tree air-freshener. She could taste the chocolate Kit Kat, feel the wrapper beneath her nail as she ripped it open. Some kind of survival instinct had kicked in, searing images on her brain with crystal clarity. If she lived to be a hundred, she thought, she would still remember every detail of that room.

She could hear the Fox psychologist saying, *Ultimately, everyone she comes into contact with is going to have a price*, and thought about the storekeeper who didn't have a price.

Two blocks further on, the press of people came to a halt. The police cordon had pushed out. The exclusion zone had doubled in size since they had last been there. Massed ranks of riot police, clear glass shields up, barred the way. They weren't getting through. In front of the police line, the crowd was hundreds deep.

Winter jumped up on a trash can, one of the circular green metal ones, and craned over the heads of the crowd.

'I might be able to get through the cops,' said Avril's mum. 'People know who I am. I could say I have important information from *Colosseum*. Everyone recognises me.' She sniffed. 'Everywhere I go, people recognise me.'

Winter said nothing. She was looking down at Avril's mum as if she was weighing her in the balance, taking her apart and assessing each piece.

'OK,' she said. 'You can try. It's wrapped in a bathrobe, in the dumpster in the alley to the right of the hotel. The Senator can't go anywhere near the police.'

'No problem,' said Avril's mum. She took off the hoodie and did a twirl. 'How do I look?'

'Great,' said the Senator.

'Pink,' said Winter.

They pulled back into the doorway of a building and watched Avril's mum walk into the crowd. They saw people register who she was, react and step out of her way. They could track her passage from the turning of heads. She was going to make it to the police cordon. Would they let her through?

Winter turned on her heel and headed back up the street, and the Senator ran after her, slipping and sliding to keep up. The pavements were slick with the damp, reflecting back the lights. Manhattan was so lit up you would be able to see it from space. She imagined looking down and seeing the dark bulk of North America, pinpoints of light here and there, then the eastern seaboard, a necklace of dancing lights and Manhattan, the brightest of them all.

'Shouldn't we wait?' said the Senator, panting.

'No.'

'She might get it.'

'She won't,' said Winter. 'And it's not safe here anyway. We have to get off the street.'

'But what else can we do?'

'We can go up and over.'

Up and over, thought the Senator. *Rooftop. No problem.*

I can't believe I just thought that.

CHAPTER 23

MIDTOWN'S ROOFLINE WAS a dark parkour course of possibilities.

The Senator looked up at the huge wooden water tower beside her. She put a hand on a rusty iron strut. It was ice-cold under her fingers. She looked down at her feet, another roof covered in scrubby weeds. The bulk of the water tank over-shadowed everything. It towered thirty feet or more above her. It was a wonder any plant could survive such hostile terrain.

Maybe she could hide in the tank. She remembered the homeless man who had lived in the conical roof space of a tank and had frozen to death in the sub-zero winter. The building's residents' committee had been outraged by the hygiene implications. *The State of New York's drinking water is a national crisis*, a newspaper had said. *It is not fit for purpose. What are the authorities doing about it?* The image consultants had been very concerned about the possible political fallout.

Now she thought, *What about someone freezing to death because they had nowhere else to go? Why didn't more of us say that?* It's what Anna would have said. She looked up at the dark bulk, green where water was oozing through the seams. There was something very totemic, emblematic about New York's water tower skyline.

Before this evening, she had always pictured Manhattan's roofline as flat, but of course it wasn't – it was an assault course of brownstone split levels and air-conditioning ducts and iron RSJs supporting the water tanks. Like crossing a mountain range – peaks and valley floors and slow going. Drops of ten foot or more only to move forward a few feet.

It was a whole other world that nobody ever saw. New York was crowded, but its rooftops were as wide and empty as the sky. Not that you could normally get near New York's rooftops. Security were always on the lookout for extreme sports fanatics treating the skies as their playground. She glanced at Winter, standing in shadow up ahead, watching the street. Tonight was different. Tonight, every security professional, from the NYPD to hotel doormen, was holding people back on the streets.

The breeze blew in her face. It was colder up here. The rooftop world that had been so alien was familiar now. She was learning to read the sharp, dark angles, the empty spaces. And the edge of the roof ahead was not empty – it was crawling with movement where there should have been stillness. Dark shapes were clustering beside the low brick parapet, peering down into the alley below. The alley with the dumpster. The Senator's heart thudded. *Hunters.*

Winter was moving towards the group. The Senator cringed into the shadows of the water tower. She clung to the rusty girder. She wanted to shout, wanted to warn her. Terror held her still and quiet. Then her eyes read the messaging, the story each individual was projecting: the body stances, the baseball caps, the jeans, the makeshift weaponry. African American. Hispanic. White. Not hunters.

Vigilantes? Organised crime? Good Samaritans?

Her politician's radar tried to process them, pin them down. Classifying, slotting them into their voter demographics.

There was something unprofessional, makeshift about the group. Like they were there to have a go. Watch the show. Career criminals would have less obvious but a whole lot more effective weapons. One of them was carrying a broom handle with a knife taped to the end of it. She pictured him solemnly removing the bristle head.

The group peering over the edge turned sharply as Winter came up to them. Dark faces looked her over. One guy had camouflage paint on his cheeks. It wasn't working. If anything, it made him more visible.

Eyes tracked over Winter and went back to staring down into the alley. She had been read, processed and accepted. Dreadlocks, jeans, and the indefinable but powerful message of sharp cheekbones, green eyes and long legs.

'What's going on?' said Winter, jumping up on the edge and looking down. Hands pulled her back, voices hissed. Winter peered over the ledge and down the side of the building.

'Oh,' she said.

The Senator sidled up. She had to stand on tiptoes to see over the edge.

A metal fire escape zig-zagged down the building. Their route downwards. Their means to an end.

A storey below and more than the height of a storey because of the stone roof, was the top floor of the fire escape – a balcony made of metal – and lying on the balcony was a hunter. No injuries were visible under all the body armour but he was almost dead. The Senator couldn't have said how she knew – it was just there in the way he held his body, his breathing coming fast and shallow and bloody.

For a moment, no one said anything.

'What's the plan?' said Winter.

'We were gonna get him to talk,' said camouflage guy, 'only …'

'Only he fell off a building,' said Winter.

'Yeah.' Camouflage guy laughed and it was a laugh that said, *I would have preferred to kick him to death but watching him bleed out, caught like a rat in a trap, is a close second.*

And the Senator thought whoever said, *My enemy's enemy is my friend*, had no idea what they were talking about. The hunt was the thing. The fear, the chase, the terror. Right now, this group were chasing hunters, but what would they do if they found the biggest prize standing right beside them?

'How is he hurt?' said Winter, peering down.

'He fell off a building.'

'Apart from that?'

'Dunno. He was here, leaned up against the wall, bleeding.'

The Senator looked down. There were blood stains smeared up the wall.

'Someone had already shot him,' said Winter.

'Where are you from? Australia?'

'England.'

'What? You on holiday? A little bit of Colosseum tourism?' White teeth grinned. He had a gold tooth in the back of his head.

I am close enough to see nose hair, thought the Senator. *Close enough to smell the sweat.*

'Something like that,' said Winter and climbed back up on the ledge. Her tone had changed. It was arctic. It carried an unmistakable warning. It made the Senator want to bend at the knee. Winter turned to face them like an avatar from a game. Her hair blew in the wind. The long, black gun was back out. She held it loose at her side, its barrel pointing downwards like it was an extension of her arm.

The Senator felt rather than heard the reaction around her: the back pedalling, the reassessment. Winter's gaze swept the faces looking up at her. Her gun hand tensed just slightly.

'We have this book in the UK,' she said. 'I don't know if you have it here. It's called *The Gruffalo*.'

She paused like she was waiting for a reply. There wasn't one.

'To paraphrase: I am the scariest thing in this wood. Anyone wants to come up here and make something of it, fine. Otherwise, back off and leave this to me.'

The Senator watched the faces around her. The decision-making, the hesitation. It could go either way. Then she felt their focus shift to her. Small, nondescript. The soft option.

'Who's this?'

Winter had dropped down onto the ledge and was sitting with her feet dangling into the alley.

'She carries my shit,' she said, without looking.

Yeah, the Senator wanted to say. She stood there, the picture of loyal devotion. Like some kind of caddy, a homunculus trailing along in the wake of the warrior.

Winter clenched the barrel of the gun between her teeth and turned onto her stomach. She looked round – she was preparing to climb down. An impractical way to carry a gun. Maybe it was for show.

'Doesn't she speak?' camouflage guy said.

Winter's armpits hugged the edge. She took the gun out of her mouth. 'No.'

The Senator peered over the edge. The drop was immense, the alley floor sixty feet below, all but invisible in the gloom but full of bins and recycling and broken air-conditioning units and working air-conditioning units and everything else you might find in a midtown alley when the place to lawfully dispose of rubbish was miles away.

The drainpipe was right there, just under the projecting lip of stone. Metal and old and square and no kind of real support but easy enough if viewed like a ladder to the fire escape below. It was all in the mind really. Winter looked up at the Senator, a question in her eyes, and the Senator nodded.

The metal creaked as Winter swung her leg onto the strut bolting the rusty iron to the brickwork. The Senator got up on the edge. When she looked back, Winter was jumping down onto the far end of the fire escape, her eyes on the slumped figure of the hunter. The Senator turned onto her stomach and felt downwards with her left leg.

Nothing.

She extended a little further until she was hanging by her armpits. Still nothing. She remembered how easy it had been for Winter with her long legs. She extended the final couple of inches, the point of no return for her aching arm muscles, and felt it. Almost as good as a ladder. She stepped down. Transferring her weight from underarms to foot. She was standing on the top of a drainpipe over a massive drop. The panic started coming in waves. She reached down with her left hand and felt a bolt in the brick like a handhold. Maybe it had held a phone wire originally; now it was rusted but still there, embedded in the brick.

Above, she could feel movement, faces starting to stare. Starting to break free of the intimidation spell Winter had laid down. She was only just below the ledge, reachable from above. She looked across at the balcony. It was lower, and a yawning chasm away. She tried to rationalise it. Not an impossible distance. Much smaller than the roof jump at the start of the night, and she had done enough jumps now to know that lower was actually easier.

But this one was awkward. A standing start from the top of a drainpipe. She could do it. She could definitely do it.

She crouched a little, trying to get her right leg onto a foothold, but the drainpipe was narrow. A single foothold for a very light person. She felt the metal shift with the slight movement and panic flooded her. Terror, cold and pure.

Please don't let me fall. Please don't let me fall. Anna, please don't let me fall.

She looked down at the balcony. Winter was leaning over the black-clad figure. The hunter was shaking uncontrollably. What kind of injury caused that reaction? The Senator had no idea. How much strength did he have left? Strength enough to lift a rifle? She could see a handgun lying beside him, like he had pulled it out and not had the strength to use it.

What if it's a trap? thought the Senator. What if it's like hunting-pack animals that lure in smaller predators by pretending to be sick. She could see Winter wondering the same. The long, black gun was back out.

For a moment, it seemed like the hunter was saying something and then Winter was hurtling backwards and slamming up against the balcony rail.

The Senator leapt. She landed on the sharp edge of the balcony, clung on, then she was clambering over and onto the fire escape. She could feel her heart pumping, hear her lungs sucking in air and see Winter staring at the hunter like she'd seen a ghost.

The Senator didn't think, she didn't wait – she darted forwards, picked up the hunter's handgun, planted her feet square like she had been taught, braced and fired. The noise was deafening. The alley rang with it. It sounded off the stone brickwork, it funnelled down to the stone floor below and bounced back at them, a buffeting wall of sound. The kick practically pulled her arm out of its socket. The bullet hit the hunter in the neck, although she had been aiming for his face. She fired again and thought her arm might break from the recoil, then she lowered the gun.

She'd made a mess. The first bullet had entered just below his jaw and travelled upwards at a forty-five-degree angle, taking out the central cortex, the cluster of nerve cells at the top of the spine, the control unit. It had been instant. A split second of awareness and then oblivion. There had been no need for a second shot.

She caught sight of Winter. She was pressed up against the balcony rail, a strange look on her face. Was it fear? The Senator got the impression, had the rail not been there, Winter would have shot several feet out over the alley like a cartoon Winter.

'What's wrong?' she said. 'What did he say to you?'

Winter shook her head.

The red light on the hunter's headcam was still on. Could it still be transmitting to the world? Could it have survived the head it was sitting on getting a bullet? She looked into the lens and imagined a billion people looking back at her.

Suddenly, Winter was beside her, her own gun swivelling in her hand and smashing down on the camera lens once, twice, three times. When the hand came up for the third time, the Senator saw the plastic lens had cracked inwards like a smashed phone screen and the light had gone out. The black grip was covered in blood.

'Where's his phone?' said Winter. 'We don't have to go down into the alley to the dumpster if we can find his.'

It was in his hand. He must have been using it when they found him. The Senator snatched it out of his slack hold. Together, they looked at the lit screen. The map was there – Manhattan, midtown, the hotel, and pulsing on a balcony, in an alley was a familiar blue dot.

It was her.

Again.

How was that even possible?

The Senator raised her eyes to look at Winter, but Winter was staring up at the roof opposite. The edge was lined with silent black figures looking down at them, the lights of their headcams glowing like red eyes in the dark.

CHAPTER 24

FOR A MOMENT nothing happened. They stood and stared at the wall of hunters across the alley and the wall stared back. More hunters were spilling out onto the rooftop opposite drawn by the lure of the blue dot.

Then there was the clanking of metal on the stairs below, and a black figure was rising up out of the darkness and climbing onto their balcony. Winter shoved the Senator backwards and she fell against the dead hunter and his phone hit the iron balcony and toppled off the edge and down into the alleyway with a clang of metal. The body was wet beneath her. The Senator rolled and the air burst out of him like he was gasping. She wanted to scream, but now the balcony was full of hunter, and she cringed silent on the floor, cowering away from the action. The hunter was huge in full body armour, and Winter was wearing nothing but jeans and a hoodie. *David and Goliath.* But he was heavy and unwieldy and Winter was fast and flexible.

Winter leaped for the overhead metal and swung two-footed at the hunter's chest, knocking his rifle out of his hands. She twisted in mid-air, locked her ankles round his neck and threw herself at him. He went over backwards and she landed knees to his chest and smacked down where his helmet met his neck once, twice, three times.

'Go,' she screamed. 'They're all coming.'

The Senator could see running figures on the rooftop opposite, hear the pounding as hunters charged up the fire escape below her. Where was there left to go? Back up? There was a window behind her. What was it? An office? The room beyond was in darkness. The Senator reached for the dead hunter's rifle as another head appeared at the top of the stairs. Winter's foot caught him on the jaw and he toppled backwards. The Senator wondered if he had taken anyone with him. She lifted the rifle and smacked the butt into the dirty glass and it shattered with one easy blow, leaving a jagged hole. Thin, fragile, old glass. Not double-glazed, modern, safety glass. Glass contemporary with the building. She had read once that burglars hated breaking glass because of the DNA risk, and she could see that.

Winter was holding off a wave of hunters at the top of the stairs. Her head whipped round to the Senator and back again.

'Go,' she screamed.

The Senator dived head-first through the jagged opening. She fell hard on her forearms, her cheek grazed broken glass, then she was on her feet, her eyes acclimatising. It was some kind of office, old-fashioned, filing cabinets and dust. She pulled open the door. A landing. More ancient, metal filing cabinets lining the walls. Stairs down. Behind her, someone crashed through the window. She looked back. Winter had landed and come up firing. There was a second long, black gun. A pair. Where had it come from? Winter was shooting like a cowboy at a rodeo. Having just felt the kick of one, the Senator couldn't understand how those slim arms were holding two steady.

She threw herself at the stairs and heard Winter slam out into the corridor behind her. She looked back. Winter was locking the door they had just come through.

'Go,' said Winter. 'We run now.'

The Senator didn't need telling. She ran, half fell, down the flights, taking the stairs three at a time. What was this place? She had no idea. If the first climb in the hotel had been a sprint up an endless flight, this was a panicking, stumbling, falling descent. She heard gunfire as the locked door above them exploded. Winter was on her heels, shoving her forwards and hauling her up bodily when she fell. She gripped the bannisters and the pain was sharp – her palms were bleeding. Windows smashed in hallways beside them as hunters worked out she was in the building and started to come in through the sides. They were never going to make it out alive.

'Out the front,' said Winter. 'We're within the police cordon. Police marksmen are out there. It will slow them up.'

The Senator had no breath to answer. Her lungs were gasping, there was pain in her chest like she was having a heart attack. This was it then, the last terrified dash of the cornered fox.

They burst out into the lobby and out through glass doors to a wall of sound. The Senator blinked in the glare of the blue flashing lights. The street was full of cop cars and police with riot shields and ambulances.

CHAPTER 25

THE COLD HIT their sweaty faces. The air was icy in her lungs. Winter had one arm around the Senator's neck, and the other arm outstretched holding the long, black gun. It swept the street. A police officer tried to approach, Winter shouted at him. A TV camera was pointing their way. Winter shoved the Senator at a cop car. In the distance, a couple of blocks away, they could see the police cordon and the crowds pushing for a better look.

Winter pointed the long, black gun at the driver and he scrambled out. They climbed in, Winter driving, the Senator in the front passenger seat, and slammed the door just as the chasing hunters burst out onto the street and stopped in a hail of bullets. The dashboard clock was showing 3.25 a.m.

A brilliant pink tracksuit threw itself at their bonnet.

'*Seriously?*' said Winter. She scowled at the vision in pink and shook her head.

Avril's mum pressed a phone up to the glass windscreen, her face full of triumph. The hunter's phone from the dumpster. She handed her way down the side of the car, opened the rear passenger door and flung herself in.

'Don't think you get rid of me that easily,' she said.

The car juddered, Winter released the handbrake and

the car lurched forwards, accelerating towards the police line and the wall of public. Winter yanked the wheel and swerved and turned a sharp left down the empty street running parallel with Madison Avenue. Empty because it was within the police cordon.

The radio crackled and hissed on the console. Someone was trying to hail them, but the system required a response from their end. Would it be the FBI or the NYPD? The Senator could only imagine the political jurisdictional nightmare that was going on. Technically, the FBI had the lead, but in New York with New York citizens in danger and the target in an NYPD land cruiser, it was too close to call.

'What happened to you two?' said Avril's mum. 'I went back and you weren't there.'

'We have to keep moving,' said Winter. 'We haven't got any choice. They're tracking our location. We can't stay still for a second.'

'How am I still transmitting?' whispered the Senator. She could hardly bear to say it out loud.

'Internal,' said Winter. 'Inside.'

'An inside job you mean?' The Senator didn't understand.

'Inside, as in, *inside your body*. The tracker of last resort. Only activated if all else fails probably.'

She just couldn't process this.

'Any dental work recently? Any operations?'

Now she got it. She felt a sudden sharp wave of nausea.

They turned left again and now they were running parallel to 85th Street. The cordons here had fewer spectators. All the action seemed to be on the Central Park side.

'Appendicitis,' she said. 'I had a suspected appendicitis six months ago. It turned out to be nothing. They went in, then sewed me back up again.' She tapped her lower stomach where the tidy scar was still a little raised.

Winter glanced down. 'Lower abdomen?'

'Yes,' whispered the Senator.

She felt the nausea circle and defeat slump her shoulders. The Adjudicator had been planning this for six months. She could understand how one person could hide. Even the hiding in plain sight she was starting to understand, but a tracker inside her? It was only a matter of time. It was not if, it was when.

The fourth side of the empty circuit was blocked by cop cars and ambulances. Winter had almost completely circled the hotel and they were nearly back where they had started. She slewed the car around, up on the sidewalk, down again and back the way they had come. It was no kind of a permanent solution. They were fast-moving but trapped in a circuit only a few hundred yards from the hunters.

'What about Avril?' said Winter. 'Did she have any time in hospital recently?

'Six months ago,' says her mum. 'She had her nose done. I made her wait until she had definitely stopped growing.'

Winter was staring straight ahead.

'What?' said the Senator.

'It's a fail safe. An emergency tracker. The last resort if they really lose the target. It's how they found target two in the desert. They probably never activated Avril's.'

'What does it mean for us?'

'It's a game changer,' said Winter. 'There is literally

only one way out. To do what the Adjudicator wants. We
need to find out what that is. We need to make the call and
tell him you never got your challenge.'

Avril's mum looked down at the hunter phone.

'No contacts,' she said after a moment. 'No texts, no
apps. It's just a map and a phone.'

'A GPS device,' said Winter. 'For them to track the
target.'

'It has received one call.'

'Dial it,' Winter said, 'and put it on loudspeaker.' She
fumbled with the phone dock on the dashboard.

Avril's mum passed the phone over and it slotted home,
the screen lit up and a dialling tone like an old-fashioned
telephone filled the car.

Bring, bring. Bring, bring.

It was answered almost immediately.

'*Colosseum*,' said a woman's voice. 'How may I direct
your call?' The voice was young and sing-song. A receptionist. The very essence of receptionist. They could picture her,
read her entire history from the one sentence: slim, bright,
cheerful, not that successful at school, sitting behind a high
marble counter in the wide, echoing, marble lobby of a
multi-national corporation. A big organisation, outposts in
Europe, an HR department and a Boss – not an outlaw or a
Lord of Misrule, but a man in a shirt and tie. Organising,
arranging, planning.

For a moment, no one said anything. Outside, sirens
screamed, but inside the car, they all stared at the phone on
the dashboard. There was an organisation behind *Colosseum*?
What had Winter said back at the convenience store? *Think
of the logistics.* And here it was – the mothership – handling
the logistics.

They looked at each other. The Senator could see Winter's face in profile. She looked like a manga drawing. All hard angles and planes. The nose ring glinted in the light from the dashboard.

Winter leaned towards the phone. 'Put me through to the Adjudicator,' she said, her voice iron calm.

'And who may I say is calling?' The voice was still bright and sing-song.

'The target.'

The line cut away to hold-music. 'New York, New York'. Someone at *Colosseum* had a sense of humour. It went on a long time. They went all the way through the four-minute extended track version and most of the way through it for a second time. Then it stopped abruptly.

Silence.

'Hello, Senator.' The Adjudicator's voice was heavy with electronic distortion. Some kind of voice manipulation. She couldn't even tell if he was American.

Bastard.

'Halt game,' said Winter. The words were clear and clipped and ringing like a marching order.

The Adjudicator laughed.

'Nice try,' he said. 'Very nice try. I am starting to like you, Senator. Or is that in fact not the Senator?'

Winter put one finger to her lips in the half-light.

The Senator kept her mouth shut.

'I never received my challenge,' said Winter slowly and clearly. 'If it was an email, it was deleted from my account.'

'Well, that is very unlucky for you,' said the Adjudicator. 'It *was* an email. Who would delete an email from your personal account? Who would do such a thing? Are you asking yourself that question, Senator?'

'Yes. I am,' said Winter. 'But I am also asking how I can rise to the challenge and overcome my flaw, if I don't know what it is? Please send it again.'

Overcome my flaw. It seemed like a strange thing to say.

Silence.

'This is very irregular,' said the Adjudicator, and even with the electronic distortion, they could hear his irritation. 'I am going to have to give this some thought.' There was silence for a moment. 'I'll call you back. Don't go getting yourself killed now.'

The line went dead.

'What the hell was that about?' said Avril's mum.

Winter was staring straight ahead. 'He's gone to check the email account.'

'How can he do that?' said the Senator.

'I can't imagine it will give him any problems. He will see your story is true. The question is, what does he do about it? What is his next move?'

'Why should he do anything about it? Why would he give the target any chance at all?' said Avril's mum.

'Because these are challenges not hunts. I know from the outside it looks like mindless public entertainment, but there is much more going on here. The hunts have been planned very carefully, six months in advance by an expert, tailored specifically to the target.'

The Senator shivered.

'And ultimately, he will be annoyed something has gone wrong in the planning. It affects the game. Stunts it. It can't unfold as it should. You can't rise to a challenge you never got. I think he will send it again. But he is not going to be happy about it.'

The Senator looked out of the window. They were almost back where they had started. Winter would have to U-turn again.

They had seen behind the veil and the Adjudicator, instead of being a mindless monster, turned out to be a planner and an organiser, an anticipator of problems, a finder of solutions. In some ways, he was more like her than she had had any idea. She wondered what it would be like to meet him.

The phone rang in the silence.

The Senator pressed the button.

'You have until 5 a.m.,' said the Adjudicator, 'to solve a riddle. If you can give me the answer at that time, I will send the challenge again.'

'Will you halt the hunt until 5 a.m.?' said Winter.

'No.'

Winter scowled. 'We accept your terms.'

The Adjudicator laughed. 'Of course you do,' he said. 'Now pay attention. I am only going to say it once.'

CHAPTER 26

T HE RIDDLE WAS twelve lines long.

The phone went dead. Winter's face was lit up suddenly by a street light. It looked carved. There were police cars behind them. It was going to be harder and harder to U-turn – they were getting trapped. Any minute now, a hunter was going to come out of a side road with an assault rifle.

'What the hell did that mean?' said Avril's mum.

'We need to get out of here,' said Winter. 'We are getting boxed in. Can we get underground? It will disrupt your signal for a bit, buy us some time until 5 a.m. I need to think.'

'Subway,' said the Senator. 'It runs all night. We need 96th Street.'

Avril's mum leaned forward between the front seats.

'You should put your seatbelt on,' Winter said.

*

THEY CAME AT the police cordon on the south side where the crowds were lightest. Police and spectators dived out of the way, and the plastic tape caught on their bonnet and was gone under their wheels. They turned right and right again and a cop car, sirens blaring, got ahead of them, carving a path through the traffic. North along one-way Madison Avenue, left onto 90th Street, past the Church of the Heavenly Rest, then their escort was crossing Fifth Avenue and leading them into the park.

Trees stretched tall above them on either side, dark skeletons against the dark sky. Winter curved round the top of the park and headed south down the West Side with the cop car leading the way like the pacemaker in a marathon. The Senator glanced back, they still had their escort behind them – lights flashing, sirens screaming.

She stared out at the dripping trees. The park was deserted. Not a single soul, no one sleeping rough. Then she got it. This was the NYPD's solution. A clear circuit of road inside the park where they could keep circling. The cops had seen them circling the block round the hotel – they had understood she needed to keep moving and this was their solution. Somewhere that was less likely to endanger New Yorkers. It was a good idea, but it was never going to work for long. It was obvious to everyone where she was, even without the tracker.

There was a cop car blocking their exit onto the 97th Street transverse.

'We need to get past that car,' the Senator said.

Winter slewed the wheel, their car went up a slight bank, round and past. The wheels hit tarmac, *clunk-clunk*, with a jolt that made all the teeth in her head rattle. There was a screeching of brakes and a shrieking of sirens as their escort scrambled to follow.

Now they were on 97th Street and exiting the park. The traffic was slow-moving, and they had lost their police pacemaker carving the way but the sirens behind were helping. Cars pulled up on sidewalks to let them pass.

Christmas was everywhere. They turned left on Columbus Avenue, right on 93rd and right onto Broadway. *Christmas on Broadway.* It was practically iconic, like something out of a movie.

'Coming up in two blocks,' the Senator said.

'We're gonna dump the car and run for it, OK?' said Winter. 'Count it down for me.'

They nodded.

The Senator could see the lit curved roof of 96th Street station up ahead, a block away. Beyond it, further up the street, the traffic was stationary. A wall of red brake lights. She could picture their car coming to a stop and a second later, cops surrounding them, forcing her out, taking her into protective custody.

'A block away,' she said, eyes on the stationary wall of cars ahead.

'In feet,' said Winter.

500

400

200

100

The Senator counted it down till they were level with the subway, the car screeched to a halt in the middle of the lanes, they threw the doors open and leapt out. A taxi in the inside lane slammed on its brakes and leaned on its horn and they handed their way across its yellow bonnet to the sidewalk.

Behind them, their escort of cop cars screeched to a halt, sirens still blaring.

The lights flashed above the subway entrance. Then they were inside and Winter was grabbing her arm and yanking her forcibly through the turnstiles. Alarms rang.

'Cops,' said the Senator, choked and breathless. 'Right behind us.'

They pelted down the steps to the platform. It was forty years or more since she had been in this station, but nothing had changed. Ninety-sixth was still dingy, the pillars still a grimy red. There was a train standing at the next door platform ready to leave. Winter pulled the Senator towards it. Behind them, she could hear Avril's mum catching up.

'No,' said the Senator. She shook herself free and hurried down the platform to the far end. Halfway along, she broke into a run.

How fast can you run? Can you even run at all?

Winter was on her shoulder, just keeping pace, making no attempt to stop her. The Senator got to the end of the platform, got on her stomach on the dirty stone, hung her legs over the edge and jumped down.

Winter landed beside her, Avril's mum copied the Senator's stomach slither and all three of them ducked out of sight just as pounding footsteps came down the steps at the far end of the platform. The cops.

Winter and Avril's mum were wide-eyed, their faces right beside hers. Sweaty in the listening silence. They were so close she could have touched them with her nose. When had she last been this close to someone? When had it got to the point that she was hiding from her own police force in her own town?

She hated the subway. Claustrophobic. Confined underground, the weight of the earth pressing down on her. It was almost as bad as being underwater. She hadn't ridden it for forty years. But she remembered how. She remembered being a carefree student and taking the subway, and she remembered what lay between 86th Street and 96th Street.

The stuff of nightmares.

Halfway between the two stations was *another* station. The 91st Street. Abandoned nearly a century ago. Sealed up, no way to it except down the live line.

She shuddered. She knew all about New York's abandoned stations from meetings with the city council: the vermin risk, the graffiti, the danger. The homeless who died on the live line trying to reach them or who died on the silent platforms, hidden forever from sight.

There was no way to hide from *Colosseum* forever, but maybe for an hour or so. Because right now, that was what they needed. Time away from the cops and the hunters. Time to solve the riddle. Time to think. There was a path through the maze. Winter had been right. What they needed was time to figure it out.

Could she cope with the claustrophobia? Would it send her over the edge? She was about to find out. The tunnel yawned pitch-black in front of them, the signal on red. According to the overhead, the next train was in fourteen minutes.

'Follow me,' she said, and stepped onto the track. 'And keep off the live third rail if you don't want to die.' She turned on the torch on the hunter's phone and started to run.

CHAPTER 27

T HE SENATOR SQUATTED on her haunches, feet flat to the floor and watched Winter. She was pacing up and down. Avril's mum was staring round at the abandoned station like she couldn't believe her eyes. 'The smell down here is disgusting,' she said.

'It's the rats,' said the Senator. *Or the dead homeless people.*

The Senator looked away down the deserted platform. She wondered what the station had looked like when it was first built. Like the one underneath City Hall, it had probably been a showpiece. Built in the heyday of the subway. The golden years when it was an engineering miracle to be proud of. She could see the mosaic sign *91st Street* in the original Heins & LaFarge ceramics. The numerals were picked out in gold. Then the trains had got longer and it was out of business. For a while, it was a regular home for rough sleepers and graffiti artists working by the red glow of the signals, and then at some point, they got cleared out and the access blocked off. Until it was completely inaccessible. Unless you walked up the live line, like they had.

The word 'curveball' was written in huge pink bubble writing on the wall. It was a work of art. Put a famous name on it and it could have been in the Met.

Her head hurt.

She stared out at the dark mouth of the subway tunnel. There were one thousand kilometres of track in the subway network, four hundred of those underground. She thought of Avril in her bunker, alone in the dark. Could they survive down here, ducking and diving, eating waste, keeping ahead of the hunters? Needing to be lucky every time.

'I wish Walter was here,' she said. 'My private secretary.'

'Were you having a thing?' said Avril's mum.

'Of course not.'

'So he just decided to take a bullet for you anyway? For the fun of it. Employee of the year. How long have you been together?'

'We were not together. I have a husband.'

'My mistake.'

It was strange, she thought – a lifetime of marriage and it was someone else she wanted right now. And Anna too, if she was completely honest. It had been a decade since she'd really thought about her, but tonight, it felt like she was here. She looked up the platform. It was almost like she could see her waiting in the dark.

'Where are you, Anna?' she whispered.

Her knees throbbed. The bruise from jumping off the roof was starting to come out.

She stared round. She didn't know if they were deep enough to mask her tracker and she didn't know if they'd been followed. She did know the clock was ticking.

'OK,' she said. 'We have under an hour left to crack this riddle. Do you want to hear it again?'

'Forget the riddle,' said Winter. 'What is going on here?'

'We need to know what my challenge is, so we have to answer his riddle.'

Winter seemed to be missing the point.

'You need to think,' Winter said. 'Imagine this is a test. People have to face their biggest fears. What is your biggest nightmare?'

'Dying,' she said. 'Being hunted to death like a fox, like a tiny frightened rabbit.'

Winter shook her head. 'If they gave you a hallucinogen and induced a really bad trip, what would you see?'

'Trapped underground,' she said, looking around. 'Trapped, running out of air.'

Winter stared down at her. 'Not underground,' she said. '*Underwater.*'

The Senator shuddered. 'Water. Pressing down on you. Trapping you, unable to breathe. I've always hated it. It makes me panic. I can't swim. I don't expect you to understand – someone like you. Anna understood.'

'I've played this game before,' Winter said.

'What game?'

'Why am *I* here?' said Winter.

'Because you're the Best of the Best.'

Winter stared off into the middle distance. 'Thirty-six hours ago, I was still on mission. I haven't slept properly in a while. I know nothing about *Colosseum*. I know nothing about the hunters. I have never been to New York. Am I the most obvious choice?'

'You think someone wants you dead?'

'This is a suicide mission.'

'It's me they want dead.'

'I think this is about me. Something happened to me

once that I didn't understand.' Winter stared out at nothing. '*Colosseum* is a game, a test, a trial of endurance with an adjudicator, and I've played his games before.'

The Senator felt all the hairs on the back of her neck rise. 'Where?'

For a long time, Winter was silent.

'That's the weird thing,' she said. 'In my head.'

WINTER

CHAPTER 1

I'M TRYING TO think about where it all began. It's got to the point that I don't know. That I literally don't know what was in my head and what was real. What was fact and what was fiction.

It started with Ash in the pub. Or maybe it started with the glucose shot.

I guess it started with the glucose shot.

*

IT WAS FOUR years ago, a few months after GCHQ recruited me, after Camp Alpha. I was in solitary confinement. An underground cell beneath GCHQ Bude. Bude is snoop central. The UK's huge listening facility perched on the rocky Cornish coast that monitors all the traffic that comes into the UK across the Atlantic. It pretends to be a military base. The solitary cell had bright yellow walls.

The hatch in the door slid back. Eyes peered in. Brown eyes, set in a patchwork of wrinkles. Control. The Head of GCHQ. He backed away and another set of eyes peered in. Grey. Their owner was much taller – you could tell from the angle of the face, the way he dipped his head. Erik, the ex-marine Head of Field. The guy I punched out in my interview.

I went back to staring upwards.

The ceiling in solitary was solid concrete with a road network of cracks and fissures. Good enough to navigate by when they turned off the lights. Not that there was anywhere to go. The cell was about eight by eight. Two storeys below ground level, no windows. Which they seemed to feel was a punishment in itself. Like a couple of days underground would be enough to disorientate you, break your spirit. It was a joke.

There was shuffling outside the door as if several people were pushing for a look at me – some interesting exhibit in the zoo.

'Do you know who that is?' Control was saying.

I wondered if they knew I could hear them talking through the door. It seemed like an odd question; Erik knew perfectly well who I was.

'Yes,' said Erik, annoyed. 'That is the hacker who crashed our servers. Who facilitated the Camp Alpha takedown, who has been in solitary five times in the last month.'

Back then, Erik, it has to be said, was not my biggest fan.

'They cannot break her,' said Control, taking no notice. 'And do you know why they can't break her?'

'Because they haven't tried hard enough?' said Erik.

'Wrong,' said Control. 'They can't break her because she has already been broken. Broken again and again. And forged anew until she is as hard as adamantine.'

I stared at the ceiling. *Hard as adamantine.* I liked the sound of that.

'I will tell you who it is,' Control said. 'Achilles. Half man, half god. When she joins the battle, she will turn the tide.'

I *had* to see what Erik made of this.

He was peering through the hatch, wide-eyed as if he had missed something. As if I might manifest some godlike destiny right there and then in my yellow cell.

'At the moment, she's sulking in her tent,' Control went on.

Rude.

'But one day she will come out and fight and she will win the battle for us.'

'Give me forty-eight hours with her,' said a different voice. It was a man's voice. Confident. Amused. An equal not a flunkey. Someone known to Control, like the head of some other service. 'What have you got to lose? Let me unlock that potential. She's no use to you like this.'

'Absolutely not,' said Erik. Hard and fast and defensive, like he was scrabbling to answer. 'This is a GCHQ recruit. We are not subjecting her to your programme of illegal hallucinogens.'

'You know the thing about Achilles?' said the amused voice, as if Erik hadn't spoken. 'He had a *heel*.'

'You won't be able to break her,' said Control. 'I guarantee it. She is flawless. Hard as adamantine.'

'It's all there in her psych report,' said the amused voice. 'Her Achilles heel. *Subject seems incapable of backing down.* Overconfidence, that's her flaw. That is how I'll break her.'

'We'll see,' said Control.

'Forty-eight hours,' said the voice, and I could hear the smile.

CHAPTER 2

FOOTSTEPS CLATTERED ON stone as they walked away down the corridor. I pictured them climbing the stairs. No lifts.

Ten minutes later, the bright-yellow cell door opened and a woman doctor came in. White coat. Heels. Great legs.

I hoped she wasn't going to kick me out of solitary before feeding time. *Feeding time at the zoo.* Sometimes they spat in it, which made me smile.

'D'you want the good news or the bad news?' she said.

'The good news,' I said. 'Always.'

'You're getting out of here – there's a VIP down from London to see you. He's come all this way, just for you.'

'So I heard and the bad news?'

'There's a VIP down from London to see you.'

She was holding a syringe in her hand. She inserted the needle tip into a bottle of clear liquid.

'What's that?'

'Glucose shot,' she said. 'You'll be missing dinner. You don't eat much where you're going.'

Figured.

The shot was in my leg, which surprised me. She got me to roll over on my side, facing the wall, to slide down my jeans. I could smell her perfume as she bent over me, and I was going to ask her to get me off while she was there but thought better of it. The shot went on a long time. A lot of glucose. She pulled a cotton ball out of somewhere, ripped off some surgical tape and stuck the cotton ball over the puncture.

She watched me pull up my jeans, fasten the buckle on my belt, and there was a look in her eyes. Appraising. A hint of speculation.

'You must be something special if he has come all this way just for you.'

She unlocked the door and stood aside to let me pass. She smelt of jasmine.

'Good luck, Winter,' she said.

I TOOK THE grey, institutional stairs up the four flights to ground level – solitary is the lowest point, literally and metaphorically. The fire door had a push-bar exit. There was no one around.

Rain was hammering down, lashing against the grey military buildings as I scuttled across the recreation yard towards the canteen. The portacabins were in darkness. I wanted to eat and I wanted to get laid. In that order, but I wasn't fussy.

White T-shirt, jeans, Converse trainers. I was seriously underdressed for the Cornish weather. I rounded the corner. The canteen was in darkness. I couldn't believe it. The canteen never closed. Bude was a twenty-four-hour facility. There was always something going on. You could eat a meal and read the newspapers any time, day or night. Surprise saw me stand stock-still and stare. It was weird. Very weird.

It didn't take me ten seconds to reach a decision.

GCHQ Bude perches on the Cornish peninsula, squatting over the heavy pipework that comes up from the Atlantic, like a malevolent mother hen. It is home to Prism and Tempora, the giant snooping programs that check all the data into the UK. Back when that was a plausible proposition. For one of the most secure facilities in the UK, it is ludicrously easy to break out of. I managed it in my first week and they hadn't mended the gap in the fence since.

Half an hour later, I was walking into the only pub in a thirty-mile radius. A low, white-washed Cornish bar with a log fire and a rough-hewn wooden counter and fishermen in chunky knits. The door creaked open like a haunted house in *Scooby Doo*.

The rain had poured down all the way and my T-shirt was soaked. Water dripped from the end of my nose. It seeped through my jeans. White cotton clung, soaking wet, to my six-pack. I don't work out. I just do a lot of sport. Or I did before GCHQ hijacked my life.

I crossed to the fire. The mantelpiece was high and wide from the days when the fire was used for cooking. I leaned my forehead against the blackened wood and toasted my front. I was dripping on the hearth. Wood smoke filled my lungs, stung my eyes, my face burned. When I was warm and wet as opposed to just wet, I straightened up and headed to the bar.

The pub looked down, drained their collective drinks, cleared their throats, tried to pretend that they hadn't been watching.

The barmaid met my eyes and looked away. A Cornish native. Dark-haired. Blue veins under pale skin.

At the sight of me, a tide of pink worked its way up her impressive cleavage. It had been four weeks, but she remembered. I remembered too. The heft of her full breasts, the weight in my hand. The way she watched me, eyes wide, as I undid her buttons.

'Coke,' I said.

She didn't ask me for any money, which was just as well because I hadn't got any.

My eyes slid sideways to the guys propping the bar. Fishermen. Straggly beards, knackered working boots, dirty fingernails. Genetic twins to the barmaid. I looked in the mirror at my sharp, pointed face. Nothing like me. I could be a different species. Two of them were head-down in their pints, but the third... his eyes flicked my way, his stance altering, his body language projecting loud and clear.

The pub had deep windows set in its thick cob walls. Outside, night was already falling, coming down suddenly like a blanket. The rain had stopped. Which was typical.

Behind me, the door opened and someone else with a wet T-shirt came in.

I checked him out in the mirror behind the bar. Someone else playing hooky from Bude, and he couldn't have been there long, because there was no way I would have missed him – dark hair, sharp cheekbones, ripped jeans and a wet T-shirt. Lithe and slim as a teenager just coming into his muscles. He was soaked to the skin and the T-shirt did nothing to hide what was underneath.

Criminally, mercilessly appealing.

I watched him shake the water out of his dark hair. I looked at the curve of his jaw and the smooth, strong chin. He was exotic as a snow leopard in a farmyard. The sort of looks that make everyone slightly breathless and punch drunk. The sort of looks that elevate their owner straight to the top.

He came up to the bar beside me.

'What are you drinking?' he said.

'Coke.'

The barmaid glared, but he didn't seem to notice.

'Did you just arrive?' I said.

'At this pub or at Bude? Yeah,' he said, when I didn't answer. 'Yesterday. For the training programme.'

In the mirror behind the bar, he looked like a dark version of me. My photo negative. My own genetic twin.

'Call me Ash,' he said.

He carried our drinks over to a table in the corner, just assuming I would follow.

I followed.

'What are you here for?' he said.

I shrugged. 'This and that. You?'

'Likewise.'

His strange silver eyes flicked over me. They were pale grey with a dark charcoal line round the iris. Alien. He had a coin in his hand. He flipped it with his thumb and it spun in the air, catching the light. He was everything mothers warn their daughters against. Or so I imagined. I hardly knew my mother and I don't remember her warning me about anything.

'Well?' he said.

'Well what?'

'Do you want to play, Winter?'

CHAPTER 3

'ALWAYS,' I SAID. I slouched back against the wooden trestle bench. The furniture looked like it had been hewn out of some mighty oak about eight hundred years before. 'How do you know my name?'

'Wouldn't you like to know?'

I rolled my eyes. 'Yes,' I said. 'That's why I asked.'

He laughed. 'You've been described to me. I heard you just got out of solitary. Where you seem to be a lot. I heard you broke someone's jaw.'

I shrugged. *What can I tell you?*

He watched me over the top of his beer bottle. Silver eyes stared into mine and the familiarity was so strong, the connection so powerful, it left me short of breath.

'I heard your motto is fight it or fuck it.'

The room was still. Nothing moved. It was as if the whole world had gone into slow motion. Except my heart rate.

'So?' he said, and it was long, drawn out and lingering. A lifetime. A world of possibilities in the one word.

'So?' I said, and it was hard to get the word out against the weight of those possibilities. I knew what he was going to say before he said it. This photo negative version of me.

'Do you want to fuck?'

Another lifetime went by.

'Or fight?' I said.

He smiled down at the beer-stained wood as if I had passed some test. As if my response was exactly what he'd been expecting. As if anything else would have been disappointing. Years of wet pints had left ring marks on the wood.

'Let's play it now,' he said. 'The fight it or fuck it game. The next person through that door, you have to do one or the other. Your choice.'

There was something about him. Something alien and yet so familiar, so achingly familiar, that I was literally incapable of refusing his challenge. Of walking away. Of backing down.

I looked around at the bar's clientele. At the Cornish fishing types, straggly beards and chunky knits and weighed the options. No particular hardship to do either. The dirty-fingernailed fisherman had just gone out through the door to the toilets, which meant in about two minutes he would be coming back the other way.

'Which door?'

'Whichever.'

I lounged back in my white T-shirt and low-slung jeans. The back of the slatted bench was hard against my neck. I was a hundred per cent confident with either option. 'What do I win?'

He caught the spinning coin out of the air and slammed it down on the stained wood.

'My lucky coin.'

His strange eyes smiled into mine, and for a moment, it was like looking in a mirror.

'Seems fair,' I said.

The door to the toilets opened and the fisherman appeared.

'Let the game begin,' said Ash.

*

I COULD SEE it in the fisherman's eyes the moment he entered. They panned round the room seeking me out, checking that I hadn't gone. That little look of relief when he saw I was still there.

I put down my drink. 'Get your money ready,' I said.

I gave the fisherman my patented *I am really interested* look. Then I got up, slow-motion style, stretching, drawing attention to myself.

'Is that it?' said Ash.

'Yeah,' I said.

I headed for the bar and swung by the group. I held the fisherman's gaze and jerked my head towards the toilet door. Universal body language for *follow me*. He stared, pint halfway up, and his face did that little grimace that says *me?* And I nodded ever so slightly and headed for the door.

As I opened it, I threw a full *come hither* look over my shoulder in case he hadn't got the message, but he was right behind me.

I stopped in front of the two doors with the stick drawings of a man in a top hat and a woman in a triangle dress.

'So,' I said. 'Your place or mine?'

He stared like he couldn't quite believe what was happening, so I took hold of the front of his woolly and hauled him into the ladies.

There were two cubicles, which was good because you don't want people having to wait.

I dragged him into the one on the right and locked the door. He looked bemused, so I pushed him down on the toilet lid and pulled off my trainers and unbuckled my belt. I slid my pants and jeans down and stepped out of them. He reached two, big, heavy fisherman's hands for my hips.

'Turn around,' he said.

I leant forward, bracing my hands on the door, smiling as I got what he wanted. I wiggled at him, circled my hips, snaked a slow undulating figure of eight while his fingers explored.

'Wider,' he said, his voice thicker, more distant, and I leant forward some more and spread my legs some more until I heard him unbuckling his jeans. There was a grunt as he freed himself, then he was gripping either side of my hips and dragging me backwards. I hovered over him just touching, teasing while he bucked and strained and twitched. Then I relented and relaxed and he sunk into me.

'Fuck,' he said.

I leant back and felt his beard against my neck and his jumper scratchy in the small of my back. His hands pulled my legs wide then they were probing and pushing and I sighed as he hit the spot and rested my head on his shoulder.

He buried his teeth in my neck as I came, throbbing and twitching inside me.

'Stand up,' he said, and we stood, awkward, joined together and shuffled round in the space until I was bending over the toilet, hands on the seat and he was standing behind me.

He started to go for it, his belt buckle bouncing as he slammed into me, gripping my hips and working me backwards and forwards as fast as he could. The toilet seat clanked, echoing in the narrow space, his breathing came loud and fast but not loud enough to drown out the slap, slap, slap of skin on skin and the crazy jingling clink of the buckle. He pulled out just as he came and I felt him spurt, hot and wet, over my lower back. It trickled downwards.

'Fuck,' he said again and collapsed on top of me, soaking up the wet with his chunky knit.

After a bit, I shoved him off and he stumbled backwards, banging up against the door.

I sat down on the toilet seat and put him back together, zipped up his flies, buckled his belt, unlocked the door and gently pushed him out.

I heard him stumble through the main door and I leant against the partition wall, my cheek on the paper dispenser, and closed my eyes.

A soft knock made my eyes spring open.

'What?' I said.

'Winter?'

It was the barmaid. Big-breasted and willing and needy. Did she see him leave? Was she checking I was OK? I opened the door and sat back down.

'What?' I said as she stood there, twisting her hands.

'I wanted to see you,' she said, eyes widening as she clocked my naked bottom half. 'What are you doing?'

I considered giving her the honest answer.

'Changing.'

I picked up my clothes and backed her out into the main part of the Ladies with the sinks and the hand dryer and the tampon dispenser. Now she was really staring, chewing on her bottom lip like she was getting ideas.

'Wait,' she said as I put one leg into my underwear, and she dropped to her knees and put her face to me tentatively. The tip of her pink tongue came out, darted at me and went back in. My hips flexed into her face. I couldn't help myself.

'Take your top off,' I said.

'What if someone comes?' she said, looking over her shoulder at the door.

'Then they'll get a load of your phenomenal assets.'

She pulled the T-shirt over her head and sat back on her heels.

'And the rest.'

Slowly, she put her hands behind her back and un-clipped her bra. She slid it down one arm and then the other, shrugged and those heavy, full breasts came free.

I reached for her head and leant back against the wall, facing the door.

After a while, I lifted one leg and hooked it over her shoulder.

CHAPTER 4

'THAT WILL BE mine,' I said to Ash as I caught the coin mid-air.

'Longer than I expected,' he said. He leant back, his eyes giving nothing away.

'Two for two,' I said.

The coin was thin and light and old. I peered at it. 'What is it?'

'Priceless. There are only ten in the world and the other nine are in museums.'

'Are you sorry to lose it?'

'No,' said Ash. 'Not to you.'

I flicked the coin and it somersaulted over and over. I caught it out of the air and slammed it down on the table just like he had. Tails was a building, a round building.

I gave him a look from under my lashes.

'I'll give you the chance to win it back,' I said. 'Fair's fair.'

He stared like he didn't see that coming.

He put his drink down. 'Jesus. You are going to be just a world of trouble.'

'Call yourself a gamester?'

He smiled a long, slow smile like a cartoon wolf. 'You have no idea,' he said.

'In your own time.'

He glanced round the room. 'Were you planning on going out and coming back in again?'

I shook my head. 'Nope.'

'Fine,' he said, getting up. 'Fight it is.'

'You'll have to go three to win. Two, and we'll call it a score draw and I get to keep the pretty Roman coin.'

He lounged over to the bar and said something to the three fishermen. They looked at me then back to him. One of them stood up.

Ash shook his head and half jerked it towards the door. *Outside.* He walked to the door, lifted the latch, dipped his head and was gone. One by one, the fishermen drained their pints and followed.

*

IT HAD STOPPED raining and was just cold. Bone cold. Cornish coast cold. The sky was huge and starry. The kind of sky you only get near the sea. The fishermen were nowhere to be seen. A moment later, they appeared round the corner of the building holding wooden mallets. Heavy, wooden hammers used for stunning fish. Ash was propped up against the wall, looking relaxed.

The lead guy hefted the mallet from hand to hand, and I could imagine him using it, a quick, fast strike that could break a limb no trouble. A short-range, heavy weapon, an extension of his arm. He had been hefting that mallet every day for ten years. He was going to be pretty handy with it.

He charged straight in, mallet at shoulder-height, going for the arm break.

Ash levered himself off the wall, rolled round the fisherman and ended up behind him. His right hand landed on the back of the fisherman's neck and his left leg extended, horizontal, and caught the second fisherman full in the gut. He stepped over the second fisherman bubbling on the ground and landed a double punch on my fisherman coming in last, still a little wobbly on his legs. It was all over in less than five seconds.

And I thought *I* was good.

I had never seen anything like it.

*

INSIDE, ASH LEANT back against the scarred wood of the trestle back, spinning the coin, his eyes giving nothing away. Silver eyes with dark rings around the irises. Wolf eyes.

'Who even has silver eyes?' I said, giving the game away that I had been dwelling.

'You like what you see,' he said, and it was not a question.

'Sure.'

'But not enough apparently.'

His outline was dark against the white wall of the pub. As I stared, the outline wavered, coming in and out of focus, like looking through rippling water. The silver coin spun, glinting as it caught the light. He tossed it in the air and it turned over and over. I tried to put a hand out to catch it and missed. The whole room shuddered and blurred as if it were a stage set melting away as another scene began.

My hand was coming in and out of focus. As I stared at it, the table rose up to meet me.

CHAPTER 5

S ILENCE. A KIND of dank, echoey silence. The table had changed beneath me – I felt it immediately. It wasn't wood anymore, sticky with beer, it was more like cool, hard plastic. Formica. Like an office table or the tables they used in the psych assessment unit. The air was stale, artificial – air cycled many times through an air-conditioning unit, not warm with wood smoke and booze fumes. The pub was gone. There was someone with me and I could tell it wasn't Ash.

I opened my eyes.

I was in a room – small, square, no windows, tiled in white, and there were funnels and channels and drains on the floor. There was a huge mirror built into the tiles and I knew immediately what it was – not a mirror, an observation window. I was in a GCHQ interview room, and on the other side of that mirror, someone was watching and assessing me. They had been doing it on and off for weeks since Camp Alpha. Lame-ass psych profiling. At first it had been amusing to mess with them, then it just got annoying.

Except it didn't feel like a GCHQ interview room with their trademark grey and black rubber skirtings. There was something different about this room. It was tiled almost like a bathroom, and there was a drain like there was a lot of liquid run-off.

In the corner, hanging from the ceiling, was a meat hook.

My imagination is pretty good, but I was struggling to think of any acceptable reason for having a meat hook hanging from the ceiling of a tiled room.

A man was sitting at the table opposite me.

Young. Thin. Glasses. I looked closer. The arm of his glasses was held on with masking tape. Actual brown masking tape. I had never heard of anyone doing that. He was wearing a grey jumper and an open-necked shirt. A total boy-next-door type. I knew if I could see his trousers, they would be kind of beige, and that if he was standing, he would be tall but skinny. If I had had to sum him up in a single word, it would have been 'scruffy'.

Scruffy but gentle. I looked into his brown eyes and knew there was no doubt about that. The fear eased off a little. Not in this world or another million identical universes was this someone to fear. I knew this like I knew myself.

And if I had had to apply a second word, it would have been 'no one'. A low-level grunt.

He was watching me wake up.

'Hi,' I said. 'What time is it?'

That was the key question. Not, where am I? Not, where did the pub go? I had been moved, that much was obvious. I was in a GCHQ assessment unit for purposes unknown but, no doubt, shortly to be revealed.

He shrugged, and that annoyed me far more than it should have, and I realised it was because I trusted him instinctively, and his refusal to answer bordered on deceptive, duplicitous even. He was part of some scheme to trick me, and it felt even more important to try and nail down the timeline. I think Alice felt the same when she pitched down the rabbit hole.

How long was I in the pub? Two hours? Three hours? I didn't feel tired. Ergo it was somewhere between 10 at night and 2 in the morning And yet the boy-next-door didn't look like it was the middle of the night. There was no sign of that air of fundamental fatigue that surrounds doctors on the night shift. He looked like it was a regular, normal day. Like he had just pitched up to work. Not a Monday morning, more like a Tuesday, still the whole week to go.

'Imagine there are two of you in a locked room,' he said. 'And only enough air for one person to survive. What would you do?'

'Stop imagining,' I said. 'This is a riddle, right?'

'OK,' he said. 'There's a fat man waiting at a station for a train and the train is going to crash into the platform, killing a hundred people on board unless it is stopped. What do you do?'

They had been trying to get me to answer a variant on this question since the events at Camp Alpha. The 'correct' answer being that you push the fat man in front of the train. The one to save the many. It was so excruciatingly, embarrassingly, insultingly obvious I couldn't bring myself to play along. There was also something fundamentally weird about the situation.

'How long are you going to sit there and ask me riddles?'

'As long as it takes,' he said. 'The train is going to crash and a hundred people are going to die.'

'Are you serious?'

'Yes,' he said. 'It is a very serious situation. A hundred

people are going to die. What do you do?'

You are faced with a scruffy Boy Next Door sucking away your youth and vitality. Do you:

Smile coyly and say, 'I can think of better ways to spend the next hour.'

Smile coyly and say, 'I can think of better ways to spend the next hour … know what I mean?' Wink, Wink.

Say, 'Do you want to fuck?'

Answer: Three.

Obviously.

'No,' he said.

'Liar.'

He looked down at his papers. Shuffled them about a bit. Glanced towards the two-way mirror. I could see him going slightly pink.

'So,' he said, regrouping. 'What do you do?'

'Exactly a hundred people? Bit of a round number.'

'OK,' he says. 'Ninety-nine people. What do you do?'

'Why have the brakes failed?'

'Unknown.'

'Because train brakes are highly unlikely to fail. Just saying. And even travelling at a relatively slow incoming speed of 20 kph, fifty tonnes of modern engine is not going to be stopped by a twenty-stone man on the line.'

The Boy Next Door opened his mouth.

'Or even a forty-stone man on the line,' I said.

He closed his mouth and glared at me. 'You think you are very clever, don't you?' he said.

'I *know.*'

'You know what?'

'I *know* I'm very clever.'

'What you are is a pain in the arse.'

'Don't you wish?'

'No,' he said, gathering up his papers in front of him and tapping them on the table. His fringe flopped with the jerky movement. 'I find your brand of in-your-face sexuality terrifying. My idea of a dream date is a quiet dinner, maybe a movie, maybe a little hand holding.'

I grinned. It was the best thing I'd heard in weeks. Disarming. Totally disarming.

'I apologise,' I said. 'I will answer your question.'

He looked up, hope in his eyes, and laid his sheaf of papers back on the table.

'You will?'

'You want to know if ethically I condone the murder of one person to save the many, whether my moral compass finds that acceptable and as an important appendix to that, you want to know whether I am quick enough to make that judgement under time pressure and in the face of oncoming danger and finally, whether, given the first two, I have the strength of mind to act on what I believe in a timely manner.'

'Yes,' he said, staring.

'Let me take them out of order. I think I would be quick enough to see and assess the parameters.' He nodded. 'I believe I would act on my beliefs in the moment of crisis, but it is hard to predict behaviour under the influence of adrenaline.' He nodded again more enthusiastically and started to scribble on his notes. 'The problem lies with the first question. The moral, ethical conundrum which the majority of people, once they have hummed and hawed for a bit, tend to decide in favour of the many, i.e. yes, it is right to sacrifice the one for the many. Your follow-up question will then involve members of my family. Not a fat man but someone important to me: a mother, a lover, a child.'

He stared at me.

'In my case, the question does not apply. Not only do I not have anyone more important to me than a stranger, but that stranger's life is already too valuable in my eyes. I would not kill the one to save the many.'

'You wouldn't?'

'No.'

'That is the first time anyone has ever said no.'

'You can't get many religious types here.'

'Is that your reason?' He looked disappointed.

'No.'

Silence.

I stared into his earnest face. It was very personal what I was going to say. Like I was giving a piece of myself away, but there was something about him that pulled the truth from me.

I sighed. 'In the event that it could be known, without question, which it couldn't by the way, that a body on the line would stop the train and, by implication, save a hundred lives, it would be my body on the line.'

'You hold your life that cheap?' he said.

I shook my head. Now we were really getting to it. 'The reverse. Your life is the most valuable thing you will ever own. I wouldn't take someone else's if my own would do.'

He nodded.

I looked at him and he looked at me and the connection between us was so strong, I realised despite all outward appearances, we were exactly the same, he and I. Almost as if he was a personification of my conscience. A manifestation of good me.

The room filled with a disembodied voice. 'Finally, Winter, we have an answer. Was that so hard?'

The Boy Next Door's eyes went to the mirrored glass and the connection was broken. The mirror had gone and in its place was a window. I could see straight into the observation room on the other side. It was in darkness compared to the brilliant white of the room we were in. There was a man standing in the shadows. I couldn't make him out. Black against the darkened room. His outline could have been wearing body armour.

A noise started up somewhere like a distant generator cranking into action. A mechanical whirring noise. A giant generator or a massive pump.

The Boy Next Door jumped to his feet. 'Please,' he said. 'Please. Don't do this.'

He crossed to the window, pressed his hands to the glass, hammered his fists against it. Someone inside flicked a switch and the mirror came back and he screamed. It spooked me more than anything else. The sheer abject terror of it.

I pushed away from the table and pulled him off the mirror. His face when I turned him round was white with fear. He struggled in my grip.

'What?' I said.

He burst free of me and threw himself at the door. It was sealed shut. No handle on our side. Like the inside of a commercial freezer. I whirled around. There were holes the size of big drainpipes halfway up the wall in each corner. There was a dankness in the air.

Not splash tiles. Not easy-clean tiles. Not drains for a bit of light run-off when the questioning gets 'hands on'.

Swimming pool tiles.

We were at the bottom of a swimming pool.

CHAPTER 6

THE GURGLING, SCREECHING sound of pipes under pressure was getting louder. For a moment, nothing happened, then water started to pour out of one of the holes in the corner. The Boy Next Door hammered on the door. He started to sob.

'Calm down,' I said. 'This is a test, right? Problem solving. Quick reactions and all that. *Let's see how quick you get out of this.* Textbook. They are not going to let you drown.'

He ignored me, kept scrabbling at the door.

OK, first things first, I thought. *Can I stop the water?*

The outlet pipe was about the size of a side plate. I pulled my T-shirt over my head. Unbuckled my jeans, pushed them down. The cotton-wool ball that had been taped to my leg had gone. Did I lose it in the pub? I couldn't remember. I kicked off my trainers. Yanked off my jeans. The water was icy. Ankle-height. It had already covered the floor.

I splashed over to the pipe, bundling my clothes into a tight sausage and fed the whole thing into the hole, squashed it in like I was filling a sausage skin. For a bit, the water fought, then the sausage expanded to fit the space and it stopped. The bung was not a perfect fit – there was still a dribble, but I knew it would take all year to fill the room that way.

I braced my back against the hole. Planted my feet, locked my knees and prepared for them to jet the clothes out. I imagined how it would go, a mighty, high-pressure hose. Powerful enough to jet a hole right through the human body. The Boy Next Door had turned away from the door to watch. His brown, lace-up shoes were submerged. His glasses were lopsided.

For a while, nothing happened. The water was cold. I shivered in my bra and pants, braced for the sudden surge of water I was expecting to blow me across the room.

Instead, it started up simultaneously out of the other three corners with a massive roaring and clanking of pipes.

The room was going to fill at three times the speed.

The Boy Next Door turned back to the door and hammered on it. He scrabbled at the seal, his fingertips scratched and bleeding and blue with cold.

I waded across to him. The water was nearly knee-high.

'Calm down,' I said. 'They are not going to let you die.'

He turned his face to me. 'You don't understand,' he said. 'I am no one. It will just get written off as a training exercise. They'll kill ten of me to find your price. They'll kill a hundred of me to break you.'

Break you.

And there it was. The thing I'd been waiting for since I arrived at Bude. The evidence that GCHQ had some grown-up tools in their armoury. And by luck or judgement, they had hit on water. My Room 101.

'What happened to good old-fashioned waterboarding?' I shouted over the wall of sound.

'You can survive waterboarding,' he shouted back, and his terror was so real, so manifest, so clearly not manufactured that I could feel it infecting me.

I swirled around. Sealed-tank room, concrete floor and ceiling, tiled walls. Point of vulnerability – glass window, which was probably a total red herring. Glass that can survive underwater is stronger than concrete. Bulletproof mirrored glass is stronger than concrete.

So, what was left?

The door. No handle. Rubber seals. Strip the seals away and the water would leak out, but probably not enough and not fast enough.

The water was knee-high now, heavy against my legs. I knew there must be a way to survive. It was a game, a test. So what else was there?

A metal table, tube legs, two metal chairs, leather straps, a briefcase. Hollow tube table legs hold a small bit of air, nothing much. I picked up the briefcase and plonked it on the table to keep it upright in case it started to bob, and then I felt with the tips of my fingers. Something taped to the underside of the table. Something wrapped in plastic. I ducked under to look. Black duct tape. A decent-sized package – lumpy. I fumbled and tore at the wrapping and it came free all in a rush and fell out into my hands. A breathing mask. Just the one. And a heavy, black handgun.

I checked the chamber. Loaded.

Drowning, claustrophobia, trapped under water. My biggest nightmare. How did they know?

I could feel the terror rising, the panic. I am not a strong swimmer. I can swim, but that is about it. I fought to close the panic down. Nothing is worse than your imagination. I knew that even then.

'Block your ears,' I shouted.

I levelled the gun at the corner of the mirrored glass and fired once. The bullet ricocheted off at an angle and into the water. Barely a dent.

'Bulletproof,' he screamed above the roar of water.

Figured.

'So what was the point of the bloody gun?'

I looked at the breathing apparatus and at his frightened face and at the gun. 'You have to be kidding me? I am supposed to kill you and save myself? Is that how this goes?'

He nodded, slumped against the wall.

The VIP was fucking crazy.

I waded over to him. He was blue with cold, his lips a purplish colour. His cheeks were wet, although whether it was water or tears, I couldn't tell.

I grabbed his wet face between my hands. 'Nothing would make me do that. No power on earth could make me kill you to save myself.' He stared into my eyes. 'Do you understand?'

He nodded.

'We will share the air. Like divers do when they are stuck underwater.'

'Then we will both die,' he said. 'There is only enough for one person. It will run out far too early.'

Jesus.

'There has to be a way out of this.'

'There is,' he said. 'One way.'

'How can you even be a part of it?'

He shook his head. 'I thought this place was an urban legend. I didn't know it was actually real.'

I looked into his frightened brown eyes and could think of only one way to help him.

'Start picking the black seal off round the door,' I said.

He stared at me for a moment, uncomprehending, then he turned his back and started to scratch with his broken nails at the rubber.

I spun the gun in my hand and brought it down hard on the back of his head where the base of the skull meets the neck and he keeled over backwards into my arms. I dragged him over to the table and picked up the breathing mask. I didn't know how much air was in the tank but if I left it too late, I might not be able to fit the mask. The room was filling fast. Another couple of minutes and I would be swimming. Another couple of minutes after that, and it would all be over.

I took off his glasses, closed them carefully and put them in his briefcase, hoping they would make it. I fitted the mask over his thin face, tightened it behind his messy hair, inserted the mouthpiece. He was breathing deeply. How long he'd stay knocked out I didn't know, but I was expecting at least ten minutes.

I let him go and immediately he flipped over, face down in the water, floating. I ducked under to look at his face – he was breathing freely, a little stream of bubbles leaking out of him, clustering around his mask and away. My skin was hard with goosebumps, my face cold where it had got wet. I could see myself in the mirrored glass: pinched white face, soaking hair. My eyes looked huge in my head.

I needed to ask myself a question about willpower.

There are few deaths worse than drowning – the panic, the bursting lungs. Could I do it for someone else? I asked myself the question, and it didn't take long to come up with the answer. *Not without some help.* The body goes into a frenzy, acquires super-strength, in the desperate scramble for air. I would be out of my mind.

I yanked my jeans out of the pipe, pulled the belt out of the loops, tied one end round the meat hook in the corner and buckled the other end round my wrist. A tether to keep me to my word. To keep me from him.

He was floating face down, breathing easily through his face mask. I could see the little tiny air bubbles escaping. I tried not to think about what it would be like for him when he came round.

My only interest was in keeping the table level as it floated. The underside held maybe a cubic metre of air. I had no idea how long that would last. Probably not long enough.

I floated, hair loose around me. I imagined what it must look like to the man in the observation room. The glass would have a greenish tint. It would be like looking into an aquarium. Like having his own mermaid in a tank.

No surrender.

I gave him the finger.

And then I drowned.

CHAPTER 7

I OPENED MY eyes and jerked upright; restraining straps were holding me down. I was in a white room, like a single room in a hospital, needles in the backs of both hands, bags of fluids swinging above me. The stands were on castors – they'd been wheeled in.

I lifted my head and looked down at myself. A hospital gown. The worn cotton type that has been on a thousand patients and through a thousand hot washes. The kind with no back. Someone had resuscitated me and stripped off my clothes and put me in a hospital bed. I swallowed, my throat felt fine, not like I had just been resuscitated. My brain thudded around inside my skull.

The door opened and a man came in.

He was wearing a doctor's white coat and had a face like an angel. Very perfect. I don't know why symmetry is so attractive. His eyes were deep blue and his lashes thick and black. His hands on my wrist were cool.

'Welcome back, Winter,' he said. 'How are you feeling?' His voice was completely accentless and there was something about the flat monotone that made me uneasy. I looked up into his perfect face and felt afraid.

'What time is it?' I asked.

He said nothing.

He was barely older than me. A DPhil student at best.

'What happened to the guy in the tank with me?'

The doctor held a syringe up to the light and flicked the end. The liquid was golden. A single bubble escaped and bobbed to the surface.

'Shall we begin?' he said.

Panic kicked in and I hauled on my restraints, yanked at my wrists. I was held fast. He ignored my thrashing, inserted the long thin needle into the top of my arm and pressed down slowly.

I felt it entering my veins. Burning down my arm.

'What is it?'

His blue eyes were right beside me. 'Let's see what's in the tunnels of your mind, Winter,' he said. 'Can you dream and not make dreams your master?'

And then the pain started. The burning. It spread out from the point of contact pouring through my veins. When it reached my heart or my brain or my eyes, they were going to explode.

'What do you want?' I screamed. 'What is the question?'

'No questions,' he said. 'This is the control dose, so I can get the levels right and you can experience what I can do.'

'In that case it's too fucking high,' I spat. 'Psycho.'

He smiled. 'Not high enough, Winter, by the sound of it. It's going to be a pleasure working with you. The endurance record, by the way, is held by a woman. Three hours and fifty-two minutes. But then she was exceptional,' he said sadly.

I stared up at the white ceiling tiles and focused.

*

I AM QUITE good with pain. They say it is all in the mind, and I have some mind-control tricks up my sleeve. I think they are connected to my memory. I go somewhere in my head. A special place. Somewhere I haven't been since I was seven. A mansion. There are hundreds of rooms and the doors are huge and the handles are at shoulder-height because that is how they were when I last saw them.

I focused.

And... opened the door to the mansion. Shafts of light pierced the gloom of the hallway, slanting down through the vast stained-glass windows. I closed the front door behind me and stood in the stillness. A fire raged outside, but inside, it was quiet and cool. I floated from room to room dragging my finger along the backs of sofas, seeing the dust everywhere. I wrote my name in the dust on a polished wooden desk.

Winter

Winter

Winter

Outside, I could hear shouts, hammering on the door. I turned away and headed for the stairs.

*

THE PAIN WENT.

'How did you do that?' said the Angel Doctor. He was flushed and flustered, his hair stuck to his forehead. He looked dishevelled and antsy and annoyed.

'Have you been getting yourself off?' I said.

'What?' he said.

'Are we done?'

'Amobarbital,' said a disembodied voice from somewhere.

It was the amused, confident voice that had watched me through the door. The voice that had let me drown. It sounded familiar somehow. I craned my neck to see who was speaking, but there was no one there.

'She's using a basic defence.' The voice went on. 'Some kind of mind barrier. A hallucinogen will get through.'

I had no idea what he was talking about, but it did not sound good.

'Can't we just call it a score draw?' I said.

'No,' said the Angel Doctor.

'No,' said the disembodied voice.

The doctor turned away to his trolley and pulled out another syringe, inserted it into a small metal bottle and slowly drained it. The liquid was cloudy – thick and coagulating. The idea of it in my veins turned my stomach.

*

THE MANSION WAS on fire. I could feel the heat, the burning. I ran from room to room, hearing it crackle up the passage behind me.

Run, I shouted at my tiny self. *Run.*

The pain went.

The Angel Doctor was standing over me and smiling. 'A new record,' he said. 'Impressive. I am going to learn a lot from you, Winter. You are a test case in your own right. I've never had anyone beat the system.'

'Am I done?' I said.

He smiled. It went nowhere near his eyes. 'Oh no,' he said. 'Not by a long shot. We are just having a little pause while we find you some company.'

He went out and the door slammed behind him.

Find you some company. That did not sound good. My mind pinwheeled around, spinning in the here and now, ricocheting off the fear, trying to outrun the panic. I stared at the ceiling. What was going on here? Some kind of test, some kind of challenge? I just had to get through.

The door opened. Two hospital porters backed in, wheeling a hospital bed. Behind them came the Angel Doctor. Beside the orderlies in their dirty scrubs, he looked even more perfect and inhuman.

The bed came alongside. Right up against mine. Clanging, metal on metal.

There was a man on the bed, wearing an oxygen mask. His skin looked pale under the mask. His wrists were bound to the sides of the bed just like mine. The Boy Next Door. He was alive. The relief was overwhelming. A tidal wave. The Angel Doctor took the oxygen mask off, tucked it under his arm and went out.

I lifted a finger and bent my wrist and touched the back of the hand next to me. His eyes opened. He tried to smile.

'We are alive,' he said. 'What happened?'

'I knocked you out.'

'Rather than killing me? And then you wore the mask? They didn't let me drown after all. You found a way round the test. Well done.'

'Not exactly,' I said.

He tried to get up on an elbow, but the restraints held him down.

I turned to stare at the ceiling. 'I put the mask on you and tied myself to the hook.'

'And what?'

'And nothing. I drowned and woke up here.'

'That is extraordinary,' he said. 'That is the most extraordinary thing I have ever heard.'

'Yeah, well,' I said. 'Don't let it go to your head. I would have done exactly the same for anyone.'

He was still staring at me. 'That is the extraordinary thing,' he said. 'It's unbelievable. You are the far end of the curve. The omega. The uncertainty principle.' He paused. 'Special.'

I rolled my eyes. 'Whatever. What I want to know is: What the hell is going on now? Why are you here?'

He frowned. 'I don't know.' He shook his head, and the movement made him wince.

'Aren't you involved? Isn't this all part of the programme? The next test? What happens now?'

'I just help with the psych assessments,' he said. 'That's my area.'

'Did you see the doctor?'

'What doctor?'

'Face like an angel.'

The door opened and the Angel Doctor came back in.

'Speak of the devil,' I said.

At the sight of him, the Boy Next Door recoiled, backed up as far as his restraints allowed, recognition all over his face. 'Interrogation training,' he said.

The Angel Doctor was holding another syringe of the golden liquid.

'What are you doing?' I said, but I already knew.

I watched it happen. Watched him empty the syringe into the Boy Next Door, watched the pain spread out from the injection site, burn its way down his arm. Watched him try to control it, watched him start screaming.

It went straight through me, tore at the roots of my hair, peeled my nails back.

'Stop,' I screamed. 'Please. Stop.'

'And *there*,' said the disembodied voice, 'is the way to get her to cooperate.'

The Angel Doctor lifted the syringe and the screaming stopped. The Boy Next Door stared round, wide-eyed and panting.

'I'm sorry,' I said to him. 'I'm so sorry.'

'Right, Winter,' said the disembodied voice. 'This is how this is going to go. You can take the dose again, or you can let him take it for you. Which is it to be?'

'I will take it.' I practically screamed it.

'Of course, you will, Achilles,' said the disembodied voice. 'Only this time, no mind tricks. If you don't stay with us, we will move back to him.'

'Don't you dare touch her,' the Boy Next Door shouted as the Angel Doctor moved to the head of my bed. He couldn't come alongside anymore because the Boy Next Door was in the way.

When the Angel Doctor leant over me and reached for my arm, he smelt of nothing at all.

OK. How bad can it be? I thought. *Pain is all in the head, right? Manage it, control it, close it down.*

It was bad. Like nothing I have ever experienced before or since. Worse than drowning.

This time, when the screaming started, it was me.

Through the burning, I could hear the sound of some-one pleading. The Boy Next Door was sobbing and begging.

'Give it to me, give it to me,' he was saying, over and over again.

CHAPTER 8

I OPENED MY eyes. Back in the yellow solitary cell with the cracks in the ceiling. The hospital room had gone. The Boy Next Door and his bed had gone. The Angel Doctor had gone. The restraints were still there though.

A doctor came in. White coat. Smiling. Nothing like the Angel of Death.

'Welcome back, Winter,' he said. 'That's quite an hour you've had.'

What hour?

I hauled at my restraints. My wrists were sore. Cuffs round the neck, the upper arms, the wrists, the thighs, the ankles.

'What have you done to me?'

'A hallucinogen,' he said. 'Amongst other things. Cortisol, adrenaline.' He looked down at his clipboard. 'To measure your stress response to certain stimuli.'

The door opened and the cute woman doctor with the great legs came in. The one who gave me the glucose shot. The one who told me a VIP had come down from London to see me. She scowled at the doctor.

'It is imperative that I am the first to speak to the subject,' she said. She turned to me. 'What did you see?'

'When?'

'During the programme,' she said. 'Just now. What did you see? Where were you?'

'I don't know.'

She started scribbling on her clipboard.

'From the beginning,' she said. 'As much as you can remember from me giving you the glucose shot.'

My head hammered. It felt like veins were throbbing in my eyes. My brain was slow.

'It wasn't a glucose shot,' she said. 'Clearly.'

'Are you trying to tell me I imagined the last few hours?'

She frowned. 'You didn't *imagine* it; you experienced a highly sophisticated simulation. Think of it like a 5D cinema with hallucinogens. We suggest the content and your imagination does the rest.'

I stared at her.

'So,' she said, all eager. 'What happened?'

'What? When?'

'Just now. During the programme.'

'Interrogation training.'

'Is that *it*?' she said. She sounded disappointed. 'No monsters? No aliens? No dinosaurs?'

'What?'

'You were supposed to picture your worst fears. The manifestation of your inner demons. We measure your fight or flight responses. Yours were off the chart. Your biggest nightmare is GCHQ training?' She laughed.

I thought about this. The cold, the hunger, the helplessness. Were they my biggest fears? Along with the drowning and the torture.

'I need you to describe the people you met and the tasks you faced in detail,' she said. 'This kind of chemical simulation is still in its infancy and we are collating new data all the time.'

I told her about the Angel Doctor and the disembodied voice giving instructions.

'It is a fascinating programme,' she said. 'The manifestation of your biggest fears. Peopled with ghosts. The people you see are the physical manifestations of ideals and emotions. Often there is a mirror of you. An evil twin if you like. Mr Hyde to your Dr Jekyll. Was there anyone like that?'

A picture comes to mind. A guy tossing a coin.

'I don't think so.'

What about a good version of you? Your conscience?

The Boy Next Door looks at me with earnest eyes.

I shrug.

'Was there anyone there who you know in real life?'

'No.'

'That's very unusual,' she frowned. 'It suggests you have no close attachments in the real world. You don't care about anyone.' She looked down at her clipboard. 'Or anything.'

I thought about Ash, the personification of physical perfection and the possibility that he could have been created in my head. *Nice job*, I told my subconscious.

'Then there is usually a nemesis figure. Your disembodied voice. An authority figure who is neither good nor bad but arbitrary. Fate, if you like. A higher power who can save you if he will.'

'He?'

'People rarely imagine a woman,' she said. 'He represents the innate human need for a supernatural force to appeal to. The religion urge.'

I was so not buying her bullshit. I squinted up at her. What were they giving me? Disorientating me, messing with my head. They could fuck off.

'Fair play,' I said. 'You gave it your best shot. And not surprising since it got so out of hand with the tank and the torture and all, but if you are trying to tell me I *imagined* the last few hours, you can fuck off.'

She scowled. 'Not imagined. You experienced a chemically enhanced simulation.'

'Right.' Sarcasm dripped from the word.

She looked at the other doctor. He was holding another glucose syringe. He tapped it lightly with the back of a finger to release an air bubble. She nodded.

'If you can dream and not make dreams your master,' he said.

The last thing I heard was her annoyed voice.

'It is imperative I am the one to wake the subjects, doctor. Now we will have to run the whole thing over again.'

CHAPTER 9

I OPENED MY eyes. The doctors had left. I was still in the yellow solitary cell, but this time, I was fully clothed and the restraints had gone. I stared at the familiar cracks in the ceiling. *Déjà vu.* The door was wide open. I swung my legs to the floor. My brain crashed against the front of my skull.

My jeans were the same jeans I had been wearing before, and they did not look like they'd been in a tank of water. They did not feel like they had got wet and then dried all new and stiff. They felt soft and worn like they had never been taken off. My T-shirt was the same. The leather of my belt was showing no sign of having been wet. How long would it take leather to dry? I undid the buckle and looked down at it, weighing the metal in my hand. Someone had dressed me while I was unconscious and they had got the right hole.

I stood up and my head swam with the blood-sugar low. I crept to the door and peered out.

The corridor that leads to solitary is grey and underground. The corridor I was looking at was white and lined with windows at head-height. Golden sun was shafting down, angling through the windows. It looked like afternoon sun.

I stood there, listening in the silence, heart pounding.

The air was still – no one was around. There were sounds from outside: birds chattering, an engine far off.

I turned back to look at the solitary cell, checked out the ceiling. It was the same room. Not a shadow of a doubt. I had spent minutes, hours, days, mapping the cracks in the ceiling. I knew every line, every fissure. I turned back to the bright, sunny corridor.

There was a door at the end with a camera above it.

The camera swivelled like it had noticed me. There was no way to avoid it. I scuttled down the corridor to the door and pulled it open. It was outside. Ground level.

So, they had moved me while I was unconscious, to another solitary somewhere else, that looked the same. Exactly the same. Up to and including the cracks in the ceiling.

I had fallen down the rabbit hole.

*

THE DOOR OPENED onto a courtyard of buildings. A stately home. Or a corporate testing centre. A million miles from the grey, wind-swept portacabins of GCHQ Bude in Cornwall.

The door behind me was warm under my fingertips where it had been heated by the sun. I stared round, reading the space, my heart hammering in my ears. Across the courtyard was an oak front door about five times the size of a normal door. I took a tentative step forward and then another.

The door to solitary clicked shut behind me and I was exposed, out in the open.

There was something carved in stone above the giant front door. I could just make it out.

Optimis Optimus.

The Best of the Best.

Fear held me still until I couldn't bear being out in the open anymore and I started to move, creeping along the side of the courtyard towards the giant door, hugging the wall, working on pure instinct.

I passed an archway. Stables. The stalls were still there, cobbles on the floor. No horses. The sun was shafting low through the arch. The setting sun. I crept past.

The giant door had a huge bell. I considered it and then I stepped up and pushed at the door and it opened.

Just like that.

As if someone was expecting me.

I was in a wide hallway with dark panelling and a roaring fire. The place had been built by giants. Straight ahead was a grand, wooden staircase rising in two stages to a galleried landing. I crept up the polished treads one step at a time to the turn in the stairs. Now I could see a closed door above me across the landing.

Principal's office.

I climbed the second flight and stood looking at the door. It was solid oak. The handle was round and golden. Dented with age and use. I didn't knock; I just turned the handle and went in.

The room was wide and panelled. What an estate agent would call 'beautifully proportioned'. The ceiling was carved, there was a bay window overlooking parkland and a huge partner's desk and a man standing in front of it.

He looked like a retired teacher. Early-sixties, suit, half-moon glasses.

On the wall was a massive portrait of a triumphant Caesar. There was a plinth with a white, marble bust of another Roman in the corner. So all in all, a pretty perfect representation of a principal's office.

I stood with my hand on the door handle, staring.

'Is this all in my head?' I said.

'You tell me, Winter,' he said.

I said nothing.

'If you can dream and not make dreams your master,' he said.

I closed the door behind me. 'The head of Camp Alpha used to quote Kipling. I can't say it went that well for him.'

His face twisted. 'I heard what happened at Camp Alpha,' he said. Now he was looking a lot less like a kindly retired schoolteacher. 'You will not find it so easy here.'

'And where is here?'

He went behind his desk and sat down. It was one of those massive old desks. No PC, I noticed, just piles and piles of paper.

'I heard you never back down,' he said. 'I heard even Camp Alpha couldn't break you. I heard you would rather drown in a tank than back down.'

I said nothing. I hate the military. Breaking you to build you up again. Conformity and uniformity.

'So, you have been sent here.' He picked up a piece of paper on the desk. '*Subject seems incapable of backing down.*'

Silence.

'What happened to the guy in the tank with me?' I said. 'Boy Next Door type. He was in interrogation training.'

His face twisted. 'Nothing happened to him. He is total-ly fine, because you would rather be tortured than allow yourself to be beaten.'

I stared out of the bay window at the manicured lawn sloping away down the hill.

'It will be a very interesting test case for him to write up.' He put the paper down in front of him and leant back. His jacket gaped. He was wearing a gun holster under his suit. Not very schoolteacher. 'So, Achilles, the question is a simple one. Are you staying for the programme, or are you backing down? Walking away? Conceding defeat?'

'Conceding defeat,' I said. 'I'll see myself out.'

It was worth it for the look on his face.

I yanked open the door and took the stairs down two at a time. The giant front door was still ajar just as I had left it. I stepped out into evening air. Cooler. Birds shrieking. My senses were crystal clear, focused and honed as a falcon sweeping the undergrowth for movement.

I looked out at the courtyard and the tarmac drive running down the hill away from me. The exit. I bounded down the steps and took off down the driveway.

'I never figured you for a quitter,' said a voice in my ear.

I whirled round. Ash. Out of nowhere. One minute, I had been all alone and next, he was there in jeans and a T-shirt, his wolf eyes raking me.

Memory had not played tricks on me. He was still the hottest thing I had ever seen. I pivoted on the spot and leapt for his throat and he went over, landing on his back with me on his chest.

I pushed my face into his. 'You drugged me in the pub.'

'Someone did,' he said. 'But not me. I had to cart your unconscious body back to base.'

'You never carried me? I don't believe it.'

He struggled to get up on his elbows. 'I got a cab,' he said.

His face was close to mine. The sun slanted through his hair. Up this close, I could see each black lash. The grey of his irises. Suddenly I could feel every inch of his long, hard body beneath me, the warmth of it. Heat swamped me. The air charged. He lifted a hand to my face and pushed my hair back.

'Let's take this somewhere else,' he said. His voice was lower. It pulled at me, hitting me in the gut, bypassing conscious thought. Sexual attraction. I looked up. We were lying on the driveway in full view of a hundred windows.

I got to my feet and held out my hand. He gripped it. I looked down at our joined hands and got that weird sensation again that I was looking at myself. My other half. My photo negative.

'So how did you get here?' I said.

He shrugged. 'I was only in Cornwall two minutes and they shipped me off here.' He stared round. 'Wherever this is. Nobody explained anything. Took about five hours to get here.'

'So, no one has drowned you yet? Or tortured you?'

'What?' he said. 'Tell me you are joking?'

'Have you met the Principal? Looks like a retired classics teacher.'

'The guy running the programme? Yeah,' said Ash. 'Something about tunnels of the mind, overcoming your flaws, unlocking your potential. Whatever that means.'

'It means they are going to simulate drowning to try and break you.'

'Why?' said Ash. 'What does that achieve?'

'God knows,' I said. 'And it's worse than that.'

*

'SO, I AM a figment of your imagination?' Ash said after I gave him the form.

'Apparently.'

He smiled. 'Trust me, this is not all in your head.'

'I know. Obviously. But what if you think that because I think it? Given I have created you and you are a figment of my imagination. Tell me something about yourself. Something that couldn't have come out of my head that I can check in the real world. What's your address?'

'131, Nelson Mandela Tower. I have three sisters and a brother called Moses.'

'Perfect.'

'You need to hurt yourself,' he said. 'An injury. Doesn't have to be much. In fact, better if it's quite small. If you wake up in solitary without it, you'll know this never happened; it was never real.'

I stared at him.

'That's a great idea we just had there,' I said.

'We?'

'Working on the basis that you are actually an extension of me. A personification. Did you ever see that buddy movie, where you find out in the end it was all in his head and he was actually both people?'

'*Fight Club*,' he said.

'Like that. Or like *The Matrix*.'

'If you die in the Matrix, you die in real life,' he said. 'What happens here?'

'I really don't know.'

He looked sideways. 'So, this is all about you? Every-thing here, every person, every blade of grass was imagined by you? Have you ever even seen this place before?'

'I don't think it works like that,' I said. 'You can dream places you have never actually been, right? It's just a case of what you can imagine.'

He looked around. 'I can imagine a lot worse than this.'

I didn't answer because the memory of the tank was strong and I could, too, and I didn't want to admit for a moment the possibility that I might be able to make it worse all by myself.

'So, what are you doing now?' said Ash. 'Breaking out?'

'The trouble is you can't. When you think about it – you can't outrun your own head. If this is all in my mind, it will just carry on outside the walls. I will see what I expect to see and the tests will continue. Real or imaginary, it comes down to the same thing. I need to pass their tests to get out of here.'

He looked away. 'I heard they are looking for the best.'

'Yeah, I got that memo.'

He shook his head. 'The best. As in, one person. They are only looking for one person. It means only one person is getting out of here.'

'So, what happens to everyone else?'

He shrugged. 'Who says there is anyone else? Maybe it's just you and me. The best of the best. Head to head.'

The silver coin was back in his hand. He threw it in the air. It spun over and over, glinting in the setting sun. A breeze blew on the backs of my arms. His strange eyes stared into mine.

'So, Winter,' he said softly. 'D'you think you can beat me?'

I looked out across the parkland.

'Yes,' I said, and it all went dark.

*

I OPENED MY eyes. I was in the stables round the corner from the main house. Cold on my face had woken me. I wondered whether they used ice cubes to simulate cold, and even as I wondered, I rolled my eyes at the idea that it was any kind of a simulation.

I breathed in the smell of stone and earth and hamster cage. I squinted down at the ground under my cheek, the round cobbles, the grouting, old and engrained with mud. Mud that must have come in a hundred years ago on the hooves of horses belonging to the great house. I stared at the ceiling. It was open to the rafters, an underside of black felt cladding, bits of straw, a cobweb.

Fact vs fiction. What was real and what was not?

My stomach was hollow with hunger and the fear was coming in waves. They weren't done with me yet.

I looked up and saw a nail sticking halfway out of a beam.

I HELD THE nail in my hand and tested the sharpness of the point. The half that had been in the wood was a shiny silver contrast to the dirty grey of the rest. I gritted my teeth and braced myself and scratched three letters into the skin on the inside of my wrist.

A-S-H

Blood beaded crimson.

I staggered to my feet. I could see all the way through the open stable door to the day beyond. The morning was bright and crystal clear with that pure ring in the air that comes on frosty mornings. Like a bright, sunny morning on the slopes when you get off the cable car and it is minus ten degrees and the sun is so bright it hurts your eyes even through shades and you can see across the mountain to the next valley and the blue, blue sky beyond.

What was real and what was not?

I needed the answer. The yellow room was the key. It wasn't the same room and I was going to prove it. Or if it was, I was going back. How did they get out of Narnia? They went back to the wardrobe. How did Alice get out of Wonderland? She went back to the rabbit hole. And once back in the real world, I would see whether the name of my dark twin was still etched into my skin.

CHAPTER 10

I STOOD IN the courtyard in the shadow of the stable arch, listening and watching. No one was around. The place was deserted. My legs felt weak.

Subject seems incapable of backing down.

I could see the door that led to the yellow solitary cell. The room with the answers.

The door opened easily. The corridor stretched ahead of me with windows at head-height. I stood listening for a moment in the silence. There was an echoing sound from somewhere far below, but I crept forwards towards the room at the end.

Halfway along, a door stood open. It had been shut before; I had barely noticed it, but now it was open wide. I peered round it. A stairwell. Concrete steps led down. Cold air rushed up to meet me. A dank, green smell. Cold, damp air and, far off, the sound of running water.

My heart thudded.

The tank room.

Someone else was playing the kill or drown game.

I stood at the top, balling my fists and relaxing them, looking back down the corridor at the door to the outside, turning and looking at solitary. Then I decided, and hurried down the steps, down and down into the gloom.

It was far deeper than I had expected, two storeys at least. I hurtled down, clattering on the stone, and the sound of water got louder with every step. It was clear and distinct now – the sound of a massive bath running.

The stairs ended in a stone corridor with emergency lighting behind grills. It felt old like a Victorian cellar that had been concreted over in parts but not enough to hide its original proportions. Maybe it had been an icehouse or part of the wine cellars back when this was a stately home.

There were two doors, side by side, on my right.

One was heavy and metal with a wheel instead of a handle, like a door in a submarine – the tank room from the outside. The other reminded me of the doors on the GCHQ detainment floor. Modern. High-tech. A control room door. It was out of place in the Victorian cellar.

I threw myself at the control room door and it opened unexpectedly easily, pitching me forwards into the room.

The Principal was sitting, side on to the door, staring intently through a huge plate-glass window into the brightly lit tank room. He was in darkness, but the tank room was bright.

Two people were playing the kill or drown game – the Boy Next Door, sitting against the wall with his knees up to his chest, and Ash, standing in the centre, hands on hips, looking around. The water was ankle-deep and pouring out of a single corner. Unlike me, Ash had made no effort to stop the flow. I wanted to hammer on the glass. He was looking at the window with no reaction. He was seeing a mirror.

I needed to stop the water.

The control room was full of equipment: levers and

buttons and a workstation with a PC. I darted forwards and yanked the gun out of the Principal's shoulder holster.

I levelled the gun. 'Turn it off,' I said.

'If it isn't Achilles,' he sneered. 'Come to save the day.'

His hand flashed out and hit something, and there was a cranking and a gurgling from the tank room. Ash whirled round, searching for the source of the sound as the other three pipes started up. They were going to flood the room at four times the speed.

I spun the gun in my hand and smacked the Principal across the face with the butt. I felt it connect with his cheekbone.

'Turn it off,' I shouted.

He spat blood over the side of his chair. It hit the stone floor. 'Or what, Winter?' he said.

I stared into the tank. The water was knee-high now. It had climbed a foot in a matter of seconds.

'How about you make it easy for them?' he said. 'You have such a soft heart. Drowning is a terrible way to go.' His hand hovered over a button on the control panel. 'This is a thousand volts. It would stop their hearts instantly.'

I looked at Ash and the Boy Next Door standing up now and shaking with fear and cold.

'You would kill them both,' I said.

He shrugged. 'You can't make an omelette without a bit of eggshell.'

It was weird looking in at the tank from this side, twilight green, like being inside an aquarium, just as I had imagined. The water was waist-high and Ash was pulling on the breathing apparatus.

'No?' said the Principal. 'Shall I do it for you?' His hand

went towards the button.

'No,' I screamed. I brought the gun down on the side of his head and he keeled over, off the chair, unconscious.

I shoved the gun down the back of my jeans and turned to the control panel, shaking with anger and fear. It had a medical look, like the controls for an MRI scanner or for an X-ray machine. There had to be an easy way to stop the water. There were probably several ways to make it worse.

It was hopeless. I needed five minutes to figure it out. I didn't have five minutes. In the tank, there was a foot of air left. The Boy Next Door was gasping and flailing like a fish on a hook, treading water, his face to the ceiling. I started pulling levers. Frantic. Watching the tank. Ash was floating, breathing easily through the face mask. He had had no trouble coming to the right decision. I watched the water close the gap and the Boy Next Door go under. The tank was full. I was going to watch him drown.

I could feel tears of rage and frustration on my cheeks.

I ran back out into the corridor and started to haul on the submarine wheel. My arms ached. It was huge and heavy and stuck hard, and behind it the Boy Next Door was drowning. I gave a massive wrench and it came free suddenly and I turned the cold metal, hand over hand, sobbing with the panic and the urgency. How long had it been? Suddenly, something gave and it spun beneath my hands, the giant seals unlocked, it crashed open and the wall of water hit me, smacking me up against the brick. Water smashed into me again, picking me up and tossing me down the corridor like a piece of flotsam. I scrambled to my knees, struggled to my feet as the water pumped down the corridor. I battled back, wading against the tide.

The table was stuck in the doorway and the Boy Next Door was wedged up against it. Ash had the breathing mask off and was trying to pull him through. Between us we yanked him clear and half dragged, half carried him to the stairs above the water line.

I cradled his head under one arm, cleared his airways, put my mouth to his and breathed out. I had never resuscitated anyone for real. Time passed while I battled to fill his lungs. It could have been ten seconds or ten minutes before he coughed and spluttered and choked. I turned him on his side and he retched great gobbets of water. When he was done, he flopped onto his back and stared at the stairwell ceiling. He had lost his glasses and his eyes squinted. He tried to focus on me.

'That's the second time I've saved you from drowning,' I said.

He tried to smile, but it turned into a cough.

I looked up at Ash. His dark hair hung either side of his face, dripping wet. His silver-grey eyes were ethereal. Unnaturally super-humanly spectacular.

'You were going to let him die,' I said.

'Obviously. It was the only option. What did you do?'

'She chose to drown,' said the Boy Next Door, looking at the ceiling. 'She is the far end of the curve.'

'Whatever,' said Ash. 'Where is that psycho?'

'In there.' I nodded to the control room. 'I knocked him out.'

'I'm going to deal with him,' said Ash. 'It's no good just knocking him out. He'll wake up in a minute.'

'Let's just leave him,' I said.

Ash looked at me like I was mad. 'Why? So he can

drown a new load of people?'

He was right. I knew he was right. I pushed my way through the water.

It had seeped into the control room; the Principal was lying in a puddle. He opened his eyes. I reached down the back of my jeans. The gun was surprisingly dry.

I levelled it. He stared down the barrel. It felt heavy on the end of my arm.

I lowered the gun.

'He needs to die,' said Ash.

'We can't decide that.'

He stared at me in disbelief.

I looked round at the empty tank with pools of water on the floor.

'This is a test, isn't it?' I said.

The Principal smiled.

'Is it all in my head?'

'The tunnels of your mind,' said the Principal.

'And how do I get out?'

'By overcoming your flaw, Winter.'

'Which is what?'

He got stiffly to his feet and collapsed into a chair. 'You tell me.'

'Not backing down. Overconfidence. Pride. No surrender.'

He shook his head. 'That's what we thought. We were wrong. You had us all fooled. Especially after Camp Alpha. How very deceptive appearances can be. Achilles, the super soldier, is a fraud. A fake. Achilles is all heel. Pity is your problem. Whoever heard of a super soldier who can't kill?'

I stared.

'We should have listened, you told us clearly enough your first time in the tank. You value life too highly. Life is your weakness, Winter.'

CHAPTER 11

THE SENATOR STARES at me wide-eyed.

'So now you know,' I say.

She squats on her haunches, feet flat to the platform. She is wiry and thin and determined. Dirt streaks her face. Her nails are ragged. She could pass for homeless in any city in America. A born survivor. Privileged, educated, wealthy. Strip it all away, and you get the essence of the person.

'But what about your guns? What about the people you shot tonight?'

I look away down the platform. 'Plastic bullets,' I say.

'*What?*' She splutters the word. 'So no one is dead?' She can hardly believe it.

I shake my head.

'Do they do any damage at all?'

'They have stopping power. That's it.'

'Like a stun gun?' says the Senator.

'Kind of.'

'You aren't serious?' Avril's mum says. 'You are going up against *Colosseum* with rubber bullets?'

I shrug. 'I protect life. I don't take it.'

'Jesus. What are you even doing here?'

'Protecting life.'

'You're a fake,' says Avril's mum. 'A total fake.'

The Senator looks away. Then she starts to laugh. It is the first time I have heard the sound.

'So, what happened next?' says Avril's mum. 'Because honestly, at this point, I am a bit confused. What kind of outfit puts their recruits through that sort of shit anyway? It is unbelievable. *Med-i-eval*.' The way she says it, you would think medieval is the worst thing she can think of.

'My kind of outfit,' I say. 'It went dark and I woke up in the yellow solitary cell in Bude. The very first thing I did was check my wrist. There was nothing. No letters, no sign of the skin ever having been broken. The doctor with the glucose shot was there to debrief me. She was pleased. She said the programme was still in its early stages, but my responses had been exceptional.

'"Level with me," I said to her. "Just between us girls. Was that really all in my head?"

'She smiled at me. "It's an amazing programme," she said. "I was thinking about having a try myself. Would you recommend it?"

'I thought about the torture and the drowning.

'"No," I said. "I wouldn't."

'Soon after, I was on mission and the whole episode receded. Only I know I am a fraud, that Achilles is all heel. But still, there has been this feeling in the back of my mind. This nagging feeling of being watched, as if someone was not done with me yet. Everywhere I go, even tonight, it has felt like someone is watching.'

Avril's mum stares. 'And you just accepted it? You didn't ask any questions?'

I look down the platform at the decay, the derelict underbelly so close to the lights and glitz of the streets above.

'I didn't just accept it,' I say.

CHAPTER 12

131, NELSON MANDELA Tower. I remember it like it was yesterday.

The lift was out of action. The stairwell whistled with cold, a perfect natural chimney. The air smelt of concrete and urine. I walked down the grey lino corridor. The doors must have all been the same once upon a time, but somewhere along the line, they had got customised. A small attempt at individuality. A brave statement of ownership. Lots of them had iron grills. Number 131 didn't.

I knocked on the door.

Silence.

I knocked again and there was a shuffling inside, a long way off and getting closer. The door opened a crack. It was on a chain.

'What?' said a voice, shaky with age.

Who the hell is this? I thought. I checked the number again.

131

'I'm looking for Ash,' I said.

'You're a bit late,' said the man.

'Can I come in?'

The door opened a bit more. He peered at me.

'Sure,' he said. 'Pretty lady like you.'

Here it was – concrete proof Ash existed; it all existed.

The door creaked open. He was old and grizzled. Eighty at least. His feet were in carpet slippers, his back slightly bent.

The flat was brown and dated. A lifetime of possessions piled up against the walls. The relief I felt at finally knowing the truth was immense. Justification of my senses. I should have trusted myself.

'Where is he now?' I said.

He stared at me.

'He's dead.'

So that's the line they are feeding the families, I thought. Not surprising. Takes recruits out of circulation. Either they make it or they don't, but either way, the service doesn't have to answer too many questions.

'Do you know how he died?'

He shook his head. 'I know what they said.'

'I'm so sorry,' I said. 'I knew him a little.'

The old man stared. 'Is that a joke?'

A clock ticked on the mantelpiece.

'Why would it be a joke?'

'He's been dead fifty years,' he said. 'I thought maybe you were a journalist and you had seen the article.' He rummaged around on an ancient teak sideboard and handed me a newspaper cutting. 'They did a piece about him to mark the fifty years.'

I stared down at it. A full-page spread from *The Times*. A picture of Ash just as he had been that morning. I looked at the date. Last week. My shoulder blades hit the wall. How was this possible? Could I have seen the article and it sneaked into my subconscious?

'They didn't even use the picture they took of me,' he said. He grinned a mouthful of brown teeth. 'Anyone would think I wasn't photogenic.'

'Who are you?'

'Moses,' he said. 'He was my brother.'

I backed out of the room and down the stairwell, tripping in my haste to get away, to get somewhere safe. What kind of drug could mess with your head that much? Make your dreams so real they become reality.

At the bottom of the stairs, huge industrial wheelie bins full of a tower block's worth of waste stood against the wall. I hunkered down between two great green sides as my world collapsed around my ears, and still, it felt like someone was watching.

*

'SO *NONE* OF it was real?' says Avril's mum.

I stare off down the platform. 'The woman doctor was real. The one with the great legs who gave me the fake glucose shot and the VIP who came down from London. The rest – Ash, the Boy Next Door, the Angel Doctor, the Principal – were manifestations of the programme. Ash and the Boy Next Door were versions of me. My avatars, if you like.'

'Different aspects of your personality,' says the Senator.

'That is such a creepy idea,' says Avril's mum. 'Like you can be split into different people. Broken up into parts. As if there are multiple people living inside you.'

'The training centre was created by my imagination – institutional, like a boarding school, because that is my background, so that is what I was expecting. In reality, I never left the yellow cell. There is no other way to explain it. Unless they have an identical yellow cell in two entirely different places.

'And then tonight, I was back down the rabbit hole and the feeling of familiarity, of a game, was back. And then he set us that riddle.'

The Senator is watching me. 'I get the riddle now,' she says.

> *I am hard as adamantine*
> *I am soft as snow*
> *I am a fraud and a fake*
> *I am no hero*
>
> *I am hotter than fire*
> *I am colder than ice*
> *I am wild and unbroken*
> *And I don't have a price.*
>
> *I am stronger than steel,*
> *I laugh at pain,*
> *Some call me Achilles*
> *But what is my name?*

'So what's the answer?' says Avril's mum.

The Senator smiles. '*Winter*,' she says.

Avril's mum stares from me to the Senator as the penny drops.

There is silence.

'There's no way this is any kind of a coincidence,' she says.

The Senator looks up at me. 'You are right – it is about you. It's about both of us. It has to be the same person behind it.'

It is all coming now. Like a deep scab. You pick away at it and get nothing but a little blood, then all of a sudden you get under a corner and some of it comes away and then flick, flick, your nail is sliding under and flicking off great chunks.

'I think the VIP that came down to Cornwall to test me, to unlock my potential, is the Colosseum Adjudicator. He didn't break me before and he's letting me know he's not done with me yet.'

CHAPTER 13

SOMEWHERE DOWN THE platform, water is trickling.

'The Adjudicator is connected to the British secret service. It explains why it always feels like someone is watching me. He has probably been watching me for four years. Biding his time.'

'Just for the record,' says Avril's mum to the Senator. 'This is not some kind of weird simulation. I am not a cool version of you. In case you were wondering.'

Grief is all around her, moving with her, moulding to her shape. She can crack a joke and it is still there, surrounding her, sealing her in.

In the distance, a signal changes and the tunnel glows briefly red.

'Rachel was scared of the dark,' she says. 'That was Avril's real name. Ever since she was a baby. She used to have a pink rabbit night light.' She looks down at her hands. 'She never wanted to be ordinary. Even as a little girl. That's why she changed her name.'

'Names are important,' says the Senator. 'It's how you define yourself. The person you choose to be. You don't have to be the person you were born. I choose to be a senator. More than the name I was born with.'

'Which is what?' I say. Not that I am going to stop

thinking of her as 'the Senator'.

She rolls her eyes. 'Marianna,' she says. 'Although everyone except my mother calls me Marie.' She smiles. 'I am on the run with someone who has never been to New York and doesn't know my full name.' She looks at Avril's mum. 'Avril was right to change. Like Winter. She doesn't have to be their creation. Winter doesn't have to be Achilles. She chooses to be someone else. Like I chose to be more than the name I was born with when I went into politics.' She turns to me and there is something distant in her eyes. 'You remind me of someone I used to know once, a girl called Anna. Like you, she couldn't bear suffering.' She sighs. 'She was all conscience and empathy.'

Anna sounds nothing like me, but I let it go.

'I haven't thought about her in years, then tonight, she keeps coming back to me.'

The Senator stares wide-eyed at nothing. Then she pulls herself together. 'So, where does all this leave us?' she says. 'Because our time is nearly up and I need my challenge.'

I check the phone – 4.40 a.m.

Time to go.

I head down the platform, down the service ladder and out onto the live tracks. The wicked bits of metal gleam. How long since the last train? I start moving – quick, careful strides like a gymnast on a balance beam but down the centre not on the rail, eyes front. Look down and you start to wobble.

The smog is thick in the air, clutching at our lungs. I catch myself holding my breath, then it all rushes out when I can't hold it anymore and I take a huge breath in and taste it gritty on my tongue. The red signal in the distance is like a beacon and a warning. A reminder of what might come hurtling down the tunnel towards us. We are hundreds of yards away, listening, straining for vibrations in the air. My heart is thundering and I can feel the panic starting to rise.

It seems like long minutes, hours, until we see the yellow corner of the platform on 96th Street. I speed up and hear the others stumbling behind me. Then I get something else – a buzz on the line, a whine and hiss, vibrations, a sudden tension in the air.

A train is coming.

We need to get off the track but there is nowhere to go. I accelerate for the shelter of the access ladder at the end of the platform, shouting at the two behind me. The train comes into view. Round white headlights charging towards us. Roaring, screeching, grinding, deafening. We throw ourselves at the ladder, clinging on as the train pulls into the station in a choking cloud of dust. The front carriage overlaps the end of the platform, trapping us in the narrow space in front of the ladder.

I get my eyes level with the concrete and squint along the platform. No hunters. A few night workers. They all get on. No one gets off. The train pulls out and we grit our teeth and clamp our eyes shut and cling on, buffeted by the hot air as the carriages clank their way past. I open my eyes and stare after the back of the train as it disappears into the black.

The window in the end compartment is a lit rectangle rattling away from me and looking out of it, silhouetted against the light, is the black-clad figure of a hunter. He raises his M-16. I shrink back, pressing myself against the metal rungs of the ladder, my rucksack digging into my shoulders, my arm twisting out of its socket trying to hold the other two down as gunfire shatters the back window of the train. He is firing high; bullets ricochet off the stone corner beside us. The noise is like a shrapnel bomb going off. A physical pain in the eardrum. Automatic gunfire in a tunnel. I close my eyes. It doesn't help. I open them again. My head rings with pain. I have no free hands to stuff in my ears. The next burst follows the same path and then the train has rounded the corner and is out of sight.

The Senator and Avril's mum cling on, fingers hooked into dirty cracks, sweaty and breathless in the ringing silence. Everything is blurred, muffled, a long way off apart from the ringing. My heart races with panic; I know I've taken a disabling blow – I need my hearing to detect threats, to listen out for hunters.

Will the hunter on the train try to get off? I'm guessing not. I'm guessing he waits for the next station. But what if he doesn't? What if his train stops at the signal and he prises open the doors and comes back down the tracks? In that case, he is only just round the corner. He could be seconds away. And it's not just him. There could be someone on the platform just above our heads. Even now, they could be creeping, creeping along the platform towards us and I would have no idea.

I need to raise my head back above the edge – was there anyone there when the gunfire started? I psych myself up, turn my head sideways, temple to the ceiling and ease upwards a centimetre. The smallest possible distance out in the open. I get a sliver of vision along the grey platform surface. The base of red columns, something rectangular made of galvanised steel, shiny as a mirror. There is movement beside it. A figure in black.

A hunter.

He is halfway down the platform. Black-clad and searching, stooping and peering, his assault rifle held out in front of him. He is deaf too – he swings round using his eyes not his ears. I ease back down. Trapped between a rock and a hard place. How long before he gets to the end of the platform? How long before he looks down and sees us against the wall, beached and exposed like jellyfish with the tide out? I crane into the gloom, searching for any kind of cover. Nothing.

Why is there a hunter on the platform? We passed through here an hour ago. As far as *Colosseum* knows, we got on a train, we are long gone, travelling away from this spot. Moving out from the epicentre. Counter-intuitive to be searching the origin. Which means, whoever is on the platform is thinking counter-intuitively, has been trained to think counter-intuitively. *Not good.*

I check the time. Ten to five. Ten minutes till I have to call the Adjudicator with our answer and there is no reception down here in the station. I wonder what the chances are of the Adjudicator agreeing to extend the time, of being sympathetic to the idea of us caught between a rock and a hard place.

No chance at all. I know that for sure. I cannot be late. We had our second chance. It is up to me not to blow it.

The hunter is getting closer. I can feel it.

On the edge of my muffled hearing, I am picking up stealthy movement – he is creeping down the platform, creeping towards us, getting closer and closer. Any minute now, he will get to the end and look down and see us.

The implications of the gunfire will not be lost on him. Somebody opened fire for a reason. Now he is searching for that reason, stooping and peering.

Nine minutes left. Where did the last minute go? Time is charging past. We need to get to street level to make a phone call.

He is getting closer. My hearing is starting to come back, sound percolating through the ringing and it is hard to move stealthily in body armour. The Senator and Avril's mum are wide-eyed and silent beside me. Totally still. I try to estimate his progress down the platform. Ten metres away, now five, now four, and decision time has arrived before I have made it.

I guess the exact moment he gets to the end and peers out into the dark of the tunnel, the moment he lowers the infrared visor on his helmet, and launch myself up and over the edge of the platform, the phone raised high above my head with its torch on. He doesn't go over – he was on his guard, but he was expecting a person, not bright light. He clatters back, hands to eyes and I am up and on the platform booting him hard in the gut, a move that should put him flat on his back, but the body armour protects him and then he is charging forwards and we are grappling and wrestling, the assault rifle on its webbed strap clanking between us.

My knuckles burn, the skin cracked and swollen from my last attempt at punching body armour. Adrenaline and panic are numbing the pain, but there is no strength behind my blows. For a moment, I think we are both going over the knobbly yellow edge onto the track and then I turn into him, get my rucksack to his chest and I am throwing him over my shoulder and he lands heavy and uncontrolled on the platform edge and then he is toppling, toppling in a slow-motion crash of arms and legs onto the live line. Will his armour protect him? Does it conduct electricity?

I peer over the edge. I can feel the other two behind me, hanging back. A sudden wall of warm wind hits me, full of grit and pollution, it blows through my hair and I stop breathing in the dirty, thick haze. I know what it means. My brain writes the words in flaming letters on the inside of my skull.

A train is coming.

The hunter on the line realises at the exact same moment. He is like a turtle on its back, unwieldy in his body armour. He scrambles to get upright.

I turn to face the yawning darkness of the tunnel.

Now the hunter is on his feet, clambering and clawing at the platform edge. It's not high – shoulder-height – but he can't get his leg up. The armour is restricting his movement. He claws at the edge as the twin lights hurtle into view, 200 tonnes of metal momentum bearing down on him.

I can hear the Boy Next Door, the personification of my conscience.

There is a train hurtling towards the station. What do you do?

I believe I would act on my beliefs in the moment of crisis, but it is hard to predict behaviour under the influence of adrenaline.

The moment stretches out. I feel like I have lived a whole lifetime, grown up and grown old, while the train hurtles towards us. This is no split-second decision. I have oceans of time. All the time in the world to consider, to look at my beliefs, to turn them over in my hands, to test them out in the white-hot heat of battle. All the time in the world to make the right decision.

His visor turns to me and I throw my hand out and he grips it and scrambles up the wall using my arm like a climbing rope. I brace my feet and brace my legs and lean back. The yellow platform edge is covered in raised knobbles designed to stop the commuter slipping onto the track. Specifically designed for traction. They do their job. My arm all but rips out of its socket, but my feet stay firm, and he is up and onto the platform as the train thunders into the station.

The train stops.

For a fraction of a second, nothing happens. The platform is empty. We are still gripping forearms like comrades before battle. He has a tattoo at the base of his thumb in the hollow where hand meets wrist.

Then the train doors open and a wall of armoured black hunters steps out. And the world goes slow again.

The hunter drops my arm.

I turn for the stairs. The Senator and Avril's mum are ahead of me. I try to run, but everything is slow, so slow and drawn out, like trying to sprint in deep sand. I want to fling myself at the stairs, but it feels like I am crawling. I hit the bottom step, my lungs heaving. The flight stretches away above me, miles of steps to street level. All the time, I am expecting the thunder of bullets from behind. Counting down the moments till they hit. Will I hear them before I feel them?

The firing starts before I am halfway to the top and I feel nothing. I look back, gasping and panting, subway dust thick in my throat.

The hunter that fell on the track is standing with his back to me, his assault rifle raised, firing at the wall of black.

CHAPTER 14

THE ENTRANCE TURNSTILES are ahead. The Senator and Avril's mum are already the other side. A two-handed parkour hurdle, not even slowing my stride and I'm over and we're out on the street with the sirens and the traffic and the air fresh on our faces after the warm, thick fug of the subway.

I think about the firefight going on below. About a man standing between us and the stairs. How long can he hold them off? Why would he? He will die down there and I will never even know his name.

I look up and sense them before I see them – it is there in the way the crowd parts and wheels like a shoal of fish. Hunters are coming down Broadway, 500 metres out but closing fast.

They have found us.

The Senator has broken cover and the tracker is broadcasting her location. I catch sight of her face and whirl round. There is another group behind us, a black shadow in the crowd, further out but closing in. From a distance, they look like a single, armoured creature. Hunters are homing in on our signal from all directions, not worried about the police, not worried about anything but the pursuit of their quarry.

Panic washes through me, dousing me in a fresh surge of adrenaline. I can see the fear on the two faces watching me – it's coming off them in waves. If we were on horseback, the horses would bolt. There is something very primal going on here. *Colosseum* is a blood sport and we are the hares.

Run, little hares, run; the dogs are coming.

I look at the phone – a minute to go.

There is a building on the corner of 96th and Broadway covered in scaffolding. The hoardings have been painted green and red to make them look Christmassy. Floors and floors of building site. I start to run.

It's a different woman on the Colosseum switchboard, but she has the same sing-song voice. There is no wait.

'Winter,' I say to the head of *Colosseum*. 'The answer is Winter.'

'Hello, Achilles,' says the Adjudicator. 'Cutting it a little fine there.'

My heart hammers. I stop dead in the middle of Broadway, hunters bearing down on me from all directions. 'Who *are* you?' I say. 'What do you want from me?'

'Time to run, Achilles,' he says and then he's gone.

The Senator and Avril's mum yank me into the scaffolding tunnel. The enclosed space is slightly warmer. Hoardings hide us from the street, block the wind. The far end of the tunnel stretches away. There is a site door to the building. *Strictly no admittance without a hardhat* says the notice. The site entrance has a heavy-duty combination lock. The sort bailiffs use when a house gets repossessed. My heart sinks. I am not getting through it.

I stare up at the scaffolding and the makeshift roof that

covers the pavement which doubles as a walkway for the floor above. Can we get up to it? There must be floors and floors of building site for the locator to get lost in. The hunters will be able to see where we are, but exactly which floor will be hard to judge on their 2D screens.

We have about fifteen seconds till the first band of hunters arrive.

There is a grating in the pavement. One of those long subway gratings that make you think the earth is rumbling when you step over them, that seep steam and pollution. I pull a knife, get down on my hands and knees and insert the blade into one corner and press down on the handle. The cantilever effect. I can't lift the weight, but I can lever it. My fingers slip and fumble in my haste.

More haste less speed, more haste less speed.

The grating pops and the other two scramble down on their hands and knees and together we heave in unison like a tug of war team.

One, two, three, *heave.*

The grating sticks and I imagine the hunters racing around the corner and then it gives with a sudden rush and opens up a foot or more. Pipework just below the surface. Two foot below. It runs all the way under the pavement.

Another heave and the gap is wide enough to squeeze through. The Senator doesn't hesitate; she lowers herself into the hole and Avril's mum is right beside her. She flattens herself out and wriggles along, making room for me, until we are all lying on our backs on the pipework just below ground level and I want to scream at them to hurry because unless we can close the grating on top of us, it is no kind of hiding place. We have just lain down on the floor and waited for the hunters to come round the corner.

Three sets of panicking fingers grip the square hatching and heave and yank and nothing happens – the grating won't budge and my heart hammers and then with a rush it slides into place, clanging shut.

Charging feet pound round the corner and stop abruptly.

Did they see the grating close? Did they hear it?

Silence.

I am lying so still it's like my body has stopped. Not breathing, not blinking, the stillness of death. My rucksack is digging into my spine.

Do not move, I want to say to the others. *Do not even breathe.*

We are below the surface, in the shadow, but a hint of movement and we will catch the eye like a mouse scurrying across an empty desert floor.

More running footsteps. At least six hunters now, just above us. How visible are we? I need to look at the others to tell them with my face that they must not move a muscle, must not make a sound, but I dare not even swivel my eyes.

The grating is so close I could lift my head and I would bang my nose. A sneeze and we are all dead.

'Is it another glitch?' says a Russian voice. 'Or is she here?'

I picture them with their phones out, looking at the blue dot where they are standing, looking about them, trying to make sense of it. They have been an hour without the signal, and now suddenly, it's back.

The hunter's phone is still clenched in my hand, down by my thigh, from the call I have just made. If it makes any kind of sound, gets a text, anything, it is game over. And the

Adjudicator knows where we are and he knows where the hunters are. He could just ring it.

There was a character, Dokkaebi, in a game I used to play, who could make other players' phones ring. *Your phone is ringing. Here, let me get that for you*, she used to say in her cute Korean accent while she emptied her SMG-12 right where you were hiding.

The Adjudicator could just call me right now, and why wouldn't he?

The footsteps shuffle closer. Murmuring. The hunters have their phones out – *Where is she?* I imagine them peering about, looking up at the scaffolding, looking at the site door, coming to the conclusion I want them to. They can see an obvious hiding place – a building site – and they will think she has gone up. Humans instinctively flee to higher ground; it is in the bone, left over from when we were living in trees. Not many prey animals stay right where they are, not running, lying still. It is unnatural. That is what they are going to think.

I am willing it so hard, I can picture it happening right above me, almost like an out-of-body experience, as if I have split myself in two – I am looking down on the heads of the hunters and on the grating and on the three white faces, tense in the darkness, staring upwards.

The hunters shuffle and murmur.

They are right overhead now. Boots are standing on the grating, the soles heavy, black rubber.

I wonder how deep the drop is below us, and what will happen if a burst of steam comes out of nowhere. Is it possible to keep silent while you burn? A blast of steam now could cost us our lives.

A voice is raised. The next band of hunters has arrived. The ones coming from the opposite direction. Now there are explanations. *Where is she?* The new group have charged round the corner and come up short. Come up against hunters standing looking at their phones. Not what they were expecting.

Look up, Look up. I am willing it with everything I have.

The new group has changed the dynamic. They all want the kill shot. The ones that were first on the scene have lost the advantage. And no one will want to be left behind. It only needs one of them to make a move and they will all follow, afraid of missing out, afraid of not being in at the death.

The seconds stretch out.

Then the booted feet are moving, and a moment later, there is a burst of automatic gunfire right above our heads. Someone is firing at the site door and everyone else has got out of the way. It is deafening. Not as bad as the subway tunnel with the magnifying effect of the stone, but still shockingly loud. I cringe against the pipe, dust rains down through the grating. I screw my face up, a totally involuntary reaction, but no one is looking down; they are all staring at the locked door. There is a heavy crash as the site door falls backwards. They drilled out its hinges.

Booted footsteps cross the grating and push through the open doorway and then they are all following. Pounding after the first guy. Pounding up the building. No one wants to be left behind now the hunt is on. They have run the Senator down, and now they are going to scour every floor looking for her locator. A 3D problem. How long will it take them to search? How many floors are there above us?

Silence.

The pavement above us is still. There is only ringing in my ears.

I let out a massive breath and turn my head. My neck is stiff – I was holding it so rigid. Avril's mum is right beside me, wide-eyed and sweaty in the silence.

I try to estimate how many hunters just went into the building. More than twenty, less than fifty, which means there are plenty more out there. Some may still be held up by the FBI, bottled up in hotel corridors, but that isn't going to last. They could blast their way out and be back on the street and heading our way.

I put my hands up to the grating and push like I am bench-pressing. Nothing. The other two start shoving with me. The sudden feeling of claustrophobia is overwhelming. We can't go up, we can't go down. We are stuck like pot-holers with the tide coming in. Feverish panicky fingers grip through the lattice work and heave.

Nothing.

Trapped.

We are going to be boiled alive like prawns on a griddle or shot from above, peppered with holes through the grating.

We give a third mighty heave and it suddenly frees. Another heave and the crack is big enough to get through and I am already moving, gun out, because if ever we are vulnerable it is rising, half in and half out of the ground.

CHAPTER 15

THE SENATOR STRAIGHTENS up as she clambers out, she has dirt on her face. Avril's mum's pink tracksuit is streaked with black. The site door is wide open. Sounds echo down from the building – boots on boards, the clanging of scaffolding.

We come out of the hoarding tunnel and stumble round the corner, half running, half walking. Any minute now, the hunters might realise their mistake.

Broadway is packed, the air still full of sirens. There is an ambulance parked up in front of the subway entrance. I head away from it, moving through the crowds, eyes darting round, looking for the black armour and movement that will tell me hunters are coming. You can read it in the crowd's behaviour. The way people shy away. The ripple effect, as those further off catch on. At the moment, there is just excitement in the air, *carnivale*, spectators slightly out of control, slightly feverish. It wouldn't be hard to start a street fight. The crowd is on edge, pumped up, drunk on bloodlust and excitement.

The Senator's white-hot gaze sweeps the busy street – round and back, round and back. Her fear is gone and in its place is a molten core of determination. The strength that has propelled her through political life has been repurposed, honed anew, refound. She is morphing into a whole different person, stronger. Or maybe that person was always there and tonight is bringing it out. The Colosseum makeover. Fulfil your potential. Be the person you were meant to be.

I think about the other targets and how I could have got any one of them to protect, and how I got the weakest, the oldest, the one with the least chance. And how deceptive appearances can be.

Target least likely to survive Colosseum.

Then I think about the crowds and the bloodlust and what will happen if she is spotted. It is human instinct to care for the vulnerable, but crowd behaviour is hard to predict. She could get protected by the herd, or she could get torn to pieces. I am not going to put it to the test.

'Calm down,' I say. 'You'll give yourself away.'

On the hunter's phone, the blue dot is back blinking on Broadway. Out in the open. We are not going to survive the next five minutes, never mind long enough to complete a challenge. The problem is lodged deep inside her and I know what I would do if it were me. Is she strong enough?

'What are you like with pain?' I say.

'Good,' she says.

I step out into the road. Hand up like a traffic cop.

STOP

A blue Chevy screeches to a halt. A saloon. An old model, the styling is square. The interior is black plastic, sweaty and torn. I yank open the door and shove my gun in the driver's face. He scrambles out, arms raised – hands by his ears. I slide behind the wheel. There is a Christmas tree hanging from the mirror. The Senator gets in the front seat.

Avril's mum gets in the back.

I fumble for the shift and take off before they've got the doors closed, screech a U-turn across 96th Street and head downtown.

'Where are you going?' says the Senator, as I take a right.

'Nowhere,' I say. 'We just have to keep moving while we do this.'

'While we do what?'

'Not optimum,' I say. 'Better than an emergency trach obviously.'

'What?' says the Senator.

'Tracheotomy. Hole in the windpipe.' I run another set of lights. 'Tell me again about how good you are with pain.'

'Pain is in the mind and my mind is considerably stronger than my body,' she says.

I lean down and pull a blade and pass it to her.

She turns it over and over in her hands as the penny drops.

If she is looking for sympathy, there isn't any.

I glance in the driver's mirror at Avril's mum. She's not who I would have chosen for this job, but you make do.

'Show me your fingernails,' I say to her.

The bright pink nails match her tracksuit, or they did before it crawled along a subway track and hid in a grating.

'You see the nail on your little finger?' I say.

She nods.

'That is how far you can go into her gut. Mark it on the blade if you can't do it by eye. Any further and she bleeds out. Get the overhead light on and use the phone's torch.'

I pass it back.

The Senator stares.

I shrug off my rucksack.

'Now get the medical kit out,' I say. 'Field dressing with the green writing, disinfectant, swabs, strip of red painkillers.'

Avril's mum is far quicker and more competent than I would have expected. Her deft nimble fingers have the contents of my rucksack laid out on the black plastic beside her in a second. A sharp, acrid smell fills the car – she has started using the disinfectant.

'Instruments and hands,' I say. 'Thoroughly as you can.'

'On it,' she says.

It is probably all the beauty procedures. She's used to the idea of keeping stuff sterile.

Beside me, the Senator is silent. I glance at her, she is staring out at nothing. A kind word and she will crack.

'Get in the back,' I say, my voice hard.

She hesitates for a moment, then she unclips her belt and scrambles, face and knees first, and falls through the gap between the front seats. She swivels round and gets herself up into a sitting position.

I glance in my side mirror. There are two blacked-out four-by-fours a few cars back. We have a tail already and I have just lost my navigator. I swing right down a side street and pray I don't meet something coming the other way.

There is rustling and movement from the back. I crane in the driver's mirror, but all I can see is Avril's mum. Her pink velour tracksuit has a solid black line where she was lying on the pipe. She looks like she is yanking at something.

'What *are* these leggings made of?' she says.

'Woven Kevlar,' I say. 'Fireproof, stops a blade and some bullets.'

'Nice,' says Avril's mum.

There is more yanking and the pink back suddenly sits up.

'Commando,' she says. 'That's a surprise.' She turns to pick up something on the seat beside her.

There is a loaded, breathless pause.

'Ready?' she says.

'Yes,' says the Senator.

It will be better and worse than the Senator is expecting. Self-administered pain, at the hands of another. You let it happen, you brace for it, you anticipate it. A lifetime of anticipation. Better and worse when the knife finally goes in. It is almost an anti-climax.

Almost.

The Senator screams.

'Hold still,' says Avril's mum. Her voice is thoughtful and detached, like a false lash has inadvertently got in the wrong place and stuck hard and now has to be lifted off. It's like having open-heart surgery performed by a beautician. Not ideal but could be a lot worse.

I take another right. I am going round in a circle. The seconds stretch out.

'Well?' I say, my eyes huge in the rearview mirror. The Christmas tree swings.

'I've made the cut,' says Avril's mum. 'But I can't see anything – there's too much blood.'

'Pinch it end to end and then swab fast.'

I picture the bright pink nails squeezing the skin. The pain will be immense. Much worse than the initial cut.

'Fuck,' says the Senator.

I have never heard her swear before, and she has had plenty of cause tonight.

'I can't really see,' says Avril's mum. 'But just before it welled up, I got a look, and there was nothing but bands of gristle with one bit slightly raised.'

Could be scar tissue, could be the tracker. I think about the man who put all this together. Not an amateur. Someone who knows what he's doing. Someone who has done it eight times before. It is going to be lodged pretty deep. I stare at the road. Risk and reward. Risk now versus certain death later.

'I'm going to use my earring,' she says. 'Just the post, to see if it's in there.'

'Disinfectant,' I say.

'Way ahead of you.'

There is another crowded silence. I picture her leaning over, trying to see, trying to hold steady, swabbing the blood away.

The Senator screams. I crane in the mirror, but I can see nothing. Suddenly, the pink back sits up.

'It's there,' she says. 'Below the gristle. Hard. I definitely felt it. No question.'

So what are the options? Dig it out in the back of a car and she almost certainly dies. Go near a hospital and the hunters will catch her and she dies. Do nothing and they catch us and she dies. What other choice is there? There has to be another way.

'We need something small and copper,' I say. 'To disrupt the signal. If we could get something copper into the wound, right over the tracker, we might partially block it.

Distort it slightly. Worth a try. It might give us a chance.'

Something small and copper. Not really the kind of thing you carry around with you. Packing my kit for tonight, I wasn't thinking, *I know, a plain copper disc, that's what I'll need.*

'What sort of thing?' says Avril's mum.

'A disc like a cat has hanging from its collar. Only, made of copper.'

'I have something.' She fumbles round her neck under her tracksuit and pulls out a pendant on the end of a chain. She passes it forwards. An oval with the name *Rachel* engraved on it. The copper has gone verdigris green in the air.

Rachel was Avril's real name. The person she was before she decided to become Avril.

If that isn't fate taking a hand, I don't know what is.

I turn it over: *For mom.*

I can see a small, pigtailed version of Avril giving it to her. Maybe for her birthday. A cheap bit of jewellery, the sort of thing a child might manage to buy.

There is something about that that makes my eyes burn.

'Yes,' I say. 'Perfect. Swab it down. Get it inside the wound then smack the field dressing hard over the top, tight as you can. No hanging around.'

The smell of disinfectant is back. She is swabbing the disc.

'You'll have to hold the light,' she says to the Senator. 'Don't move. Don't try and get up, just hold it steady.'

The Senator is holding the light for her own operation. That is surgery in the field for you.

There is a ripping sound like material tearing as the field dressing comes out of its sterilised packet.

'It's just like masking tape,' says Avril's mum. 'I thought it would be soft.'

There is a second of crowded silence as she gets into position.

'OK,' she says. 'I'm going in.'

I can tell the moment it happens. There is a sharp intake of breath from the Senator and then an audible smack as the dressing comes down. Avril's mum took me at my word.

'*Fuck*,' says the Senator who must have sworn more in the last five minutes than she has in the last sixty years.

'Well?' I say.

'I did it,' says Avril's mum. 'Inside the slit. Right over the lump. Then closed it up with the tape.'

There is a pause while she swabs. Clearing the blood away from the field dressing, trying to see if there is any new blood.

'The bleeding has totally stopped,' she says. 'That tape is amazing.'

I let out a breath I didn't know I'd been holding.

'You need surgery to remove it,' I say. 'It's that good. Better than skin. Now give her two of the red pills.'

'Did it work?' says the Senator. Her voice is croaky, like it's coming from the back of her throat. I can see her trying to move. Gingerly easing herself upright to take the painkillers.

'I don't know,' says Avril's mum.

I hold my hand up by my ear and she passes me back the phone. I look down, checking to see if the blue dot is still there, to see if the tracker is still transmitting. My heart sinks. The blue dot blinks up at me as strong as ever. The disappointment is sharp. I didn't expect it to work, but I thought it might. The chances were good. Maybe thirty per cent. I thought it might.

I look in my side mirrors to check our tail. Nothing. Somehow, we seem to have lost them. The blue dot is on a street called West 86th. I take a right and keep watching the mirrors. Nothing. I look down at the phone. The blue dot is still on West 86th.

'Where are we now?' I say.

'Upper West Side,' says the Senator.

'No, precisely.'

'Columbus Avenue and 76th,' she says.

'So not West 86th?'

'No,' she says. 'We are ten blocks from 86th.'

I yank the wheel and slam on the brakes and the Chevy lurches up against the kerb and comes to a stop. I stare down at the little blue dot. It is still moving. Travelling down West 86th.

I feel my face breaking into a smile; the blue dot is lagging. Not by much, but enough. A few precious minutes. This is why we've lost our tail. I hold the phone up and show them the screen.

'We did it.'

'It thinks I am still on 86th?' The Senator says, catching on quick.

'The signal is disrupted. Lagging. Not keeping up with you. How long since we were where the blue dot is now?'

The Senator considers. 'Five minutes? Is that good?'

Not long, but enough. A lifetime in fact.

'Very good. If we keep moving, we will *always* be ahead of where they think we are. They will never catch us. For the first time tonight, we are ahead of the game.'

CHAPTER 16

I PULL AWAY from the pavement.

'I can't believe it,' says the Senator.

'How are you feeling?'

'Like someone just dug a hole in my gut and then stuck masking tape over it.'

'I should have been a paramedic,' says Avril's mum.

'Now we are ahead of the game,' I say, passing the phone back. 'Let's keep it going. Log back into your e mail. We need to find out what your challenge is.'

There is silence while the Senator scrolls. There is not a shadow of doubt in my mind that it will be there now, that he will have sent the challenge again.

'Nothing,' she says.

There is disbelief in her voice. I am not the only one that expected him to play fair. I remember Avril being afraid of the dark and the power failing. Maybe he doesn't play fair. Then I think about him knowing we were hiding under the grating and keeping quiet. Not tipping the hunters off, letting them lose themselves in the building, letting us escape. We were saved for a reason – to give her a chance to rise to the challenge.

'Look again,' I say. 'Go back to the night of the announcement. There will be something.' I know it like I know myself.

'Got it!' she says suddenly.

Finally, we are going to get some answers.

She is silent while she reads.

'Go on then,' says Avril's mum. 'Let's hear it.'

'I don't get it,' says the Senator.

'It's probably a riddle,' says Avril's mum. She snatches the phone and reads it out.

Where is Anna?

Walk on water, first lady, before the dawn to find her.

Some seasons are colder than others, tread carefully in the tunnels of your mind.

Love Colosseum

'Not much of a riddle,' she says.

'Is that the same Anna?' I say. 'The one that you said was like me?'

The Senator is silent.

'That's the stalker, isn't it?' says Avril's mum.

'What stalker?' I say.

'She wasn't a stalker. She was a member of staff. A student from Columbia. A junior staffer. She worked in my husband's office and then she went crazy and then she died. She wasn't Anna.'

'She took a potshot at her,' Avril's mum says.

'That definitely qualifies as crazy. What happened?'

'I was at a fundraiser. She fired at me, I stumbled and my husband shot her. He saved my life. He was quicker than anyone, quicker than my own security.'

Avril's mum is leaning between the seats. 'Maybe they

were having an affair. Got out of hand.'

'They were *not* having an affair. And if they were, why would he shoot her?'

'Maybe she gave him an ultimatum – threatened to expose him. Maybe he was tired of her. Maybe this was just a good way to shut her up.'

'You don't understand what it's like for him,' she says. 'Women throw themselves at him all the time. He only has to look at a woman and everyone thinks they're having an affair.'

'Funny that,' says Avril's mum.

'I think I know my own husband.'

'He's a tart,' she says. 'Sorry.'

'He is not.'

'Yeah,' says Avril's mum. 'He is. Take it from me. I've had more than my fair share. To be honest' – she leans between the front seats, talking to me as if the Senator isn't there – 'I would say her husband is her biggest weakness. She has no clue. Ask any woman and they would agree with me. Don't put your faith in men who look like heroes, with their five million Twitter followers and their Botoxed faces. Put your faith in people who act like heroes. It's not what you look like or what you say. It is how you *act.*'

'You don't understand what it's like for him,' the Senator says again. 'He has been dogged his entire political life by stalkers and obsessive fans and the press. He only has to stand next to a pretty girl and the speculation starts. It's the downside of the halo effect. He hates it.'

'You don't know much about men, do you?' says Avril's mum.

'OK,' I say. 'This is all beside the point since that woman wasn't actually Anna. *Who* is Anna?'

'No one,' says the Senator. 'We were close once, like I said. She went away a long time ago.'

'Where did she go?'

'I don't know.'

'So tell me about her. What was she like?'

'Brilliant,' she says. 'Top of the class. Razor-sharp political brain but a dreamer. Impractical. Superstitious. She would toss a coin to see what it said. Checking in with destiny, she used to call it. Putting herself in the hands of fate.'

I know the type. The GCHQ research department is full of them. Max, the Head of Research, has a lucky cat and a Magic 8 ball on his desk. He has even been known to ask it operational questions. The Magic 8 ball, not the cat.

'So basically brilliant but a bit nuts. And what happened?'

'She got increasingly angry. She thought we weren't achieving enough. Helping enough people.'

'So, an idealist as well as brilliant and nuts. What about *Colosseum*? Was she interested in *Colosseum*?'

'This was long before *Colosseum*, but I know she would hate it. It would be one of the things she would think I should be shouting louder about.' The Senator looks out of the window. 'She would probably be right.'

'And when did you last hear from her?'

She shrugs.

'Ten years ago.' She sighs. 'She couldn't see a cause without throwing herself at it. A total bleeding heart. She was literally drowning in good causes and she felt them all so keenly and her own powerlessness. She couldn't cope with the pity she felt. Totally unsuited to front-line politics. She went mad with empathy and the enormity of the task. So many causes needing a champion. She had a breakdown in the end.'

'And what happened to her after that? Where did she go?'

'I don't know,' she says.

There is something very weird about this. Why does her challenge involve someone she hasn't seen for ten years?

Who is Anna and what happened to her?

Anna

10 years ago

SOMETHING IS WRONG. Terribly wrong. I can feel it in my unravelling bones. I can hear it in the voices on the wind. I can smell it in the air. I have turned to meet my destiny and it is not there. There is only void. Nothingness. The emptiness of eternity.

Dark water.

The sun is coming up above the horizon, hot and red and angry and too late I remember what the solstice really is. A turning point, a time of change, a time of rebirth, but also, a time of death. I shudder and shake and fight as I am pushed to the edge. But you can't fight fate. You can't escape destiny. I, of all people, know that.

Dark water presses against me, down my neck, presses against my eyes. As I sink into the depths, I know the next breath I take will be water.

He is there in the dark with me, but he is a strong swimmer, and I am not.

I understand. Too late I understand.

Baptism by dark water.

Death by dark water.

CHAPTER 17

'ANNA'S BEEN COMING back to me all evening in fits and starts,' says the Senator, 'like she is connected to events somehow.'

'Well, there's obviously some mystery,' says Avril's mum. 'Or she wouldn't be your challenge.'

I am silent. I cannot picture how an estranged political staffer and her fate could be of any interest to the Colosseum Adjudicator. It is totally unfathomable.

'OK,' I say. 'Leave Anna. What about the rest?

Walk on water, first lady, before the dawn to find her.

Some seasons are colder than others, tread carefully in the tunnels of your mind.'

'First lady – that's obviously me,' says the Senator. 'I was just about to announce I was running for President.'

'I knew it,' says Avril's mum.

'Before the dawn is easy too. Sunrise is at 7.17 today.'

'How the hell do you know that?'

'Walter and I were talking about it this evening.'

I check the time. 5.30 a.m.

'It's not actually as straight forward as that,' I say. 'It's light before sunrise. You have astronomical dawn, nautical dawn – which is what the military use – and civil dawn, which is when it is starting to get light, but the sun is not officially up.'

I can feel them both staring at the back of my head.

'But for the purposes of *Colosseum*, and given that it is the solstice, I think we go with sunrise as our definition, which is the moment the sun hits the horizon. It's what they'll be using at Stonehenge.'

I glance in the side mirror. Still no sign of a tail. Sooner or later, they are going to realise something is wrong with the tracker.

'OK,' says Avril's mum. 'What's next?'

'Water is my biggest fear, so that's probably what's in the tunnels of my mind. Some seasons are colder than others. Winter is the coldest season. It can't be a coincidence. But that suggests the Adjudicator knew Winter would be with me a week before I called her. How is that possible?'

'I have no idea, but I think you are right about the water. This man uses it to break people.'

'I can't swim,' says the Senator. 'I never learned.'

'I think he probably knows that,' I say. 'In fact, I'm sure he does.'

'Why can't you swim?' says Avril's mum. 'Was there some reason?'

The Senator looks out at the night. 'I've always been too scared,' she says. 'Since I was a little child. It used to drive my mother mad.' She frowns like she is trying to remember.

'So, you never had lessons?' says Avril's mum.

She thinks about this. 'Not that I can remember. To be honest, I can't even remember trying. Every time I think about it, there is just a blank.'

There's a red flag right there.

'Maybe something happened to you,' I say. 'A long time ago. Put you off and your mind has thrown up some barriers. If I say "water" to you, what do you see?'

'A bottle of water.'

'If I say "swimming lesson", what do you see?'

The Senator thinks about this. 'Nothing.'

'If I say "drowning", what do you see?'

'Dark water,' she says. 'And I can hear a dog barking.'

I feel the chill up my spine. Something happened to her long ago, I would bet on it.

'*Walks on water*,' she says. 'But where? America is a big place. There is water everywhere.'

The street lights flash by, showing her in profile. She is focused. A problem to solve. Something she can do. Totally in control. I check the gauge. The last thing we need is to run out of gas.

I feel like we have all the pieces here in New York. They are all here, ready and waiting to slot into place. I turn them over and over. In New York. It is not a coincidence she ended up here. It was intended.

'The President is not the First Lady,' I say. 'Who is the most famous first lady of them all?'

'Jackie O,' says Avril's mum. 'Obviously.'

The Jackie Onassis Reservoir.

We have some of the pieces and they are clanging into place.

'I couldn't understand why the hunters left us alone at the reservoir when we were hiding. Do you know what they said? *That's the no-go area.* I think the reservoir is your Tito's Bunker. Your safe space. It is where you have to go to do your challenge. *Colosseum* didn't touch Avril in the bunker and they won't touch you there.'

'They have probably filled it with something,' says Avril's mum.

'Like what?'

'Sharks.'

'Sharks are saltwater creatures,' says the Senator.

'The worst things are in your head,' I say. 'Conjured up by your own imagination. Your mind can pull worse stunts than the Adjudicator. That is what he does – pitch you into your nightmares.'

Dark water, it just had to be; there is some kind of ghastly, perfect symmetry to it.

'But what does the Jackie O have to do with finding Anna?' says Avril's mum.

I have a very bad feeling about this.

'I can hazard a possible guess,' I say.

'Maybe someone bumped her off,' says Avril's mum. 'Maybe her body is in there.'

The Senator stares out of the window.

'Maybe the same person who deleted the challenge.'

'And who was that?' I say. 'Because it becomes a lot more relevant now we know what the challenge actually is. *Who would delete an email from your private account, Senator?* said the Adjudicator. *Are you asking yourself that?* Pretty specific. Like he wanted you to work it out.'

'There are only two people who have access to that account – my husband and Walter,' the Senator says.

'Did Walter know Anna?' I say. 'Did they work togeth-er?'

'No,' she says. 'Anna was before his time.'

'And yet, he's the reason I am here. He's the one who

talked you into going on the run with me instead of staying with the FBI.'

'He took a bullet for her,' says Avril's mum. 'It's not going to be him.'

'What did he say about me exactly?' I say.

'He said you were the Best of the Best and that, if anyone could get us through the tunnels of the mind, it was you.'

Tunnels of the mind.

'Who is he? How did you meet?'

'It was at the Human Rights Campaign benefit,' she says. 'Ten years ago. The Marriott Hotel on Broadway. He was with the British embassy. It was summer and there were flaming torches in the ninety-degree heat. He came up to me afterwards.' She goes silent. 'You know how you just get talking and really get on?'

'Not really.'

'Like you know what they think on a thousand subjects without needing to discuss them?'

'Soulmates,' says Avril's mum.

'Then what?'

She shrugs. 'Then nothing. We met a couple more times and I offered him a job. Simple as that. I could have offered within ten minutes of meeting him.'

'And he accepted? Turned his back on his illustrious diplomatic career?'

'He never had an illustrious diplomatic career,' she says. 'Someone like that never does. Too thoughtful. Too gentle. I think he was a trade attaché.'

'Really? How old is he?'

'You met him.'

'He was wearing a balaclava when I met him,' I say. 'He could have been twenty for all I know. We never saw his face when he was in the corridor waiting for the hunters.'

'Early-sixties, I guess. Now I come to think about it, I don't honestly know. I should know.'

'Is Walter his real name?'

'No,' says the Senator. 'How in the world did you know that? He changed his name when he came to America. Apparently, his old name made people think he was a woman. He called himself after his favourite poet.' I can hear the smile in her voice.

I am silent, joining the dots. Doing a bit of basic arithmetic. Putting two and two together.

'What?' she says.

'Early-sixties, self-effacing, inexplicably junior despite his manifold talents? Still working? Nothing strike you as weird about that? Did he go away at all? Every couple of months for a few days?'

'He has to visit his family in the UK,' she says. 'He is very devoted. I hate it when he goes. Sometimes, he has to go very suddenly.'

'I bet he does.'

'What?' she says.

'He's a spook,' says Avril's mum. 'It's like that episode of *West Wing*.'

The Senator smiles. 'No, he really isn't. We had his background checked very thoroughly. He was squeaky clean. Not even a parking ticket.'

She has no clue. Absolutely no clue at all. That was why he was wearing a balaclava. I probably know him.

'MI6 probably,' I say. 'Not us. We would have left the parking tickets. Too unsubtle. Didn't it seem odd that he could pick up the phone to the head of the British secret service when you needed help?'

'They went to school together.'

'I'm sure they did.'

'I don't believe this,' she says.

'Is he the reason you stayed in New York?'

She thinks about it. 'Not really. The safe houses were a bust. It was never the plan to stay in New York. When I agreed to run with you, I thought we would leave New York, but you didn't arrive in time.'

'I arrived at precisely the time he told me to. To the minute. He *meant* for you to stay in New York.'

The streets slide by.

Could *he* be the Adjudicator? He has a clear link to the British secret service. I ponder the point. It doesn't seem very likely. He has been unconscious for most of the night.

'Where was he during the other Colosseum hunts? Was he away?'

'No,' says the Senator. 'He was with me the whole time. What are you suggesting?'

'Two men,' says Avril's mum. 'One of them deleted your challenge. One of them wants you dead. Which is it?'

The Senator is silent.

'It has to be one of them,' says Avril's mum. 'And the Adjudicator wants you to work out which. Like it is connected, part of the jigsaw. Like they have a role to play. Although, how that's possible when one is locked up in an emergency bunker and the other is on the operating table, I don't know.'

Dawn ticks nearer.

'Whoever deleted the challenge,' the Senator says. 'I couldn't do it anyway. I couldn't search the Jackie O. I can't swim. I couldn't do two minutes. Never mind two hours. And the Jackie O is massive. Ten acres.'

'But not deep, I'm guessing. Scuba kit and some kind of light,' I say.

'How long would I have to be in there? Until dawn?'

'As long as it takes.'

'This is it,' says Avril's mum. 'This is your nightmare. Your challenge. You're just a few hours behind the game, that's all.'

'But what if they come for me while I'm in there?'

'They won't,' I say. '*Colosseum* will wait to see if you rise to the challenge. They will be there, but they won't interfere. Just like with the running man and Avril. We need to get some kit to help us. Scuba gear and powerful diving torches. Where can we do that in Manhattan?'

'There *has* to be another way.'

'I don't see another way,' I say. 'And we are running out of time. We have a tail, five minutes behind. If I stop, they will be on us.' I turn to look at her. 'Dawn is coming.'

CHAPTER 18

THE SENATOR IS staring out of the window.

'What is it?' says Avril's mum. 'Have you remembered something?'

'It's nothing,' she says. 'I was thinking back to the night of my birthday and the Colosseum announcement. I was on the stage and the room felt wrong and I caught sight of my husband looking at *Colosseum* on the big screen and he had this strange look on his face. I had seen it before – I just couldn't remember what it meant. And then in all the panic and noise I forgot about it.'

'Other things to worry about,' says Avril's mum.

'Yes. I just remembered that's all. Where I had seen that look on his face before and what it meant.' She falls silent.

'Well?' says Avril's mum. 'The suspense is killing us.'

'Excitement,' she says. 'Like something good was about to happen. I last saw it on election night. He knew he was going to win, but he couldn't let it show.'

She looks out of the window. Thinking about her husband. The love of her life. Her photo negative. Seeing him in a different light, through a different spectrum, the prism of Avril's mum. Not a view she's used to. Not the kind of woman she ever comes into contact with normally. Her husband looks quite different in this light. Her definitions of hero are out of date, and she is wondering why she never questioned his version of masculinity. She is weighing him up, weighing up every past look and gesture, every comment by a member of her staff. Wondering if he really is her photo negative. She looks stricken.

'Scuba gear,' I say, as gently as I can.

The Senator pulls herself together. This is her area. 'Down on the water, not far,' she says. 'School of Diving. It's going to be shut at this time of night though. And how can we stop?'

'We will just have to be really quick,' I say, trying not to think about the massive amount of kit you need for diving. 'In and out. And there are three of us to carry.'

'Any problems, and you two can take off and leave me,' says Avril's mum, 'and I will follow you with the kit.'

I am silent thinking about what I would do if I was a hunter who knew the target needed diving equipment.

It is almost impossible to act randomly.

'How many other places in Manhattan have diving kit?' I say.

'None, as far as I know,' the Senator says. 'Apart from the cops obviously, but we don't want to go near them.'

None.

The enterprising hunter, instead of staying ten blocks behind, is going to be thinking ahead. And one destination in particular is going to come to mind.

'You think hunters may already be there waiting?' says Avril's mum.

Yes.

I shrug. 'It's not inconceivable if they realise something

is up with the tracker. How will you get tanks and wetsuits and all the rest of it to the reservoir if we leave you?'

'Give me some credit,' she says. 'I got into the quarantine zone and got the hunter's phone out of the dumpster, didn't I?' She puts a hand on my shoulder. 'You can trust me to do this,' she says, 'if it comes to it.'

And what choice do we have?

Walk on water, first lady, before the dawn to find the truth.

Dawn is approaching and we are out of options.

I meet her eyes in the rearview mirror.

'The maiden, the mother and the crone,' says Avril's mum. 'It is practically mythic.'

'Less of the crone,' says the Senator. She tries to smile. 'I reckon I can get away with fifty. After my Colosseum makeover.'

'I'm just fine with maiden,' I say.

I can see Avril's mum checking the Senator out.

'It's because you're so slim,' she says to her. 'Nothing ages you faster than fat. What work have you had done?'

'Two lifts,' says the Senator. 'Nose and teeth.'

In the rearview mirror, Avril's mum nods. She strokes a finger along her own jawline. 'I was thinking about having a second one,' she says.

The Senator gives me directions. It is like having a massively overqualified satnav in the car. Her local knowledge is encyclopaedic.

'When we get there, always supposing the hunters are not there already, we will have to be quick. In and out. No messing about. We have to break in, get what we need and be out of there in four minutes. Do either of you know anything about diving?

'No,' says the Senator.

'I did a week once,' says Avril's mum. 'Before Avril was born.'

A week.

How can a total beginner do a night dive? A total beginner who can't even swim? I think about the dark and the silt and the disorientation and my heart sinks.

'OK, so I will find the stuff and you two help me get it into the car. Wetsuits, face masks, fins, weigh belts, regulators, tanks and harnesses. Everything else – hoods, boots etc. – are great but not essential. And time is key here. In and out. No messing about. We are on the clock.'

'It will be freezing,' says Avril's mum. 'Stone-cold, stop-your-heart, freezing.'

She's not wrong. Stone-cold dark water. The thought makes me shudder.

'It'll be fine,' I say.

'Coming up on the left,' says the Senator.

Up ahead is a row of shops like a high street. Half the frontages have shutters down. Graffiti scrawled across the metal. Windows with ancient displays of fishing tackle. *Get your maggots here* says a sign.

I slow to twenty mph, then ten mph, then stop. Nothing is moving. A wrapper blows along the gutter. Unlike the centre, which is teaming with action, this quiet corner of Manhattan is deserted. I count the seconds down.

Visibility is good for yards and yards behind and in front.

There is one of those diving suits in the window like they used to wear a hundred years ago that make you sink to the bottom of the sea.

Five seconds, long enough. Why would anyone wait? If they were here, they would just mow us down with their assault rifles.

I open the car door and listen.

Moment of truth.

Nothing. Nothing moves in the shadows; no one jumps out of an alley.

Wind whistles between the buildings, it is colder here and there is the smell of something in the air – the harbour. We are close to water. You can just tell.

I ease out of the car and straighten up.

Still nothing.

I cross the five metres in the open to the shop door. It is sealed down tight, no one has been through it – modern locks, decent alarm system. I spend the first couple of seconds having a look and, by the end of the third second, have come to a conclusion. Nothing I have in my rucksack is getting me in. I head back to the car.

'Belts on,' I say. I swivel in my seat with my arm on the headrest beside me. The back window of the Chevy gives a letterbox view. I stretch my neck and crane to see, wrench the gearbox, searching for reverse. Look down at the shift. Find reverse. Put my foot down, the Chevy lurches as its back wheels hit the kerb, then it surges up and over onto the pavement and I yank the wheel hard over until the car is pointing straight at the shop front. They stare at me from the backseat.

I turn to face forwards, psych myself up a little, get my hands level on the steering wheel and slam my foot down on the accelerator. The Chevy surges forwards with a roar of engine – two tonnes of metal accelerating towards a solid immovable object. Twenty-five mph on impact equals whiplash. Thirty mph equals possible broken bones. Forty mph could be fatal. The key is to already be braking on impact which, in turn, means accelerating over the theoretical safe speed in order to hit with enough power to achieve one's objective. That's the theory. I did a week of it at Camp Alpha, but like so many things at Camp Alpha, it was a question of practise. The best stunt drivers in the world have been doing it a lifetime. Smoking doughnuts are harder than they look.

I brake just before impact, my ribs slam against the steering wheel, my head rocks back and forth on my neck and the bonnet rams through the shop window with a mighty crack of glass. The window doesn't break – the safety glass does its job – it cracks into a million tiny pieces. Textbook. Even the Camp Alpha CO would be impressed. The airbags don't go off, which is a pretty good indication I got the speed about right. I ease back and the Chevy's crumpled bonnet comes free and the window collapses downwards like a guillotine, with a deafening crash of glass. There is a fraction of a second of silence, then the shop's alarm goes off, all guns blazing, shrill and urgent as a school fire alarm.

I reckon we have already had a minute. Maybe a minute and a half.

I back the car out onto the street and we jump out, hearts racing and clamber up through the ruined shopfront, crawling over broken glass and the wrecked display of fishing paraphernalia.

The smell of live bait is everywhere; somewhere they have tubs of maggots. They are all about fishing. There are cheap cameras on the wall, so you can photograph your fish after you have caught it, and scales with hanging nets, so you can weigh it.

The interior is dark and seems to be given over to rods and nets and all things fishing, and I am wondering whether the Senator has led us astray – easy enough to make a mistake about a place like this; *School of Diving* could just be a name – when we find a corridor leading to the back.

It opens out into a wide locker room spanning the whole building. A fish tank hums in the corner, casting a blue glow. Face masks line shelves, wetsuits dangle from pegs, there is a huge plastic container of fins. There are certificates on the walls –instructors' diving qualifications. The floor is wet. The smell is unmistakable. *This is more like it.* In the corner, there is a metal table with high-pressure hoses coming out of the wall ready to fill tanks. The tanks are on racks over by the back door.

I yank the bolts on the door just in case. Tradecraft rule number 1 – scope out your escape route. Always give yourself somewhere to run.

Below the metal table are a dozen tanks sitting on the floor. I heft one up. Standard one hundred cubic feet. Full. Ready and waiting for a trip out in the morning. A tiny bit of luck.

I start grabbing wetsuits, the Senator scoops up fins. I push everything into Avril's mum's waiting arms.

'Come back for the tanks,' I say.

She hurries out to the car and I swing round looking for torches. Without light at night, we will see nothing. I am expecting them to be in the back part of the shop – the front end is merchandise, a retail outlet, items sold from a till.

The back is the other business, connected but separate. Diving lessons and excursions. There are cubby holes like a locker room and all manner of stuff, but no torches.

Surely *any* diving around here, even in the day, would have to use torches, lights of some kind, maybe headcams? The Hudson has to be murky. I whirl round, but there is nothing. Maybe the excursions around the bay are for fishing, and the diving is done indoors in some kind of aquarium. In which case, we are in real trouble.

I go out into the front of the shop, starting to panic. I reckon we have already had five minutes. Avril's mum is back from loading and I am hefting about twenty kilos of tank when the side wall of the shop is lit up by the beams of a car.

I freeze.

A black four-by-four is coming down the road, slow and cautious, like it's looking for something. Like it is trying to get a lock on a signal.

We have been too slow.

The hunters have caught up with us.

CHAPTER 19

T HERE IS NO need to say anything. I drop the tank and we lunge out down the corridor, scrambling into the back room, scrambling for the door. No fumbling with bolts, no locked door trapping us in. We are out of the building within three seconds of seeing the headlights.

We are in an alley. Dark after the blue fish-tank glow of the back room. The smell is strong and I wonder how close the water is. There are bins of fish guts and bins of rubbish and a canoe and a rusty outboard motor. I imagine car doors opening, out on the high street. I close the door behind us, banking on the siren to muffle the sound.

Hopefully, they check the building before they go out the back. Her locator is going to show her still in the shop. We edge down the alley and out onto the street. The high street with the shop fronts is round the next corner. The other two keep a couple of paces behind me, close but not too close. Perfect formation. They are both naturals. The street we have come out on is much like the high street but without any shops. Offices with their lights off. If it were residential, lights would be going on all along the street. If they had ever gone off. Everyone is watching *Colosseum*.

It feels exposed. Only doorways for cover. There is nothing to get behind – nothing but grills and shuttered frontages the whole way down the street. A metal backdrop for a gunfight. The noise would be immense.

There is a shop on the corner, its metal roll-down shutter covered in graffiti. It could sell anything – there is no clue from the frontage. I think about the Chevy loaded with kit and the oxygen tanks still inside and the missing torches. I peer round the corner into the high street.

Two black four-by-fours are parked up behind the Chevy, their doors wide open, their occupants already in the building. I can just picture how it went – the tracker told them the target had stopped; they pulled up, saw a diving shop with a smashed window, heard the alarm, knew they had caught her and leapt out of the car. They probably left the engines running.

There is movement up the street in front of the four-by-fours; a hunter is standing beside the Chevy.

Damn.

He is going to check it out, find the kit and know we can't have gone far.

I turn back to the other two.

'I'll stay,' says Avril's mum as soon as she sees my face. 'The moment you go, this place will be deserted. They will all chase after you. When the coast is clear I'll bring the stuff to the reservoir.'

'Torches,' I say. 'There is no way we can search something that size without them. They have to be there somewhere. I just didn't have time to find them.'

She nods.

'As soon as you get to the reservoir, get the other side of the fence and shout. The Jackie O Reservoir is the safe zone.'

'For her,' says Avril's mum. 'Not necessarily for us.' She grips my shoulder briefly. For some reason, it reminds me of a Croatian cliff path and a mother saying goodbye to her daughter, and my eyes prick. 'And I'm OK with that,' she says, and walks away up the street. A moment later, I see her step into a doorway, hidden from view.

I turn back to watch the front of the School of Diving. The problem is, the hunter is still looking in the Chevy, checking it out. He is practically inside it. He is bent at the waist, his whole body in the car. Any minute now, the hunters searching the building will be coming out the back. We need to get out of here before that happens and our escape route is blocked.

Caught between a rock and a hard place. *Again.*

I look at the Senator, then I look back at the hunters' cars standing behind the Chevy with their doors open, and then I look back at the Senator again. I don't have to take the Chevy – Avril's mum can do that. I can take one of the cars behind it.

It would be the craziest call in an evening of crazy calls. No one in their right mind would be dumbass enough to try it. I can only imagine what the training officers at Camp Alpha would say.

I count to three and break cover round the corner and hustle at a low, speeding crouch to the back of the four-by-four. The Senator is right behind me. We peer round the boot. The driver's door is open. I look at the metal by my nose. Armour plating. I slide down the side, knees bent, my back to the car, praying the keys are in the ignition, praying there isn't anyone in the back sitting it out. Any minute now, the hunters are going to do what we did – go out the back way, come down the alley. A second later and they will be out on the street with us.

There is a sudden ghastly moment when we are out in the open, beside the car. Fully visible, the point of no return. And then we're level with the driver's seat and the car is empty and I can see the keys and I am throwing myself inside and turning the key in the ignition and the Senator is scrambling in behind me. I slam it into reverse and we screech backwards up the street, all our doors wide.

The hunter with his head in the Chevy straightens up and stares open-mouthed, but before he can get his gun up we have turned the corner and are gone.

CHAPTER 20

THE SENATOR WHOOPS in the back like a crazy teenager.

'I can't believe we just did that,' she says.

I can hear her clambering about slamming the doors.

'Careful,' I say. 'Mind your stomach.'

I crane in the rearview mirror. She is leaning over the back seat looking into the trunk area. Her top half disappears from view. I get a picture of the field dressing holding her gut together and wince.

A moment later, she is climbing through the gap between the front seats, an M249, the American version of the FN Minimi, in her arms. The sight of her with a fully loaded squad automatic weapon is shocking. She is smiling in the light of the dashboard.

'Have you totally lost it?'

'It makes me feel better,' she says.

I look in the side mirror. Still no tail. 'Do you even know how to use it?'

'Sure,' she says. 'Know your enemy. I did a course.'

It doesn't surprise me. She is nothing if not thorough. I can imagine her earnestly taking notes while some West Point sergeant showed her the form.

'Just put it in the footwell, carefully, and leave it alone.'

It is the para version with the collapsible metal stock and, by the looks of it, a fully loaded drum. She pushes the manual safety to the right and I get a flash of red telling me the weapon is ready to fire.

'*Right now*,' I say, wondering why the hunters have machine guns with them. They are prepared for a massive firefight. Neither the police nor the FBI could handle this. It would take an army.

I check the side mirror again. Still nothing. The digital clock on the dashboard is showing 6:05 a.m. An hour and twenty minutes till dawn. Not long to find the answer to a question we don't even understand.

Where is Anna? Walk on water before the dawn to find the answer.

Walk on water? What does that mean? The Senator is terrified of water. And her fear is in the bone, instinctive, old. It has been there for decades. Since she was a child. She can't swim. So maybe it is connected. Some old childhood trauma she has to overcome. That would be very like the Adjudicator. I bet the whole challenge is designed around the fact that she can't swim. But black water? A night dive? That is enough to scare most people, never mind a non-swimmer. I can feel the cold sweat creeping up my own spine at the thought.

'How is your gut?' I ask, glancing over at her.

'Great,' she says. 'Those painkillers must be really powerful.'

She's not wrong.

She taps the field dressing. 'It feels like I'm wearing a corset keeping everything in.'

'You are,' I say. 'It's keeping your insides in. Field dressings are designed for mortal injuries far behind enemy lines. They hold you together for as long as they need to.'

'Right,' she says. 'And how long will that be in my case?'

'About an hour and twenty minutes.'

I make a quick right, watching the road behind in my rear mirror. Nothing. The five-minute lag is still functioning.

'Do you think she'll be OK?' she says.

I stare out into the night. 'I don't know.'

'We are leading them away from her at least, like the Pied Piper – the rats will be streaming after us. Shouldn't we get rid of the hunter's phone?'

'No.'

'Isn't it another means of tracking us? You said we couldn't have a hunter's phone on us because it would give us away.'

'The hunters can see your tracker; only the Adjudicator can see a hunter's phone.'

'What am I missing here?' she says in a you-have-to-be-kidding-me tone of voice.

I am silent.

'Well?' she says.

'The Adjudicator won't give us away.'

'How can you possibly know that?'

I look out into the middle distance. 'I understand him and how he operates. He makes sense to me. There are rules here. This is a game but not in the conventional sense. Did you ever see that movie where they find themselves in a computer game?'

'No.'

'They have to complete a mission and in the process they became stronger, sharper, faster, braver. They come out the other end better versions of themselves. The best they can be. That is what is going on here tonight.'

'So, he's doing me a favour? Is that what you're saying?' she says.

'Doing both of us a favour.'

'You don't have a challenge.'

'*You* are my challenge. Keeping you safe, protecting you. He wants me to step up.'

She is silent, thinking about the implications of *step up*.

'It's all about finding the balance between you and Ash,' she says. 'A synthesis of your two sides. Ash represents the darker side of you. The person you could be.'

'There's no scope for balance. I can't deliberately take a life. It goes against the very essence of me. Who I am. It would rip out my core. I don't expect you to understand. In politics you have to compromise what you believe in all the time to get ahead.'

'I do understand,' she says. 'We are more alike than I would ever have imagined.'

'Once I deliberately take someone's life, I will never be the same person again – I will be Ash and not Winter.'

'But you would be a better agent.'

'I know,' I say.

'It's a very clever programme,' she says. 'Your training programme. Using your own strength against you. That's what happened back on the balcony with the hunter, isn't it? He asked you to kill him.'

I am silent.

'Empathy is an awful thing,' she says. 'You get trapped

in it. It can drive you mad. Believe me, I know.'

I seriously doubt that.

'You get trapped in the tunnels of your mind,' she says, 'paralysed by pity. It's one of Walter's favourite phrases: *capti in cuniculis animi.*' She sighs. 'I wish I could speak to him one last time. There is so much I never said.'

I think about her private secretary. The man who would have taken a bullet for her, the man prepared to be gunned down at her side, and I think about the unmistakable anguish in his voice when he spoke to me on the phone. Who is he and how is he involved? Does he know the Adjudicator from way back? Were they working together? Whatever his motivation, there was no doubting his sincerity.

'He begged me to come,' I say. '*Please*, he said to me. *Please come. I will do anything. I'd take her place if Colosseum would let me.*'

'What?' She frowns. 'You actually spoke to him? He didn't say.'

'He thought you would never agree if you knew I was a woman.'

She is silent. She stares out of the window. We are back in the centre.

'He was probably right,' she says.

I accelerate through the lights and horns blare.

'I wouldn't beat yourself up.'

'No,' she says. 'There are plenty of people waiting to do that for me.'

My lips curve. I can't help myself, and she grins out into the night.

I AM STARTING to recognise parts of this tall town. We are
on Central Park West, the park on one side and apartment
blocks with their elegant awnings out over the pavement on
the other and I am glued to my rear-view mirror. We *still*
don't have a tail and that is making me very uneasy. If I was
a hunter who had lost the target and knew which car they
were driving, I would be hanging out round the reservoir
waiting for them to pitch up, and that gives us a problem. If
they are already there, how are we even going to get out of
the car? The moment we appear, they will be on us with
their M-16s and what chance will we have against automatic weaponry?

'You know your riddle?' she says. '*I am wild and unbroken,
And I don't have a price.*'

I say nothing.

'He knows you pretty well, whoever he is.'

'We need to get as close as possible to the reservoir,' I
say. 'The shortest possible distance for us to cross. Out in
the open, we are fair game. Once we are the other side of
the railing, they won't touch us.'

'You hope,' she says.

She's right. It's all hope and speculation. A plausible
scenario built on nothing but air.

'86th Street,' she says. 'It crosses the park.'

'Are you sure?'

I can feel her roll her eyes.

'Yes, I'm sure. This is my city. The south gatehouse is
up a bank above it.'

'We don't want a bank. Where is it lower?'

'Further on. About a hundred metres to the water I
would estimate.'

'How fast can you run?' I say. I wait a beat. 'Can you

even run at all?'

She smiles. 'I guess it depends how much I want to live. And no, I've never had a woman.'

'A hundred metres is too far. What about the steps we came up before? With the guy with the gold head?'

'Bronze,' she says. 'Mayor Purroy Mitchel.'

'We'll drive in the gate and up onto the pedestrianised area. You get out the far door, leg it up the steps and over the railings. They will be chest-high on you – difficult to get over in a hurry. Don't stop to worry about the spikes, just get to the other side.'

'And the moment of truth,' she says. 'Because there is absolutely no cover there.'

I look across at her. 'Get you and your *no cover*.'

'You know what it comes down to?' she says.

'No?'

'How much I want to live.'

'I will give you the best cover I can,' I say.

'With your rubber bullets.'

'Any type of bullet hitting a tyre causes a whole host of problems for the driver. I will swerve hard, slam on the brakes and fire. You will get out of the opposite door furthest from them and leg it. You'll have the body of an armoured car between you and the hunters. Get to the steps and crouch down behind the stone.'

'They'll open fire on you,' she says. 'They'll mow you down with their assault rifles if they don't plough into you.'

She's not wrong. I'll be a sitting duck unless I can take out the lead car. Olympic-standard marksmanship. And lucky.

'Don't worry about me,' I say with a confidence I'm not feeling. 'They're only interested in you. I'm just here for the ride. They will pour after you like soldier ants. Remember them in the hotel corridor? You'll be leading them away from me. Just get the other side of the fence and wait for Avril's mum.'

We are on Fifth Avenue and yards away when two black four-by-fours come at us from the side. They have been lying in wait. I swerve, the car skitters, horns blare and I step on the accelerator. They are right behind me; I can see them in my side mirrors. Too many to lose.

We make the right into Central Park through the stone pillars and lurch across the inner track and round a flower bed. The monument to Mayor Mitchel is ahead with the stone steps going up on either side.

I buzz down my window and the car fills with the roaring of revving engines and the squeal of tyres. Cold air hits my face. Wet. I can feel the reservoir beyond. I can see her eyes in the dashboard light. The heater is going full blast and suddenly I don't want to get out into the night.

'Winter,' she says. 'About Anna.'

But it is too late for whatever she was going to say. Behind us, the pursuit is making the turn into the park and they open fire in a deafening blast of sound, drowning everything out. Sound as a weapon. The wheel pulls, the tyres skidding on the smooth surface covered with fine grit.

I hold the wheel, yank on the handbrake, and the car slews around in a spray of gravel.

'GO!' I shout.

Behind me, I hear the car door open, but I am already steadying my arm and firing through the open window.

CHAPTER 21

I THROW MYSELF out of the car and up the steps, bent double. My long guns graze the stone. Where is the Senator? Bullets ricochet past me, my heart pounds and then I am at the top crossing the running track and hurling myself over the iron railings into the dark. The spikes catch on the underside of my hoodie and I tear myself free, slide down the steep lip of the reservoir and land, scratched and winded and panting, just short of the water.

There are boots on the stone steps behind me.

They are coming.

Dark water laps my feet. Pitch-dark and ice-cold. I imagine hundreds of bullets thudding into my chest as I fall backwards into the water. I am drowning again in the dark.

My ankle buckles under me as I try to stand on the sloped edge – I wrenched it vaulting the fence. I grab out at the railings for balance and a hunter appears at the top of the steps. No more than ten feet from me. He is wearing body armour and a helmet and carrying an assault rifle in his arms. I freeze on instinct.

This is it, the moment of truth. Am I safe this side of the railings? Is the reservoir the safe zone in tonight's game of *Colosseum*?

His visor is shiny black – reflective. I can see nothing of

his face, but I know he is looking at me. For a moment, he does nothing. We just stare at each other, but his M-16 stays lowered and then he looks up the track away from me searching for the target.

He wants the Senator.

I start to move, hand over hand, leaning backwards, propelling myself along with my arms, while he walks beside me. I turn my head to look back and they are all coming, pouring out at the top of the steps onto the running track. All dressed the same, all heavily armed, all well-equipped, not shivering and bleeding in the dark and the cold.

I accelerate hard, the panic making me fast, lending energy to my tired muscles. My biceps ache. Above me on the path, the hunter is keeping pace with me easily. The running track is smooth – he is not scrambling along a near vertical slope covered in scrub.

We round the gentle curve. The stone walls of the south gatehouse are near enough for me to throw a stone at and there is no sign of the target, the woman I am protecting, and the panic grips me again and I accelerate. Beside me, the hunter breaks into a jog.

I slam up against the stone side of the gatehouse with the forward momentum and reach for the ledge. It is wider and lower than at the north end. I let go of the railings and pull myself up and edge along, out over the reservoir, expecting at any moment to hear them opening fire behind me. Just before I round the stone corner, I turn my head.

All along the railings, as far as the eye can see, hunters are standing, watching me. Tens, maybe even hundreds, of them. I round the corner out of their sight and there she is, sitting on the little stone balcony facing the water, her knees up to her chest, the FN Minimi beside her. I can't believe she brought it. Her Kevlar mesh is dirty. She has a leaf stuck to her face and a long scratch on her cheek. She watches me edge my way along to her.

I drag air into my lungs and collapse down beside her on the stone. In front of us, the reservoir lies huge and black and impossible. Wind whips the surface. I shiver. There is enough space to sit with our knees up. Just above the waterline.

'Do they know where we are?' she says.

'Yes,' I say.

I look out at the flat expanse of dark water. Way ahead, out there somewhere, is the north gatehouse.

'This is it then,' she says.

I lean my head back against the stone. I want to close my eyes. 'I don't see we have any choice but to wait. How could anyone search that without gear?'

How could anyone search it with gear? I am thinking. Now I can actually see the task ahead, it's impossible. *Before dawn.* It would take a team of professional police divers a week to search. There is something impossibly Herculean about the task. Like cleaning the Aegean stables. It just can't be done by an ordinary mortal.

'How long until dawn?' she says.

I check the phone. 'An hour. Give or take.'

'We still don't actually know what I am supposed to be doing. It is all extrapolation. *Walks on water* – what is that supposed to mean? We haven't really cracked it.'

'We are in the right place. The hunters' behaviour proves it. If we weren't in the right place, we wouldn't even be having this conversation. We would be tiny particles of carbon smeared on this medieval stone.'

'1864,' she says.

'What?'

'The southern gatehouse was built in 1864. It's not medieval.'

I look out across the dark water at the whole of Manhattan lit up on the skyline. It's spectacular. There's a big screen over the water on our left with what looks like a stage for concerts. I look to the right, towards the east. Somewhere out there, the sun is rising, its golden fingers creeping across the sky.

'The longest night of the year,' she says.

'Figures.'

'Dancing to the tune of the Lord of Misrule.'

'The who?'

'The Lord of Misrule,' she says. 'From the Roman Saturnalia. Their equivalent of the solstice. I need Walter to really give you the details.'

'It's no coincidence it's the solstice,' I say. 'He chose it deliberately. A hunt in the depths of midwinter. A sacrifice to make the sun come up. It has been going on for millennia.'

'In Rome, the masters waited on the slaves,' she says. 'It was the time when everything turned on its head and the natural order of things was reversed, when the Holly King and the Oak King swapped places. Although some traditions have them as two halves of the same person.'

'Are you a good Senator?'

She is silent.

'Not really,' she says after a while. 'My intentions were good.'

'The road to hell is paved with good intentions.'

'And never more so than in politics,' she says. 'You let things go, thinking you will make up for them in the long run, thinking you mustn't jeopardise the big goal. Then one day, you look behind you and see all the things that you let go, and they are as high as a mountain.'

I lean my head back against the stone and close my eyes. Suddenly, I am very, very tired.

'Although once you are in the running for a presidential nomination, you don't do a whole lot of anything for anyone. Politics is one long exercise in not doing or saying anything that could be deemed controversial. You kid yourself that you are only playing along with it for now, keeping your nose clean, eyes on the bigger prize, but when do you reach that prize? It was what Anna always used to say: *When do you stop worrying about appearances and say enough is enough, I take a stand here. This is where I stop acting and you get to see who I really am and what I really believe.*'

'Tell me about Anna,' I say.

'She's been coming back to me all evening,' she says. 'In fits and starts. I've been remembering.'

'Don't fight it. Try and remember. What can be worse than being hunted?'

'Dark water,' she says. 'I already know what's worse.'

I look at her. Manhattan's lights reflect in her eyes. She is terrified of water, no question, but there is something else going on here. Who *is* Anna, and what happened to her?

'Anna loved the solstice,' she says. 'She thought it was lucky. The luckiest day of the year.'

'And your husband,' I prompt. 'Do you think it is possible they were sleeping together?'

'In the early days,' she says. 'He didn't like her much, he thought she was too needy.'

I look out across the dark water. They were having an affair; he tried to break it off; Anna gave him a jealous ultimatum; he killed her. And somehow, *Colosseum* found out and dumped her body here. What a perfect test for her.

Anna

Now

I AM SO much happier now that I'm dead. I am sure I read that somewhere. And isn't it meant to be true? The perfect afterlife, the golden void, suspended forever in space and blissful solitude. Not that there is any solitude. I have never been alone my whole life. A bit of solitude would be nice.

It is strange being dead. One minute you are there walking and talking and the next, you are gone, snuffed out like so many millions of pointless lives before yours, and the world carries on as if you were never in it. All the things you were going to do. All the plans you had. Gone.

Drowning is a terrible way to go – the panic, the terror, the battle for air, and it was not my first time. I remember that early baptism. The dog barking and the choking dark water.

Is it possible to hate someone more than yourself? No doubt many useful research dollars could be spent by graduate students on the subject. It is a question that fascinates me, and I have had a long time to think about it. Ten years is a very long time. A lifetime, in fact. So, I have had time to give it a lot of thought, and on the whole, all things being equal, I would say, yes, it is possible to hate someone more than yourself.

I hate her pragmatism and her pointless hypocrisy. Her thoughtless, wasteful use of her time. Her whole life a pointless travesty of the human experience. I hate that she has forgotten me. Shoved me away, relegated me to some distant attic in her mind, not thought of, barely remembered. How dare she?

How dare she forget what she did to me.

*

'I THINK MAYBE your husband killed Anna,' I say, as gently as I can.

The Senator shakes her head.

'I killed her,' she says. 'I had to.'

I stare.

'Only she's not dead. She just went quiet.' She looks out across the water. 'This was the last place I saw her. I chose the solstice deliberately. The luckiest day of the year. I have a superstitious streak a mile wide. If you unravelled me end to end, spread me out on the floor, entrails and all, there would be mile upon mile of black cats and magpies and bargains with fate.'

A faint breeze ripples the surface of the water. It raises all the hairs on the back of my neck. She looks unearthly in the dim light. Ethereal.

'*You* are Anna.'

'Of course,' she says.

CHAPTER 22

MariANNA. Although everyone except my mother calls me Marie.

My head aches. I lean back against the stone. 'So there isn't a body in the water. There isn't anything to find?'

'Except perhaps metaphorically.'

If that isn't just typical of *Colosseum*.

'There have always been two of us,' she says. 'Marie and Anna. I walked into the water ten years ago, knowing one of us had to die.'

'Why did we leave Avril's mum getting scuba gear? You knew there was nothing in the water.'

'I wanted her away from this. Safe. We are sitting ducks here. It's only a matter of time.'

The breeze whispers across the water.

'Can you hear that?' she says. 'On the wind?'

Anna, Anna, Anna.

'It has come back to me now. The first time I saw her.' She looks at her hands. 'It was the day I drowned.'

She stares out across the reservoir. 'I was supposed to be learning to swim, but I was afraid. I wouldn't go in the water.' She hugs her knees to her chest. 'I had a dog when I was young. A border collie. We have a boating lake at home with a little island. My mother tied him up on the island. *All you have to do is swim out and untie him,* she said. Like a game. I think she thought it would break me of my fear.'

I am silent.

'I couldn't do it. The dark water. I was afraid. I begged and begged her to untie him. *You must do it*, she said. *Find the courage.*

'The whining was awful. It went on all day and all night. Dogs can't go long without water. I knew that even then. I stood on the bank watching him wagging his tail hopefully and whining. I couldn't bear it – it did something to my head.

'The next night, the whining had stopped and he was lying down not moving. I remember his tongue sticking out of his mouth all swollen and dark and his eyes blinking against the flies and his breathing coming fast and shallow and knowing it was nearly too late.

'I stood on the grass, my feet just short of the water. The wind was cold on my wet cheeks and the fear was everywhere. My face felt stiff and strange; the crying had left salt tracks. I crept forward till my toes touched the black and the dread soaked through me and the panic rose so hard and so fast it made my legs buckle. I forced myself into the water, one desperate step at a time, my nightie flapping against my bare knees.

'The black water crept up my legs, icy against my stomach, icy under my arms until the ground fell away, and suddenly, the bottom was gone and the lake stretched out deep and dark before me.

'I launched myself forwards and splashed my arms and kicked my legs and it didn't work. I knew it wouldn't. Nothing but total despair had made me try. I couldn't swim and no amount of willing it was going to make it happen. It was hopeless.'

She pauses, staring at something only she can see. Lost in the horror of her memories, trapped in the tunnels of her mind.

'Drowning is a terrible way to go,' she says finally. 'The panic, the terror, the desperate fight for air, the pain in your lungs.

'Then through the dark and the panic and the fear I saw something moving on the island. My dog was on his feet. He was tearing at his chains, fighting to get to me.' She looks down at her jagged nails. 'He strangled himself trying to reach me. He choked to death on his own collar. I remember the dark water and the bursting lungs and I remember the sound of him dying and then nothing.'

'And Anna?'

'When I woke up, she was sitting on the end of my bed. Empathy enough for the whole world, pity enough to drown us both. She drove us mad in the end. I couldn't cope with the misery, the pain of human existence, so much suffering and my own helplessness.'

'And the solstice?'

She looks out across the water. 'I had to do something – she was driving us mad. I wanted to send her back. I waited till I saw my husband on the track, then I walked us both into the water. She never even saw it coming. And it worked. She has been gone a decade, and I have been able to function. And then *Colosseum* started up, and she has been coming back, breaking through in my dreams, writing messages for me and leaving them on my desk. I have no idea how the Adjudicator found out about Anna, but he must know I can't swim.'

Walks on water.

'I wonder if you are meant to drown yourself.'

'Again,' she says.

I glance down at the hunter's phone. It is nearly dawn. An hour has gone. Flashed past in the time it takes me to turn my head. Her whole lifetime gone.

It is nearly dawn and I have failed. I have failed her like she failed her dog all those years ago as a helpless, powerless child. I close my eyes. I am exhausted.

Darkest before the dawn.

We are sitting ducks here.

I open my eyes.

Just below us, on the water, ducks are roosting in a line. They were there in a line before we arrived. A *perfect* line. They rustle and mutter and stir, indignant heads coming out from under wings. I stare. They're not floating on top of the water – they are sitting on something. I peer down into the dark, following the line of ducks out towards the centre. Flashes of white feathers on the water.

'What are the ducks sitting on?' I say.

'A wall,' says the Senator. 'The Jackie O is actually two reservoirs divided straight down the middle. There is a dividing wall running the whole way from the gatehouse in the north to the gatehouse in the south, just below the surface. Literally about six inches below. Not many people know that.'

I stare at the ducks, clearly in a perfect line now that I know.

'So technically, you could walk down the centre of the reservoir?' I say.

'If you were nuts,' she says. 'What if you fell off?'

'*The first lady who walks on water,*' I say.

And the final piece clangs into place.

She shakes her head. 'I can't,' she says. 'Dark water. It's my nightmare. Worse than being hunted, worse than anything. You don't understand. It will send me mad. I'm not that far from it in any case.'

I look up at the stars.

'When I was in the tank,' I say. 'The last thing they did as the air ran out was turn the lights off. It was pitch-dark when I drowned. I don't think I can do it either.'

I lean my head back against the stone wall. I'm all out.

The Senator stares at me wide-eyed. The fear in her eyes is gone. Instead, there is something else. Something in the very depths. She puts her hand out – it is small and frail with ragged nails.

I look down at it. She is trying to lend me her strength.

'Together,' she says.

CHAPTER 23

I T IS BEYOND cold. Ice-cold. Cold in the bone. Sharp.
My breath catches and I feel it across every molar. She
slips and slithers and slides and the ducks squawk and flap.
The water is no more than ankle-deep on the wall but like a
knife. She edges her way forwards with me just behind her.
The cord is knotted round our waists. I haven't the heart to
tell her I am not a strong enough swimmer to hold her
weight as well as my own. If we go in, she will drag us both
down to the depths.

The stone is slippery with duck droppings and weed.

Up ahead of us, the big screen on the water blazes into
life like it was waiting for us to set foot on the reservoir, to
make the leap of faith. Something is playing on the screen,
but we're too far away to make it out. A final countdown
maybe.

The whole thing feels staged. The scene is for us, and
now we have entered. The stars of the show. The wall is at
least a foot wide but difficult to see. I put my hand out and
grip her waistband. Across her shoulder, the FN Minimi
clanks.

'Don't bring it,' I had said to her. 'It just weighs you
down.'

'It makes me feel better,' said the gun control campaigner, and I let it go. If it is acting like a comfort blanket, it is serving some purpose.

We have edged a few yards out into the reservoir, and all along the banks, I can see the silent figures of the hunters. A blast of automatic fire over to our right has my head swinging round. Some of the hunters are pointing out towards the park, keeping away any attempt at rescue. Not that there is likely to be any. They are silent and watchful. A black army. Drawn up in formation like Roman centurions. No one is getting past.

'Don't turn around,' I say, but I am too late.

She turns and sees the wall of hunters standing on the east bank watching her, and she freezes stock-still. Catatonic. The sky is lighter behind them.

Dawn is coming.

Wind whips our hair while we stand out on the spine in the middle of the reservoir.

She is wavering; I can feel it.

'Just look ahead,' I say.

She starts to shake. Arms. Torso. The Minimi clanks. If it spreads to her legs, she is going in.

'I don't think I can do it,' I say. 'You will have to help me.'

She stills. Straightens. 'Hold on to me,' she says. 'We do it together. One step at a time. Slow and steady.'

The surface is inky black around us. Manhattan's skyscrapers light up the skyline. It's beautiful. Like a poster. She is a Manhattan poster child. She could probably name every single one.

'What is that building ahead of us?' I say. 'The one with the double towers?'

She looks up. 'The Eldorado.'

'And that one?'

'The Ardesley, and beside it The Turin.'

'And the tall one in the distance?'

'The New York Times building.'

We are a third of the way across the reservoir, and now we can make out what is playing on the big screen. *Colosseum.* The feed is coming straight from the hunters' headcams. The picture in the centre is much clearer and closer.

I look up.

Somewhere right above us, is a drone. I can't see it, but it is there. The hunters are all just an illusion. For the theatre of it. The Lord of Misrule could take us out with a drone strike, any time he likes. We are only alive because he is allowing it. I picture him watching me drown.

'Is this a test?' I say to the sky.

'What?' says the Senator.

We are halfway, right out in the middle of the reservoir, the furthest point in any direction. Suddenly, she stops and stares. She drops to her knees. The Minimi on its webbed strap clanks against her back. My numb fingers slip from her waistband.

'What?' I say. 'No time.'

Then I see. There is a light below the surface. A brightly lit rectangle – brilliant white in the black. An iPhone attached to the dividing wall. Ten foot down under water, maybe more, it's hard to tell.

'It's a phone,' I say. I peer some more. 'And it looks like it's ringing.'

Where is Anna? Walk on water before the dawn to find the answer.

And here is the answer.

I pull out the hunter's phone, switch on the torch and hover it just above the surface. I can't make out what's holding the iPhone to the stone.

I stare down into the dark water and the fear rises. Maybe it was never that far below the surface; maybe on this longest of nights we are closer to our superstitious selves than at any other time. The dark water laps at our feet and I can almost taste the fear. The primitive urge to get out of the water, to run, is so strong it claws up my throat, choking me with my own panic. A breeze blows in my face. I am cold to the bone, shivering and shaking in the dark.

The streets of New York feel far away, the sirens muffled. There is only the breeze on the water and the silent watchful hunters.

A room is filling with water and someone is going to drown.

Then there's a sound from the east bank – a single movement made by hundreds of arms. I look up. The hunters have raised their weapons to their shoulders. Behind them, the horizon looks light. Dawn is nearly here. I turn to the big screen. A countdown has started.

'You have to go in, I think,' I say. 'You need to answer the phone and answer the question. The hunters are getting ready. I think this is your challenge. If you don't do it, or if you're too slow and the sun comes up, they're going to open fire.'

She looks round. 'I can't do it,' she says. 'I will lose my mind. Quite literally. It will kill me. You don't understand.' She sees my face. 'OK, maybe you understand.' She stands, wretched and terrified.

'You won't die,' I say. 'You will still be in her, like she is in you now.'

She looks away. The seconds stretch out as the internal struggle goes on. The final battle. As she faces down her fear.

I can see it, the moment it happens. The power radiates out of her. Pull her skin aside and it would blind the whole world.

'I can't swim,' she says. She shrugs off the Minimi and it hits the wall with a splash. 'You will have to pull me back up. I'll tug on the cord.'

She sits down on the wall, the water lapping her Kevlar thighs, then she turns onto her stomach and she's in and I am planting my feet, bracing all my body weight, leaning backwards holding the cord and remembering her turning on her stomach on a balcony saying, *I can't do it*, a hundred years ago.

I take a great big breath and hold it.

I can't see what she's doing, I am too busy trying to stop myself being pulled off the wall. My back is aching, the cord is cutting into my numb hands and there is no way I am going to be able to tell if she is tugging it or not. When my breath gives out, I haul on the cord. For a moment, nothing happens and panic hits me, then I feel it start to shift and I get down on one knee and lean my hand down and she grabs it and a moment later she breaks the surface with a massive, gasping, flailing gulping for air. I haul her half out onto the wall, stomach first, her legs still dangling down and collapse beside her. She has the phone in her other hand.

She swipes right, lying on her stomach, watching herself on the big screen.

'Hello, Senator,' says the Lord of Misrule.

She doesn't reply. She lies gasping and panting.

'Where is Anna?' he says.

She gets slowly to her knees, then to her feet. She straightens up. She stands tall. Something has changed – the line of her jaw or the cast of her shoulders – she could almost be a different person.

She stares out across the water.

Nothing moves. The hunters on the east side are still, the wind has dropped, even the ducks flapping and rustling on the wall are silent.

'Here,' she says.

The line goes dead, but on the big screen, fireworks are going off.

Target wins! it says.

A cartoon senator is doing a victory dance in the middle of the screen. Ribbons and confetti are raining down on her avatar.

I get up on my elbows and look towards the far bank and the wall of hunters – they are lowering their weapons. The assault rifles are pointing at the ground.

We won. I can't believe it.

Colosseum let us win. There was no sting in the tail. No trick up his sleeve. I roll on my back and stare up at the sky. There are stars. The water is ice-cold on the back of my neck, it laps at my temples. The longest night. And here comes the dawn.

'Is this a test?' I say to the stars.

'Yes,' says Anna.

She picks up the machine gun, brings it to her shoulder, lowers her chin and starts firing.

The FN Minimi squad automatic weapon can fire 1,000 rounds a minute. The wall of hunters across the water collapses. Pink mist fills the air. Some turn to run. Others try to get their guns back up. She mows them all down. Indiscriminate. Not a moment of hesitation. Right to left and then left to right. The shattering noise fills the whole world. The gun kicks against her shoulder, spewing casings. On the big screen, *Colosseum* has switched back to the live televised feed. A giant ten-foot version of the Senator is standing firing like an angel of vengeance.

I curl into a ball as the machine gun thunders above me. Jam my fingers in my ears. Shaking with the noise and the violence and the cold.

CHAPTER 24

SHE LOWERS HER weapon. There is nothing but bodies on the east bank. Piles and piles of bodies. Hundreds of them. She's killed them all. I lift my head and turn to look behind us. The big screen is carrying the single feed from the drone; all the headcams are down. She is standing there like a warrior with me curled up at her feet.

Under the screen, I can see movement. Faces are starting to appear on the west bank. First one or two, then a dozen or more. Cautious, wide-eyed faces, not helmets and body armour; New Yorkers peering at the action. They can't believe it.

Beneath us, something moves. A slight tremor, like a minor earthquake. The wall trembles. The stone vibrates; the wall is wobbling. We stare down. She says something, but I can't make it out over the roaring in my ears from the gunfire. I feel rather than hear the explosion. A plume of water in front of the south gatehouse shoots hundreds of feet into the air. Something sparks on the firework barges and the south gatehouse collapses in a mighty blast of brick. Like a demolition job on a derelict tower block, rushing downwards in a cloud of dust. The dividing wall we are standing on buckles and I am up and dragging her behind me, running the buckling spine to the north gatehouse.

The power of the second explosion as the north gate-house goes up knocks us off our feet. Beneath us, the wall collapses and we topple backwards, fighting and flailing into the icy black.

I hear the hiss as the smoking barrel of the Minimi hits the water, then she is beneath me, dragging me down, down into the black. The cord tightens around my waist. The panic kicks in and kicks in hard. Arms and legs flail. My lungs heave.

Black water.

As it closes over me, I imagine the Lord of Misrule laughing.

Of course the Adjudicator was never going to let us win.

CHAPTER 25

I CHOKE UP water, spewing and heaving and gasping. I roll onto my front and get up on my elbows and hurl into the sodden earth. My hair hangs down soaking. There is a hand on my shoulder. A man's voice tells me to take it easy, but I can hardly make out his words. My hearing is muffled, like I am listening through fog.

I fight to speak, but I can't control the choking heaving. I empty great gobbets of water out of my lungs. My throat burns as my stomach spasms. My mouth is full of stomach acid. I rest my forehead on the wet leaves. And fumble at my waist. The cord comes up free. Not attached to anything. It has been cut.

Where is the Senator?

I turn my head, but I can't see past my rescuer's legs. His trousers are soaking wet. He went in fully clothed. Then the legs move and, a little way from me, I catch sight of medics clustered round a figure on the ground covered in silver foil. Avril's mum is with them. Her pink tracksuit is dripping wet and she has a scuba mask pushed up on top of her blonde hair. She got here. Beside her on the grass, the beam of a powerful torch shines through the leaves. I picture Avril's mum standing on the west bank, hands on hips going, 'Why didn't you wait?' She must have plunged straight in. She can't have wasted any time, given it any thought.

As I watch, the Senator sits up and thrusts the foil cover aside.

My rescuer says something about hypothermia and getting me a foil blanket. He orders me not to move. *Do. Not. Move.* And it is so familiar I wonder for a crazy moment if I know him.

Then I dismiss it. My brain is playing tricks on me. My heightened senses making connections that aren't there. He saved my life, so I trust him. It's as simple as that.

I turn and watch him hurrying away from me down the bank to the ambulances. There is something familiar about his legs. I screw up my face, trying to make him out more clearly, but he is just a black silhouette against the lights of the emergency vehicles.

I turn my head to the water. I am on the west bank, the other side of the railings between the big screen and where the south gatehouse used to be. The inky black is still and silent, but the other side of the reservoir is full of the flashing lights of ambulances and police cars. I turn my head back the other way. The NYPD are keeping the crowds at bay on my side. More ambulances and police cars. A makeshift cordon of police tape. A Fox News camera crew. I can't see my rescuer – the Good Samaritan. I get up on all fours and then up on my knees. My head swims. I hear sirens, but they sound distorted, as if they are coming from a long way off. A helicopter hovers overhead, I can feel the *thud-thud-thud*, the air is pulsing with vibration, but I can hardly hear it.

I get one knee up and press down and heave and get the

other foot up. I am drenched and shaking with cold, but I cannot leave it a moment longer. This is not over. The Adjudicator is still out there.

I stagger forward, one step, two steps, and I am in the shelter of the trees. I look back. There is no sign of my rescuer.

I skirt the car wreck at the Engineers Gate. Leaves crunch under my feet. I stuff my hands in my pockets, head down, and keep walking. On Fifth Avenue, one of the buildings is wrapped in red ribbon with a massive bow. Like the whole building is a present. Its windows are bright with baubles. The department store next door has its windows smashed. The Christmas display is walking out the door, looters taking advantage of the chaos – the police all tied up with *Colosseum* and crowd control. I climb up into the window, yank a ski jacket off a model and pull it on. Thick and warm, probably $500 worth. I leave the orange bandana and the goggles for another looter and get moving.

THE RONALD O. Perelman Center for Emergency Services is a squat square nestling like a small child at the feet of the giant, glass skyscraper that is NYU Langone Health. Steel bollards line the forecourt where the ambulances pull up. There are five of them pulled up now. Strange and boxy in unfamiliar colours. Purple – *NYU Langone Health Emergency Medical Services*. Blue and orange – *Mobile Stroke Treatment Unit*. People are coming and going. The place is as busy now as it is in the middle of the day.

The Senator's husband is completely innocent. One man deleted the email and it was the same man who called me for help. Maybe he was never injured at all. Maybe he faked it. He would have no reason to fear the hunters if he was in league with them. Maybe the Adjudicator is an old friend. I cannot begin to imagine his motives – if he wanted the Senator dead, there were much easier ways – but Walter, her mild-mannered private secretary, has some urgent questions to answer.

A harassed-looking nurse mans the front desk. There is no Christmas here. Not even the mandatory tree in the corner.

'Bellevue,' she says. 'He transferred four hours ago. Out the door, turn left, four hundred yards.' She says it like she has said it many thousands of times before. She is already moving on to the guy behind me.

I back out into the cold of the forecourt. I am knackered. After the warmth of the building, I notice the cold. I turn left and start walking. Past the Tisch building on the left then the Arnold and Marie Schwartz Healthcare Centre, over East 30th, past a red, Gothic building that would look right at home beside our St Pancras, cross East 29th and there it is – a modern, glass building on stilts, *Bellevue* written vertically up the side in giant letters.

I push through the glass doors. Reception here is much quieter than accident and emergency.

The nurse doesn't bother to look up. 'He's in a closed ward,' she says. 'I'm afraid you can't see him.'

I stay silent.

She glances up over her half-moon specs. Whatever she sees, causes her to rock back in her chair.

I catch sight of my reflection in the mirrored glass behind her.

I look like one of those movie posters. Zombie apocalypse. *Return of the Living Dead*. My eyes are huge in my head.

My hair hangs in drowned rat's tails. My lips are blue with cold. My clothes are wet and torn except for the ski jacket, which still has its labels hanging off it. The heavy round security tag bumps against my waist.

'I'll call the ward for you,' she says.

She picks up the phone.

I turn and lean up against the counter, looking out through the main entrance. There is a billboard on the street. It says, *Give them what they want this Christmas.*

The Bellevue has a massive Christmas tree in the corner decked in silver and gold. Only silver and gold. It is regimented, very perfect. The same sequence of baubles one after the other all the way up. Take it apart and you'll see wire tiers each decorated on a factory floor and then clipped together on arrival. An air-freshener plugged into a socket at its base is pumping out Christmas fragrance: pine needles and sandalwood and cinnamon. The whole thing is a total fake.

'You can go up now,' she says behind me.

I ignore the lifts and make for the stairs. It doesn't matter how tired my thighs are – I am not getting in a closed box. Cool, stale air hits me. It's all concrete and dust bunnies, just like the stairwell at GCHQ. I come out on the top floor checking my knives. My guns are at the bottom of the Jackie O, but I still have all my blades.

Standing by the lift are two suits – Secret Service, no question. Alert and competent. They get in my face, get a good look at me and stand down.

'Room 10,' they say.

I turn the corner, walk down the long corridor. Paper chains loop from side to side. Rooms and machinery and soft lighting. Some kind of a recovery unit. Room 10 is at the end. There are another two black-suited men on the door. They watch me walk up the corridor towards them.

'Hello, Winter,' says the one on the right.

'Is he conscious?'

'And expecting you.'

He reaches behind him and opens the door. No body search, no pat down, no weapons check. He just stands aside so I can walk in.

The lights are down low. A single room. Bed in the middle surrounded by beeping medical machinery. Tinsel is wrapped around the long arm of the TV unit.

I had guessed who I was going to find in the bed, but it is still a shock.

CHAPTER 26

THE PRINCIPAL OPENS his eyes. Not a figment of my imagination. Not an avatar conjured up by a training programme. Here.

'Our man in America, I presume,' I say.

He smiles. A weary, groggy, drugged smile. 'Hello, Achilles,' he says. His head is bandaged. His cheek is swollen. He is not faking it.

'Is this a test?' I say.

'You tell me.' His voice is weak and rasping.

There is a radiator underneath a long picture window. I lean up against it and cross one ankle over the other. Warmth.

'Was any of it in my head?' I say.

'What do you think?'

'No.'

He says nothing.

'Why did you make me believe it was?'

'Standard practice. Disorientation. And a security measure – someone who is really incompatible with the programme writes it off as a nightmare and moves on to gainful employment elsewhere.'

'I could have shot you in the tank room.'

'Rubber bullets.'

Ironic.

'What about the yellow solitary cell? How did that work?'

'Two different yellow solitary cells,' he says. 'With the same ceiling. One is a photograph of the other.'

Unbelievable.

'Who did I meet in Nelson Mandela Tower?'

'An actor. Something like that is easy to fake. Much easier than a skin graft to remove a name etched on your arm. And despite all our efforts, we still couldn't break you. Life is your Achilles heel, Winter. You *still* value it too highly. And even *Colosseum* and a hundred hunters couldn't stamp it out of you.'

'What is *Colosseum*?'

'We don't know. It's the brainchild of our former head of black ops. The man behind your training programme. You know him as the Adjudicator. For what purpose, we have yet to discover. He has a substantial backer from Eastern Europe. In our defence, while his methods were controversial, his results were always outstanding. We have the best network of agents on the planet.'

'Network of hitmen you mean. I thought it was *your* training programme. Weren't you the boss? Wasn't that your office at the top of the stairs? The one with the picture of Caesar?'

'No,' he said. 'I flew in that day to check out the latest batch of recruits. I used to fly in twice a year to see if there was anyone we wanted over here. Four years ago was the last time I was there. The centre was decommissioned shortly after. A raw recruit beat the system. Painfully decommissioned, I should say. Not our finest hour.'

I think about this. *Four years ago. Raw recruit.* 'Me, you mean.'

'You.'

'You should be in jail.'

'Grow up, Winter, you can't make an omelette without a bit of eggshell. Unfortunately, decommissioning smashed an unnecessarily large number of eggs.'

'So you and he fell out?'

'Spectacularly, I would say. We all knew him for what he was. That kid in the playground everyone gives a wide berth to. Not the biggest, not the toughest; the most dangerous. But that is exactly the person you need. Until they turn against you, and then you really have a problem.'

I think about the disembodied voice and the man watching me drown through the two-way mirror.

'After you beat the system, he became unpredictable, more violent, more whimsical. It was as if he couldn't get past it. He was like the Roman emperors in the late Empire – absolute power corrupts. We closed him down, but unfortunately, not terminally.'

'And he went rogue.'

'Never an ideal scenario.'

'And you just carried on running America like an international man of mystery, pushing your Manchurian candidate towards the White House. Until he came along and spoiled it.'

He stares at the ceiling. Machinery beeps.

'Nothing like that actually,' he says. 'She was never part of the plan.'

'Oh really?'

'*Dilexi tum te non tantum ut vulgus amicam, sed pater ut gnatos diligit,*' he says.

'What does that mean?'

'*I loved you, not as a guy loves a girl but as a father loves his son.* It is Catullus – the greatest of all love poets.'

'*Love* poet? You love her?'

'Yes,' he says. 'From about ten minutes after I met her. I left my wife a month later. I couldn't live the lie.'

I couldn't live the lie. Oh, the irony.

'And now the whole world sees what I see,' he says. 'When she was chosen for the hunt, I just didn't know what to do. I should have seen it coming. The gameplay was so familiar. I told myself it was a coincidence, but all the targets have been connected to me one way or another. Either agents, informers or sleepers.'

I just don't believe this.

'Are you trying to tell me Avril was a British agent? You have to be kidding?'

He shakes his head. 'She was an influencer. One of the most powerful influencers on the net. She was on the service wish list. Worth a million bots. Control a dozen of her and you can control every election in America.'

'What about the general?'

'Since his university days,' he says. 'He was a Rhodes scholar.'

Unbelievable.

'The Senator is no British agent.'

'Not the Senator,' he says. 'I went to the Marriott Hotel that night to meet a British agent with a problem. The path to the White House that we had mapped out for him had become blocked. Not by one of his many lovers, but of all things, by his wife.'

Not the Senator. Her husband.

'She had decided to run for political office. For the Senate. No one had seen it coming. We had a file on her almost as thick as his. A brilliant political mind but riddled with neuroses. Hardly the ideal political spouse. There had been an incident, a suicide attempt at the reservoir. He and his security team fished her out. If he had been on his own, I think he would have left her. He was worried she would prove an electoral liability, ruin his chances. All the reports had her down as a total bleeding heart, all hopeless charity cases and lost causes. Then suddenly, out of nowhere, she announced she was going to run for political office.'

'It wasn't out of nowhere,' I say. 'It was the solstice. A turning point. And it wasn't suicide.'

'Anyway,' he says. 'Running for office was the final straw. He wanted her dealt with once and for all. He had already made one attempt.'

'The student from Columbia? At the fund-raising event?'

He nods. 'She really did love him. He set her up to take the shot. He was going to play the avenging hero and shoot her straight afterwards. Unfortunately for him, she fired and missed. No result. That night he told me he wanted us to do it.'

'And then you met her.'

'And then I met her and my world view changed and my top priority became keeping her alive.'

'How on earth did he end up a British agent?'

He shrugs. 'Easy enough with someone like that. Trapped by his own sexual appetites and vanity. We offered him a Scottish estate. I think he believes *droit de seigneur* still exists.'

'Why didn't you tell her?'

'It has been hard but *passions are best likened to floods and streams,*

The shallow murmur, but the deep are dumb.'

'Right.'

'None of us were ever promised a rose garden.'

'What does that even mean? *Promised a rose garden?* You should have told her. For her sake, if not your own.'

'I suspect a part of her always knew but she didn't want to believe. She walled it off.'

'I think you'll find she is asking herself some pretty searching questions now. Why did the Adjudicator choose the Senator and not her husband?'

'Nothing would satisfy him more than making me watch the woman I love go through hell. He knew what was in her service file. He knew about the reservoir and the suicide attempt ten years ago. It is very hard to defend against a Colosseum hunt, even for the British secret service.'

'So what was your plan?'

'I understood the email challenge and what it would mean for her mentally. I wanted to protect her.' He shakes his head. 'Love makes people do some very stupid things. I planned to keep it from her till the last minute, but I knew we were going to need help, and I thought of the recruit I had come across four years before – arrogant, overconfident and hard as adamantine. A defender of life. Achilles in the raw.' He sighs. 'I got the Senator to stay a couple of blocks away from Central Park and I called you in to help. I was expecting to be with you, to be able to direct events.'

'You mean you weren't expecting to be clubbed around the head? Weird. So that was why you were wearing a balaclava.'

'I thought the sight of me might be a shock. I wanted a chance to explain.'

'I don't know why you risked bringing me into it. You should have used another agent.'

'He has a weakness for you,' he says. 'After you beat the system. He'd never had anyone behave like you did. It levelled the playing field bringing you into the mix. And the final line of the challenge – *some seasons are colder than others* – seemed to suggest it.'

'You know perfectly well it suggested it. You brought me in deliberately, so he could finish the job he started four years ago. A sacrifice on the Colosseum altar.'

He shrugs. 'He hates to fail. You are unfinished business, grit in his shell, and I would have given him anything he wanted to save her life. Up to and including yours.'

The medical machinery is loud in the silence. Somewhere, a fan whirs. The radiator is hot through my jeans.

'Who exactly are we talking about here?' I say. 'Did I actually meet him?'

'Don't you remember?'

I stare out into the dark as the penny drops. A talented young doctor with the face of an angel and no mercy bends over me. *I've never had anyone beat the system*, he said. *Let's see what is in the tunnels of your mind.*

'I remember. But what is it all for? He didn't go to all this effort just to revenge himself on you. There were far easier ways to do that. What is going on here? What does *Colosseum* achieve?'

He shrugs. 'Honestly, at this point, is that really the question?'

I stare down into the street. Two looters are struggling

past with a boxed TV held between them.

Yes, I think, *it is the only question.*

'So now you know, Achilles,' he says. 'The real question is – are you coming out of your tent to save the day?'

THERE IS COMMOTION in the corridor. Many feet moving fast. Someone bumps up against the other side of the door, and I picture the Secret Service standing shoulder to shoulder barring the way.

We hear a woman's voice raised in command. Impossible to disobey. A commander in chief.

'Here comes the woman of the hour,' I say. 'Unless I much mistake the matter.'

The door slams open, and the Senator stands on the threshold. She is still carrying the Minimi. Her hair sticks up in wet peaks. She clutches a foil aluminium blanket around her shoulders.

Her eyes meet mine and then they are swinging to the bed. Walter tries to sit up but doesn't get further than his elbows before she is across the space and throwing herself at him. He collapses backwards and manages to get his bare arms round her. They go white at the elbow he is gripping her so hard.

I get a picture in my head of them having sex, and wish I hadn't. After a while, he loosens his hold, and she pulls back, the gun clanking between them.

'Is that a machine gun in your pocket or are you just pleased to see me?' I say.

She turns my way. 'This is Winter,' she says. 'The Best of the Best.'

'Oh, believe me,' I say, folding my arms, 'we have already met.' My voice is brimming with the unspoken.

Over her shoulder, he meets my gaze, anguish in his eyes. The unspoken plea. Begging me, begging me on his knees not to unmask him.

I roll an internal eye as I walk to the door. *Hard as adamantine?* I don't think so.

At the door, I turn back.

'In ancient Rome, what happened to the Lord of Misrule at the end of Saturnalia?'

'He was executed on the altar of the temple of Saturn,' Walter says. 'Or "Cronus" in the Greek. Although it depends which account you are reading.'

I am silent.

'Good luck, Achilles,' he says.

CHAPTER 27

R AF NORTHOLT IS quiet. They know all about my arrival. It's 5 o'clock in the afternoon in New York but 10 o'clock at night in London. Dark again. It took six hours to cross the Atlantic in the cargo bay of a Hercules. No natural light. My whole life is taking place in the space between daylight.

A Service merc sits on the runway ready to whisk me to debrief.

Traffic is light into central London. We go down the ramp, through the titanium tube and into the GCHQ underground car park.

I get in the lift. Control's circular office is on the top floor looking out through a clock face. I press 'down'.

The detainment level is in the bowels of the building. The bright white corridor smells of TCP. I don't come down here much. I wonder if this is where Erik, the Head of Field, is convalescing after our trip to Siberia, or whether he is still in hospital. I walk past the interview suites right to the end and turn into medical. There is a reception desk and a duty doctor. He looks bright-eyed and perky, like he has just turned up for work.

'Are you the night shift?' I say.

'And raring to go. What can I do for you?'

'I'm looking for a cute doctor.'

'Aren't we all, darling,' he says.

'A particular cute doctor – face like an angel. Left here about four years ago. I just need to look at the employee files on your systems.'

He smiles. 'It's the time of year, isn't it? Christmas makes everyone romantic. Does your angel have a name?'

I shrug. 'I didn't get his name. You know how it is. Blue, blue eyes.'

'We don't have anyone like that in medical,' he says. 'More's the pity. I think I might know who you mean – works for Special projects, based in Cornwall.'

Special projects.

'He hasn't left though, you'll be pleased to hear,' he says.

'He hasn't?'

'And in even better news, he is in town this week and in the building.'

'He's *here*? In GCHQ? Right now?'

This is not the man I am looking for – the Adjudicator would not be hanging out in GCHQ.

'Lab 2,' he says. 'He doesn't do medical check-ups, but maybe he'll make an exception for you.' He winks.

'Has he got a name?'

'Everard,' he says. 'Doctor Everard to you.'

I am already striding past him. I walk on into the medical warren. Past Lab 1. The door to Lab 2 is ajar, I peer round.

It looks like a chemist's lab: white surfaces, glass distillation apparatus, Bunsen burners, test tubes and a man standing with his back to me. The GCHQ interrogation expert.

I resist the temptation to stride in and get him by the throat.

'Hello, Everard,' I say.

He turns and his eyes are confused for a second, like he doesn't recognise me, then he smiles.

'Hello, Winter. How are you?'

'*How am I?* Have you been watching *Colosseum?*'

He shakes his head. 'I don't watch a lot of TV,' he says. 'Has it been on again?'

'Yes,' I say. 'And the whole experience was strangely familiar.'

He looks at me, a slightly distracted expression on his face. 'Was it?'

One test tube is decanting slowly into another.

'It was uncannily similar to an experience I had during training four years ago.'

'Was it?' he says.

'What happens to all the dead bodies?' I say, keeping a lid on my temper. 'Just out of interest.'

'What dead bodies?' he says. 'What are you talking about?'

I stare at him in disgust. '*What dead bodies*, says the interrogation expert.'

His brow clouds over. The angel looks thunderous. 'I have *never* lost a subject. Ever,' he turns back to his experiment. 'I am a doctor.'

Doctor. He makes my skin crawl.

He gestures to his workbench. 'I work long and hard to make sure I get the results without any dead bodies. Cellular degenerator. Attacks nerve endings. You still hold the endurance record, by the way.' He turns to look at me, and

I feel his eyes crawling over me, sexless, disinterested, weighing my physique. He goes back to his test tubes. 'I think it is the increased body fat. Women's bodies naturally have a greater fat-to-muscle ratio.' He turns suddenly, like some fascinating idea has just occurred to him. His face is alight. 'It would be very helpful if you would trial this for me. You are the ultimate test subject. What a lucky chance you are here. Are you free now?'

I give in. The willpower that has held me at the door collapses. I am across the room and I have him in a choke hold.

'Where is that place? The training centre?'

'It was all in your mind, Winter,' he croaks.

That annoys me more than all the rest. I swivel, smack his forehead on the bench and drop him. He collapses on the floor.

'Surrey,' he says. 'They shut it down not long after you were there. Some kind of training accident. It got hushed up. I'm not sure what happened to the site.'

'What about the guy who ran the programme?'

He pushes himself up into a sitting position. His forehead is starting to swell. 'Who knows? I think he disappeared. It's not a surprise. You can never catch someone like that. Very talented guy,' he says seriously. 'Amazing results. He never gave up on anyone. *It is just a case of facing down your weakness*, he used to say, *and unlocking your potential. Most of us go our whole lives operating at half speed, never achieving our full potential. It's a tragedy. Be the person you were meant to be.* He designed the whole programme. Monitored the recruits himself.'

A cold sweat creeps over me. A man stares across the

table, his glasses held together with masking tape.

'Imagine there are two of you in a locked room and only enough air for one person to survive. What would you do?'

'Stop imagining,' I said. '*This is a riddle, right?*'

'Boy Next Door type?' I say. 'Floppy hair, glasses?'

'No,' he says. 'Nothing like that. Young, tall, always spinning a coin. You wouldn't have met him. He stayed the other side of the glass.'

CHAPTER 28

I GET ON the last train out of Waterloo. The location Everard has given me is surprising. This is not Cornwall or Scotland, remote and inaccessible where no one can hear you scream. This is Surrey, where you can't move for golf courses and Ocado vans.

The train is full of revellers decked out in tinsel and Christmas jumpers getting the last ride home. The guy opposite snores. I lift his phone. He doesn't stir even when I use his thumb to open it.

The station I need is tiny. It probably has two trains a day. One from London and then another coming back the other way and comparing notes. I have missed the last train by about two hours. I get off at Guildford. According to my new phone, my destination is ten miles south as the crow flies. I buy a hot sausage roll and a bottle of water from a late-night Greggs, put my hood up and start to walk.

Out of the bright lights of Guildford, the sky is huge and clear. England is colder than New York and frost coats everything, hanging twinkling in the air. The black skeleton trees creak in the cold. My white breath spirals away from me. My body clock is shot. It is 2 in the morning. I haven't slept in a bed for seventy-two hours. I am awash with adrenaline.

The moon is out and the sky full of stars. My eyes after hours of night-walking have adjusted. It is almost as light as day. A strange silvery monochrome day.

I can't explain even to myself why I am coming in on foot. Completely off-grid. Not even my own phone to give me away. I could have got in a taxi and been there in half an hour. But it feels right. Somehow, I need to find my way back to my past.

It takes me more than two hours, but when the walls come into view, I am still not ready.

The gates are locked with an iron padlock hanging from rusty chains. The driveway sweeps away up the hill. I stand outside the railings peering through the bars. It is amazing what only a few years of neglect can do. The neat parkland has gone back to wilderness. Frosted thistles reach waist-high out of the scrub. I stand for a while, feeling the cold prickle down the backs of my arms, then I climb the great iron gates by the hinge, jump down and I am in.

The driveway is silvery in the moonlight. Drifts of leaves have blurred the edges – it's half the width it used to be. Far off, a bird calls, but here inside the walls it's silent. My heart hammers in my chest. The fear is primitive, worse than the fear of being hunted. The same fear man has always had – fear of the dark, the endless night.

I glide up the drive. The house stares down at me blind – its windows are boarded. Covered in chipboard. There is a black and red notice with a drawing of an Alsatian.

24 hr. security. Keep out!

An animal scuffs the undergrowth somewhere behind me and I jump, heart racing, senses on a hair trigger.

The gravel courtyard has weeds knee-high. The door that led to solitary and the tank room is boarded. It is ghostly in the moonlight. The place is derelict. Can nature have achieved this much in such a short space of time? My rational self is battling to keep hold of reality. Is it all an illusion? Has someone drugged me again? Or was everything an illusion – the last four years, Siberia, the Senator? Am I going to wake up in the yellow cell in solitary and find I've only been gone for a couple of hours?

The huge oak-panelled front door is not boarded, but it might as well be. Unless you have a key there is no getting through it. It would be easier to go through the wall.

Optimi optimis it says above the door.

The Best of the Best.

I skirt the side of the courtyard and make for the stables. They are crumbling with neglect. One of them has a door hanging open. I peer inside. It is completely empty. The night is quiet. It feels a long way from anywhere.

I go back to the main house and stare up at the frontage. And remember the glass dome above the landing.

*

THE GLASS IS old and thin, a burglar's nightmare. It smashes down onto the landing below with a crash loud enough to be heard a mile away. I clean the edge with the cuff of my anorak and slither and squirm through the gap, feet-first. For a moment, I hang, then I drop. My trainers crunch glass. I am on the first-floor galleried landing outside the Principal's office, overlooking the hall, the grand staircase beside me.

The air is still. Colder than the outside. I can feel night invading. Little currents disturbing the stillness.

I open the door to the Principal's office. It is pitch-dark, boarded. Too dark to see my hands ahead of me, groping into the black. A plinth. Cold marble. A face. My heart races. That superstitious fear is close to the surface here. The fear of the other-worldly, the prickle of the neck in a churchyard, the dark spreading yew that bleeds. I stretch out, feeling for the wall, for some reference point and hit a heavy, carved frame. The paintings are still here. The canvas is rough, the oil textured. Who was by the door? Was it Caesar? My fingers trace the surface and hit a jagged, frayed edge right in the middle. There is a massive wide tear down the centre of the picture. Top right to bottom left, like someone has slashed down with a sharp knife.

I step back fast. I can feel the anger, read it under my fingertips as clear as if I had been there. Panic fills me. I blunder backwards, the noise terrifying in the silence, and grope for the desk. I get down on the floor and crawl under the desk into the footwell and wrap my arms around my legs and rock like I used to when I was a small child.

*

BLACK WATER CLOSES over my head. I cannot get to the surface. Someone reaches for me, pulling me into the light. I am in Sleeping Beauty's castle. A key turns in the lock. Only the prince has the key. The great castle door creaks open. The prince has come.

I sit bolt upright and crack my head on the underside of

the desk. It is day. Bright light shows round the edges of the boarded windows. Perfect squares drawn in fiery gold. The room with its dusty, shrouded furniture is clear in the morning light. My back is stiff as I clamber out of my hiding place. I get to my feet and pad out onto the landing and peer down over the bannisters to the hall below.

Sun streaks through the wide-open front door. Low, golden, winter sun.

The dawn.

CHAPTER 29

H E IS STANDING there in the hall looking up at me.
Body armour like a Colosseum hunter, dark hair.
Sun shafts across the hall. He is standing in his own
spotlight, glittering.

He is spinning a coin. Up and back, up and back, it
glints silver in the sun. Even from up here, I recognise it.
There is a round building on the tails side.

I lean over the bannister.

'That would be mine,' I say.

His fist closes over the coin. He gives his slow, cartoon
wolf smile that kicks me in the gut.

'Hello, Winter,' he says softly.

'I thought you were never coming.'

'My better half,' Ash says. 'The light to my dark. You
are the exact negative of me. You know that? My biggest
failure. Do you know what my flaw is?'

'A total disregard for human life?'

He smiles the wolf smile. 'Apart from that.'

I shake my head.

'I hate to lose.' And now there is no smile in his eyes,
only the cold pitiless depths of a winter's hunt to the death.
'I hate to leave a job half done. I came down to Cornwall
that day, intrigued. GCHQ had themselves a diamond in

the rough, a woman – a *girl*. I walked into that pub and there you were. Larger than life and twice as dangerous. I will never forget your face as you floated in that tank, your hair spreading out around you as you chose to drown. As hard as adamantine. And I couldn't get through to you. All that potential and I couldn't unlock it. I haven't had a day since when I haven't thought of you drowning in that tank, your hair floating around you.'

The sadness is so clear on his perfect face; I feel it like it is my own.

'I can't get past it,' he says.

I take a step down the stairs towards him and then another. I want to comfort him, this photo negative version of me.

Then I get an image of a girl with blonde braids pitching forward into the dirt and I stop abruptly.

'Avril,' I say.

It is just a name, but spoken now, at this time, by me, it has the stopping power of a hammer blow to the face. A wall thrown up between us. And it is not just Avril – it is all of them:

Frank who tried to run; Ian who didn't. Richard who wouldn't fight; Elliot who would. Sean, Tony, Oliver, Rachel, Marianna who didn't die.

He searches my face. He reads the rejection. The anger. It passes like a shadow across his eyes. He looks away from me. 'I wasn't happy about Avril either. But the rules are the rules. I made them. The least I can do is stand by them.'

'What is *Colosseum* for, Ash?' I say. 'What is the point? Is everything just a game to you?'

'Let me ask you a question,' Ash says. 'If you wanted to

launch Google or Amazon today. How easy would it be?'

It is so completely not the question I was expecting that it stops me in my tracks halfway down the stairs.

'It couldn't be done,' I say. 'It's not a question of hard or easy. That ship has sailed; you couldn't unseat the incumbents. First mover advantage and all that.'

Ash nods. 'I see you understand the problem. It couldn't be done. You would need an immense PR event that caught the attention of the world, or nine events,' he says.

I stare.

'Are you telling me *Colosseum* has been one giant PR stunt? To what purpose?'

'Brand building, idea association, ruthless, lethal, relentless, unstoppable. Until number nine of course.'

'Sorry,' I say.

'On the whole, I think it enhances the overall effect, and after all, the publicity has been immense. Is that love?' His silver eyes bore into mine. 'Love that burns the soul? Love that drives you out of your mind?' He shrugs. 'I don't know. Such a romantic story and who is to say she won't die in the end?'

My fists clench.

Ash smiles. 'Still so soft-hearted, Winter? A long-range rifle is very hard to defend against. Maybe on the next solstice. Or the second. Or the seventh. There would be a kind of poetry to that. An inevitability. Symmetry and justice and another demonstration of a powerfully unstoppable force. If you take the first letter of the name of every Colosseum target it spells a word. A word that is going to be synonymous with a ruthless, unstoppable hunt to the death.'

I try to work it out in my head.

'F-I-R-E...FIRE?' I say.

'S-T-O-R-M,' he finishes.

'FIRESTORM? What the hell is that?'

He smiles. 'Something that is going to change the world.'

'What are you selling?'

'*Colosseum* for everyone.'

I can't imagine how that could possibly change the world.

'*Colosseum*,' I say. 'I should have seen the connection to this place from the start.'

'You should have,' he agrees. 'I'm kind of disappointed you didn't.'

The coin spins in the air between us. The seconds stretch out.

'So, Winter,' he says, and it is long drawn out and lingering. A lifetime. A world of possibilities in the word.

'So?' I say, and it is hard to get the word out against the weight of those possibilities. I know what he is going to say before he says it. This photo negative version of me.

'Do you want to play?'

'What's the game?'

'Life or death,' he says. 'What else?'

I look at him standing there in his body armour. Gun holsters on each thigh. I look down at my empty hands, clench my fists. I am outclassed and outgunned.

'Winter.' The whisper comes from across the hall. Someone is standing in the open doorway, silhouetted against the dawn. The same silhouette that walked down the bank away from me at the reservoir to get a foil blanket. I just have time to recognise the floppy hair and the earnest expression before the Boy Next Door throws something across to me. It arcs through the air.

A heavy black gun lands in my hand and I have levelled it before Ash can move. He looks down the barrel. Then he laughs. The spinning coin crashes to the floor.

'Finally,' he says.

CHAPTER 30

THIS IS NO split-second decision. I have oceans of time. All the time in the world to consider, to look at my beliefs, to turn them over in my hands. I live a whole different life with the dark version of me, grow up and grow old staring into his silver eyes.

I remember the Senator saying, *It is a question of balance.* And my reply, *Once I deliberately take someone's life, I will never be the same person again. I will be Ash and not Winter.*

All the time in the world to make the right decision.

I pull the trigger.

It is a perfect shot. Right between the eyes.

My first.

I collapse to the floor as my legs give way. The Boy Next Door is coming across the hall.

He puts his hand on my shoulder. 'Are you OK?'

I shake my head.

'The one to save the many,' he says.

He gets down on his knees beside me and puts both arms around my shoulders. After a while, he sits down on the floor and goes back to the same position.

The bones in my backside are going numb.

'I'm sorry,' says this version of me with the messy hair and broken glasses.

'What are you doing here?' I say.

'I lost track of you in London, but I had a feeling you might come here.'

'You lost track of me? Why were you tracking me?'

'What?' He sounds surprised. 'I'm your field support. I got myself transferred to field support after ...' He is awkward. 'You know?'

'They tried to drown us. Then tortured us.'

'Yeah that. I think they expected me to quit.'

'Why didn't you come and find me, come and talk to me?'

He pulls back to look in my face. 'I thought ... if you wanted to see me, you would have popped by.' He peters out. 'We are only on the floor below.'

I look down at the gun. It feels different in my hand to my normal gun. Heft the weight of it. The power. 'I didn't realise you existed till twenty-four hours ago. I thought you and Ash were figments of my imagination, manifestations of me. Good me and bad me.' I can't look at the body on the floor.

'What?' he says.

'I know it sounds ridiculous.'

'Tell me I was bad you?'

I stare out at the sun. It is low, right in my eyes. The courtyard is white with frost. We watch as the sun comes up, slanting across the wooden floor.

'It's Christmas Eve,' he says. 'I had almost forgotten.'

'So you have been there all this time looking out for me?'

He nods. 'I ran the Siberia evacuation.' He smiles. 'I carried you unconscious across a nightclub on my first day.

It was me who fished you out of the reservoir. Me and June.'

'Who's June?'

He looks at me in surprise. 'Her daughter, Avril, was target number eight. Surely you remember?'

'I need to pay more attention to people's names,' I say.

He nods. 'Names are important. It is how you define yourself.'

Marie or Anna. Winter or Achilles.

'Thank you,' I say.

He shrugs. An embarrassed shrug. 'No problem. And then you took off.'

'You saved me from drowning.'

'Only once,' he smiles. 'You're still ahead.'

'Tell me again about that dream date,' I say. 'What was it? Dinner, a movie, a little hand holding?'

He lets me go and sits back. He is blushing. Actually blushing.

'I can't believe you remember.'

I hold out my hand. 'Winter. Nice to finally meet you.'

He looks at my hand. Then he takes it.

'Simon,' he says.

EPILOGUE

A week later

W E ARE IN the Bunker, our GCHQ underground home. Erik, the Head of Field, is out of hospital and still not speaking to me for being the one to take down *Colosseum*. He is so completely the Senator's ideal I must introduce them some time. We are watching a CNN story from yesterday, a reporter is standing on the steps of the White House waiting for the new Democratic presidential nominee to turn up and collect the Congressional Gold medal for services to the nation. Suddenly, the cameras cut to a downtown scene.

It is a courthouse and the Senator is emerging with Walter, our man in America, by her side and, on her other side, the storekeeper. He blinks in the afternoon sun. The commentator tells us she cut the audience with the White House to personally represent her friend at his eviction case. Apparently, she won. Which is no surprise. She will probably get the presidency unopposed.

I stare at her. The Senator is back. Almost. Blue suit, neat hair, long, painted nails. She waves to the crowds which have miraculously gathered.

'Is there anything you would like to say to your husband?' a reporter shouts.

She looks full at the cameras.

'Yes,' she says. The world holds its breath as, with perfect politician timing, she pauses. 'I want a divorce.'

She grins and waves as she gets into a limo and then she is gone.

'That is true love,' I say. 'It was right under her nose all along and she never saw it.'

Simon, my new quartermaster, is standing in the doorway, all Buddy Holly glasses and floppy hair, clutching bags of breakfast sandwiches in his arms. Grease has turned the paper clear. Overhead, the ceiling cooling ducts roar. We have been up all night, watching *Colosseum* and waiting. Bacon and weariness fill the air.

'Apparently, the first thing she did was change her name,' says Viv, Erik's quartermaster. 'The very first thing. I wonder why she would do that.'

'It means new beginning,' I say. 'From the Latin word for the dawn.'

'You'd think she had bigger things to worry about.'

I meet Simon's eyes across the room.

'Names are important,' I say. 'It is never too late to get it right.'

'I hear the Republicans are not going to stand,' says Viv. 'Can you believe it? She is going to be unopposed. In fact, if they announced a global president, she would probably get that.'

Something makes me look down at my PC.

The Colosseum home page has changed. A moment ago, it was black and white, now it is all the colours of the rainbow, like a beautiful butterfly emerging from its chrysalis.

Welcome to Firestorm

Cheating husband? Bitch wife? Hate your boss?

Let Firestorm take care of your problem.

Safe. Anonymous. Cheap.

The colours mimic the old eBay homepage. It is the same idea but with Dutch auctions: the hitman with the cheapest price wins.

eBay for contract killers.

Colosseum for everyone.

Now I get it.

Something that is going to change the world.

A Letter From Alex

Back in 2019, I picked up an old book from a market stall. It was called *The Running Man* and was by an author I'd never heard of – Richard Bachman. I opened the first page and started reading. Thirty minutes later I looked up, surprised to find myself still standing on the street. For a book that was written in 1982, it is astonishingly prescient. I started *Winter Dawn* that evening. In my head it was *The Running Man* meets *Fight Club* meets *Die Hard* (I like to think Winter could give John McClane a run for his money).

Fast forward a few months to February 2020 and the first Winter book, *Winter Dark* had been nominated for an Audie and Ell, my narrator, and Tamsin, my producer, and I went to Manhattan for the awards ceremony. We paced round the Central Park reservoir and discussed the gatehouses and the dark water and the wall just below the surface. The weather was beautiful and the ducks were in a row and even though Stephen King won the Audie, it was one of those perfect golden afternoons that live forever in the memory. I went back to London and finished the book.

It wasn't until some time later that I discovered that Richard Bachman is much better known by his real name… Stephen King.

I would love to hear from you if you have time to drop me a line. You can get me direct on *alex@acallister.com*.

Best,
Alex

PS. Check out my website for pictures of me, Tamsin and Ell pacing round the reservoir.

www.acallister.com

@CallisterAuthor

alex.callister.winter.dark

Printed in Great Britain
by Amazon